# LIFE AFTER

J.C. WARREN

Midnight Tide
PUBLISHING

*To my loving husband.*
*Words cannot describe what your support means to me.*

# LIFE AFTER

# YEAR 1 DGC (DURING GLOBAL CRISIS), DAY 230

## TRANSCRIPTS FROM STATION 101.5 OUT OF DETROIT

CHRIS FORESTER: All right, folks, it's officially 9:00 a.m. on Monday. We've entered the twilight hour. Today's twilight topic is climate change. We have Dr. Diego Rivera from the Climate Institute in Gainesville, Florida. Diego, you don't mind if I call you Diego, right?

Diego Rivera: I prefer Dr. Rivera, but at this point, I don't think it matters.

Chris Forester: [Laughs] Sure, sure. So, Diego, it appears your group has found a new solution to help avoid some of the predicted weather conditions. Can you tell us about your group and the research they have been working on for the last couple years?

Diego Rivera: Absolutely, Chris. We've pulled together funding from multiple sources to help mitigate the increase in dangerous storms as well as attempting to create solutions for humans to continue to prosper in the predicted harsh conditions.

Chris Forester: You make it sound like climate change is dangerous. [uncomfortable laugh] I know everyone says the storms will be bad, but that can't be possible. It's just some change in temperature, right? A little extra heat?

Diego Rivera: [Sighs] If it were that simple, the government wouldn't have signed the UN Climate Agreement. We wouldn't be working with every organization possible to combat these issues. To say this isn't real at this point in history would be idiotic. Are you just trying to get me angry on air?

Chris Forester: I'm not an idiot, but I don't see these drastic changes. Look at Florida. Everyone said they would be underwater by now...

Diego Rivera: If you think Florida is not sinking, you'd be sorely mistaken.

Chris Forester: People still live there.

Diego Rivera: [Sigh] That's like saying people are still living in the Amazon. Sure, it still exists, but that doesn't make it livable or safe. Our only viable way of life now is in areas with already established sustainable systems—Florida is not sustainable.

[End of Transcript]

# YEAR 5 AGC (AFTER GLOBAL CRISIS), DAY 235

## WINONA

WINONA KICKED HER FOOT OUT, smacking a rock off the ledge of the cliff. It was the thud of the rock against something soft, instead of the clattering of it falling down the cliffside, that made Winona look down. She looked over the edge of the cliff to the ledge below. It was the boy, sickly pale with an oversized shirt draped over him, that wouldn't let her look away.

She was still staring when the boy turned to look up, but Winona still felt the tremble of shock. She forced her mouth into a neutral line, wiping away the combination of shock and horror that probably still plagued her eyes, and gave a small wave.

"Sorry about that," she said, squaring her shoulders. "It's been a while since anyone has been through these woods."

The boy rubbed the reddish-pink spot developing on his forehead and gave her a shrug. "You didn't know I was down here. Happens."

She narrowed her eyes at him before she tilted her head toward the afternoon sun. It was getting later than she planned. Her stomach rumbled to life in agreement. She lifted the pail of salt water at her side, the one she had put down to kick the rocks, and nodded goodbye to the boy.

She had barely turned her body toward her home when his voice echoed against the rocks and into the trees. "Name's Jeremy."

She wanted to take the step, put herself out of his sight, and go home to make another bland pot of potato soup. She almost did, but the way his voice pulled her in, its soft timbre, and the undertone of excitement she hadn't felt in a long time were too much for her to ignore, despite the logical part of her screaming to get out of there or the sound of her father's voice echoing in her head that strangers were dangerous.

"Winona," she said, placing the bucket back on the ground. The sun had slipped farther down the sky in her indecision, the rays shining through the boy's T-shirt and giving her a chance to truly size the boy up. He looked like he lived off tree bark and water. His body, barely thick enough to hold him up, didn't give her the impression he was capable of hurting her. The smile he gave her showed off the chip in his front tooth that made him look younger than he probably was. It was disarming and comforting. She tried to focus on her reservations, but all her fears washed away with a tide of anxiety and the smallest ounce of excitement.

She hadn't had a meaningful conversation with anyone in years. She could let him come home with her, feed him, and then send him on his way. Just a night of company. She smiled, pulling it back so far she could feel the air on her gums and the pain in her cheeks. "Where are you headed?"

He shrugged. "Don't know. Maybe to the sea? It's salmon season…er…it would have been at least."

"No more salmon out there," she repeated awkwardly. Had it really been that long since she had spoken to someone that she couldn't even hold a conversation? It was pathetic and absolutely not how her mother had raised her. A small pain, a reminder that her parents weren't there anymore, pinged in her chest. She rubbed the spot before taking a deep breath and turning back to Jeremy.

"I went fishing yesterday but could only get a small trout, barely enough for dinner." She reached down awkwardly and held up a pail of salt water. "Plenty of water, though."

"I could go for a trout. I could go for anything right about now. It's been a few days." He shrugged again.

Winona added it to her mental list of reasons she should invite Jeremy back for company, at least for the night. The boy looked to be around her age, maybe a little closer to eighteen than she was, but he looked much closer to death than she had ever felt in her decade alone. "Didn't catch anything today, but I have some potatoes back at my house. You know how to get a fire going?"

Jeremy nodded.

"Perfect. I'll feed you tonight, but you're going to have to pull your weight." She groaned internally. Her father would be berating her, his hands swinging in the air and his face the color of a tomato.

His face lit up. "Really? Are you sure?"

"I guess so," she said, before getting on her knees and offering a hand to him. He wasn't too far down, maybe ten feet, and she knew if she focused on him instead of the rock ledge he was on, she could manage. She waited for him to throw the backpack she hadn't noticed at his feet.

He grabbed her hand, his soft fingers holding on to her calloused hand, and she started to lift him. He wasn't light, but she had been training physically her entire life, so she was able to pull him up to his shoulders with relative ease. From there, he dragged the rest of himself onto the ground next to her. She listened to him panting, struggling from the effort, and added it to the reasons this would be fine.

"Just dinner and no funny business," she reminded him,

reaching over to help Jeremy off the ground. When he was on his feet, and his backpack was slung over his shoulder, she offered up the pail. "Can you carry this?"

He took it, not responding to the question, and lifted it to his face. "Is this okay to drink?"

Winona doubled over, laughing so heartily that tears sprung to her eyes. "Drinkable? HA. Maybe in a few hours. Are you thirsty?"

He nodded. With a sigh, she unclipped her small metal bottle, which contained clean water, from her waist and handed it to him.

"Don't drink it all. And so help me, if you get any backwash in there, I'm going to leave you right here to starve." There. She had made it clear who was in charge. She looked up at the orange sky and mouthed, *See?* Her father didn't answer, but she could still feel his disappointment.

Jeremy gave her an enthusiastic grin before drinking the water with a satisfied breath. "That's the best water I've had in months. Thank you so much. It's been days since I passed that lake."

"That lake about two days south?" she asked, starting the walk back to her house.

"Yeah, that sounds about right." Jeremy crooked an eyebrow at her. "It's hard to keep track of time."

"It used to be a pond, and it's not safe to drink. Like, it will kill you kind of not safe. The ocean overflows there now." She eyed him curiously. Father always told her to clean first, or she'd never survive. How was he still alive? "Have you always been able to just drink water?"

He shrugged, and she narrowed her eyes. If she counted right, that was the sixth shrug since they met. Her dad did the same thing when she expressed concerns about the woods. It bugged her then, and apparently, it still drove her crazy. "I don't know. Mom always said I had an iron stomach, I guess."

"Interesting," she said, her voice not hiding the uncertainty she felt. She'd never heard anyone, even her parents, say something like that. It wasn't normal. "Where are your parents now?"

Instantly, she burned with an apologetic blush. What was wrong with her? She wouldn't want anyone asking about her dead family members. She trained her eyes on the dead forest between them and the blurry white shape of her home. There wasn't a living tree between the cliff and her house. The only living plants she'd seen since her parents died were the ones in her garden. She was grateful her parents had been smart enough to save seeds before things started to die off.

She listened to the sound of their breathing, just barely louder than the crunch of the forest floor, and begged him to respond. To not decide to walk away and leave her to talk to just herself again. She let her hair fall in front of her face before peeking through the brown curls to take in his stormy face. With his tumultuous gray eyes, Jeremy was fairly good-looking. His high cheekbones, sharp straight nose, and cupid bow lips were perfectly proportioned with his big eyes framed in dark lashes and thick brows.

The only thing that wasn't so perfect was the chip in his tooth and a short, dark scar that cut through his right brow like a shot of lightning parting a storm cloud. Winona didn't care if he was good-looking or ugly because if this silence kept on, he wouldn't be sticking around. She wanted to apologize, to pretend she didn't say anything, or to just melt into the forest and disappear.

Before she could do anything, he interrupted her thoughts.

"They died a few years back. Brothers didn't last much longer."

His casual tone and calm eyes released the pressure in her chest, and she took a deep breath. Winona gave him a soft smile. "Same."

Her head tingled with frustration. *Same.* Clearly, she had been alone for too long. Casual conversation was no longer as easy as it once was. Winona sped up, trying to put a little distance between herself and Jeremy as she chastised herself. When he didn't try to catch up, giving her the space she needed to wash away her embarrassment, she took a small thankful breath. They walked like that until she could see the dark silhouette of her rundown Victorian.

Winona slowed down to direct Jeremy around a rusted car that was sinking into the soft soil and pointed toward her home. "That's it."

"Whoa. All that for just you?"

She watched him take in the brown wood siding that used to wrap perfectly around the edges. It wasn't as perfect now, the wood splintering and jagged at the corners, some pieces having fallen to the ground in the last storm. But even with the broken roof and molding, it gave her a comfort she thrived in. She gave him a weak smile. "Family property—owned it for generations. Washington is all I've known—during and after. Even after they told us to leave, my parents had managed to make the property self-sustaining."

Jeremy watched her fidget with soft, troubled eyes that she resented. Her mouth curled down as she tried to imagine having to leave her home just to survive like Jeremy must have. It was hard enough to bury her family. Her eyes flicked past Jeremy to the large stones she had carved with their names over their graves, and she shivered.

Her mind reeled, pulling her memories out of the box she had shoved them in right after she finished placing their gravestones. Her parents collapsing just out of reach. The sound of their shrieks, echoing for hours, on repeat in her head for days after. The strong scent of charred flesh that forced vomit into her mouth. Even now, when she kneeled next to them and told them about her week, the smell still lingered so strongly in her head that she thought it might be soaking through the soil. A constant reminder that she should have saved them.

She knew it was a miracle the wildfires didn't touch the property. That she had survived, running out of the forest in just enough time to only burn her foot. Her foot tingled just thinking about it.

They stood there for a minute, locked in their own personal thoughts, until she finally managed to pull her mind back to the present and start walking up the house steps. Her shadow slid past her, warning her how close they were to sundown. "Come on, we have a lot to do. These woods are hard to see through at night."

Jeremy nodded, running up the steps behind her, and dropped the bucket she gave him by the front door with a few loud thumps that reminded her of her dad. She sighed, wishing it was her father following her instead of this stranger who felt oddly like a puppy she wasn't going to be able to shake.

It had been years, but he was still clear, as if he still stood in front of her. The crow's feet he developed from constantly making all three of them laugh. The softness of his eyes when he cleaned up her scrapes and cuts. His hand, double the size of hers, covering her own as he taught her to play football in the backyard. The twinkle in his eyes when she broke the glass pane on the back door. The glass was still broken, covered up with some cardboard they found. Mom had given them an earful, but the memory still made her heart ache for what was.

"Nice place," Jeremy said, interrupting her thoughts. He whistled as he looked around the dusty living room with wide eyes and a wide grin.

"It's home," she said awkwardly, trying to shuffle herself in front of the outline from where the television used to be mounted. She averted her eyes from the matching set of chairs so worn in they turned a brown that looked too close to the dirt outside. A scratched-up dark-brown square coffee table that had more rings on it than the oldest tree in the yard was nestled between them and had a thick layer of dust from lack of use. Everything had been turned from facing her to facing the bay window framed by yellowing curtains and covered in streaks from trying to clean it with dirty rags and salt water.

She wouldn't call it nice, but it was all she had left, and every room was filled with memories of her childhood she wasn't willing to give up. "Let's get started or we won't have dinner going before dark. Can you cook?"

Jeremy shrugged.

"Okay," she dragged out. She let her nails bite into her palm, a sharp reminder that having Jeremy was better than talking to yourself. "What can you do?"

"I mean, I can help fix things up around the house. Dad used to be a carpenter before. Taught me everything I know. Do you need anything repaired?" Jeremy averted his eyes as a red blush crept across her cheeks. Embarrassment washed over her.

"That could be useful," she replied, thinking about the missing step out back and the hole in her roof that leaked into the bathroom. The blush was replaced by a soft smile. "Tomorrow—you can start with the back steps. If that goes well, you can move onto the next project. For now, come help me get the firepit going."

She looked over him at the dimming light outside. The sky was turning a bloody-caramel color, and they were running short of daylight. "We need to light the candles before it gets too dark to see. We have maybe another twenty minutes."

"I…I…I can stay?" Jeremy stammered out, watching her with hopeful eyes.

*Crap.* She cursed herself. She was going to regret this. "One night. Don't make me regret this."

"Thank you! Thank you!" He wrapped her in a bear hug. "You won't. I promise."

She stood in shock, her body trying to melt into the hug, until he let go and took a step back. She smoothed out her shirt, avoiding his eyes, and said, "Just help me get dinner started."

"Yes, of course." He shuffled, pulling a backpack off his shoulders, and held it out. "Where should I put this? It's all I have left."

Her chest ached for him. Where would she be if she lost her home? Where would she be without everything that made life so easy? She shivered, her mind painting an image of her dressed in the same outfit Jeremy was wearing, her hair one knotted mess hanging behind her. She bit her nails into her palm hard enough to push the picture away.

"You can stay in the extra bedroom. Follow me." She focused on the soft creaking of the stairs as they strained under their combined weight. It was comforting, a sound she had listened to as a child when her parents would come up to check on her. It warmed her heart. When they got to the second floor, she turned away from her room on the right and pushed open the door on the left. It stuck a little but opened with a cloud of dust flying into the air.

"No one has slept here in years," she coughed out, dust hitting her throat. "It's a little musty, but everything should be clean."

Jeremy smacked her back on the way to jump onto the bed. She tried to ignore the burning, and she watched another cloud of dust fly into the air, but it was clear Jeremy was too excited to care. The room was nothing compared to hers, but it had a bed. She was sure Jeremy hadn't seen one in a long time, if ever, and his pure joy made a smile break out on her face.

"Thank you so much. I'll work my ass off to help out around here. I promise."

"One night." She straightened her shoulders and wiped the

smile off her face. "We really need to get started, or we'll never be able to make dinner."

Her stomach growled as she spun around to walk down the stairs. Her embarrassment washed away with the echoed growl from his stomach, slipping out of the guest room. She hurried down the stairs, made her way out the back door, and hopped over the broken step. She dropped to the soft ground below and walked to the shed.

She grabbed the rusted handles and gave a silent prayer that today was not the day they gave out. Not when the sun was setting this fast. When it opened, she let out a sigh of relief.

"What's in here?" Jeremy asked, his voice so close to her she could feel his breath on her neck. She jumped, her body shivering, before spinning around to see Jeremy smiling his crooked grin at her. "Sorry about that. Been awhile since you've had company?"

She nodded, and he shrugged. She turned back to the shed, rolling her eyes. She jerked her thumb at the rows of plants behind them. "Stock of candles made out of wax from the soybean crop over there. As well as all my gardening supplies. Mom loved to garden and taught me as soon as I could walk."

She fumbled for a minute, leading Jeremy into the dark shed, until she found the candles on a shelf and handed them to Jeremy. She silently cursed herself for not putting out the new candles in the morning like she had planned to. "You know, I haven't seen a garden in years. Will you walk me through it tomorrow?"

"If you really want me to," Winona said, her secret smile swallowed up by the dark shed.

Jeremy gave her a goofy grin. "Sweet! Man, you're super cool, you know that?"

She laughed softly. "Thanks, I think. Let's get dinner cooking. I should have enough supplies to make potato soup. You're not allergic to anything, right?"

"Haven't found anything I can't eat or drink yet," Jeremy said over his shoulder. He walked toward the firepit, candles stacked in his arm. Jeremy fumbled to put them down on the ground before pointing to the empty pit. "Where's the wood?"

"Fresh wood is back here," she said, hefting a load of split logs into her arms before joining him. She dropped them next to the pit. "Can you get a pyramid going?"

When he nodded, she walked away to get a handful of dried leaves she had left out in the sun for kindling. On her way back, she admired Jeremy's pyramid. It was neater than she had ever been able to create. It looked like her father had done it himself.

Jeremy took the kindling and started to work on the fire. Once it sparked, he smiled up at her. "Easy peasy."

He stood up, brushing off his legs. They stood there in silence as the fire grew into something usable for cooking. The comfort of his presence washed over her. She forgot how nice it was to have company, even if you didn't speak. All she really needed was someone to help out around the house. If he didn't mess up the back steps, maybe she'd let him stay longer.

"How long do you plan to stay here?" Jeremy asked, dragging her attention back to the present.

"I don't plan on leaving if that's what you're asking." She waved a hand around the garden. "I have everything I could need right here."

"Don't you want to see the rest of the world?" Jeremy turned his head upward and stared at the darkening red sky. "Don't you want to find others?"

"No." She snapped, fighting at the rising panic in her chest. No, she didn't want to see the rest of the world. She could barely handle this world. She could barely manage to keep herself fed, and she had an entire garden. She wanted her parents back. She wanted to not have to worry anymore. She walked off to swipe two bowls from the kitchen and then trudged silently back to the pot of soup. She handed him a filled bowl before walking to the rusted patio set.

"I didn't mean to upset you," Jeremy mumbled into his soup.

"I shouldn't have…" She trailed off. She shouldn't have been so cruel? Been so rude? Let him stay? She battled with herself while should take a slurp of her broth. It was bland, like always. "I shouldn't have snapped."

She met his eyes, her hazel searching his gray, and sighed. "I can't imagine leaving this place. This is all I have left of my parents."

Jeremy tapped his head. "Everything you need is up here. My parents and brothers, they live up here."

He took a sip of the soup. Eyes lighting up, he gobbled it down before going to get a second bowl.

"Don't you miss them?" Winona asked when he returned to the table.

"Of course, I miss them, but that doesn't mean I can't keep living. They would want me to. I think they would be proud of me for finding someone so capable. I mean, look how well you're surviving." Jeremy waved his spoon at the house before digging into his second bowl.

She nibbled on a potato and contemplated his words. Her parents would want her to keep living. But did that mean she needed to keep moving? She had everything she needed here. "Why keep moving if I'm surviving so well here?"

"Because we need to find others. We aren't meant to live our lives in solitude or in pairs."

She knitted her eyebrows at him. "There's a lot of we in your statement."

Jeremy gave her a wan smile. "I guess I was hoping we could stick together. You know?" He shrugged.

"If we're sticking together, I have ground rules." *Like no more shrugging.* She picked up the empty bowls and started toward the kitchen so he couldn't see the excitement she was trying to shove away. The idea of having someone to spend time with, even if it's this boy, made the world suddenly less difficult.

Jeremy followed on her heels as she made her way to the kitchen. "Like what?"

"For one, you'll need to pull your weight like we talked about. Then you're going to need to learn personal space boundaries. And I definitely don't want to leave here unless we have to." She eyed him as she washed the dishes in a bucket of water. It was the best she could think of.

"I reserve the right to add more," she added, before Jeremy could speak.

"Do I get some too?"

"No." She gave him a look.

"Come on, it's only fair."

"The world isn't fair anymore," she pointed out, before racking the bowls. When he didn't respond, she walked out toward the dying flame with the remaining sink water. The bucket was heavier than usual, and she tripped. The water spilled out in front of her, just barely licking at the fire, and she moaned.

"Unfair. The world is unfair," she added as she stormed past him toward the bucket of salt water she had collected today.

Bucket in hand, Jeremy placed a calloused hand on her arm as she headed back, and water sloshed out. She muttered a curse before dragging her eyes to his meek smile. "If you want to save water, you can use some of that dirt out there to smother the flames. It'll save you a lot of water."

She gave him a begrudging smile. Her father had told her something similar when she was younger, but she could never remember when she got around to shutting everything down for the night. She placed the bucket on the ground. "We'll clean this up after you dry out the fire."

He squeezed her arm softly before heading outside with an empty bowl. She watched him scoop up dirt and spray it over the fire. It died easily, and he turned to give her a bow. She clapped, an easy laugh slipping out.

Perhaps this was going to be better for her than she thought. She couldn't remember the last time she laughed so much. Or even laughed at all.

## WINONA

It had taken Jeremy a full day to fix the steps out back since he had to track down the supplies he needed from around the house. Winona wasn't a lot of help since she didn't know where a lot of her father's tools were. She never really helped him as a child. But once Jeremy had what he needed, it didn't take him long to finish up the stairs while Winona made them another pot of vegetable soup.

They spent that second dinner talking about what different chores Winona needed help with and what projects she wanted done around the house. Things like the creaky step on the way to the second floor or the holes in the roof that leaked into the house. Not that it rained to cause a leak, but she stayed hopeful, which meant the holes would need to be fixed.

Talking to Jeremy, after that first night, was easier than she expected and more enjoyable than she was willing to admit. She liked to hear his voice after so many years of silence. She didn't realize how much she hated the silence until it was gone.

Winona agreed to let Jeremy stay another few nights, asking for his help with the daily fishing and water-gathering chores she normally did. They had just finished for the day, the sun starting to set, when they returned without fish but with a full bucket of water. She watched Jeremy place it on the floor next to the sink.

"What are you going to work on next?" she asked when he turned to look at her.

His eyes widened, and a smile broke out on his face. "So you were serious? I can stay?" He wrapped his arms around her, and she stiffened, but he didn't notice. "I'm so glad. I really hope I can be helpful enough for you to keep me around."

She untangled herself and pulled away from him. "Having you around so far has been good, and I desperately need the roof repaired."

"Is that where you'd like me to start?"

She frowned. "Let's do that a little later." Jeremy's smile grew. "I was hoping you could help out in the garden first. One of the beds broke, soil has gotten everywhere, and I need it repaired so I can plant in there again. If we're going to have two of us, I will need to start planting more food now, so we don't run out."

"Speaking of food," Jeremy hedged, his face dropping slightly, "I was thinking that maybe I could help with dinner? I just think you're doing a lot—with the garden and the fishing and the water. I used to cook for my family."

She narrowed her eyes at him. It was the first time he had offered her any information about his past. "Do you not like my dinners?"

He frowned. "No, that's not it at all. I just...I want to be helpful. I was hoping to take on some more work. I don't want you to think...I just want to be helpful."

She shoved the negative thoughts about her cooking out of her mind, it wasn't like she thought she was particularly good at it anyway, and focused on Jeremy's nervous wavering. It was clear he was really hoping to provide value, and she didn't see a reason to say no. "Fine. You can cook tonight, and we'll see how it goes. How does that sound?"

Jeremy nodded enthusiastically. "Will you walk me through the garden so I know what's ready to harvest? I want to make sure everything I use is safe."

"Safe? Why wouldn't it be safe?" She quirked an eyebrow at him as he nervously rubbed his palm with his thumb.

He shrugged, a poor attempt at looking nonchalant. "I don't know. I just want to make sure I know what I can and can't use, that's all. I want dinner to be perfect."

"It's getting dark out there so let's go out now, and I'll show you around." Winona headed outside, Jeremy in tow, and walked through the garden. She pointed out which peppers were ready as well as some of the beans that were okay to use. Most of the garden was ripe, with beautiful vibrant greens, reds, and yellows scattered throughout. She pointed to the broken bed off to one side of the garden. "This is the one I'd like repaired. Do you see how one corner deteriorated? We should have replacement wood somewhere in the stockpile over there."

"I can get that rebuilt out in a day or two," Jeremy said, walking over to toe the broken pieces. He turned around and looked at her. "I would be happy to."

They shared a brief smile before Winona turned to point to the soybean plants on the other side of the garden. "Besides the soybeans here, I have already made tofu that can be used with dinner. I try to use it as a protein replacement when I don't catch anything."

"I'll be sure to add it to tonight's dinner. Are you good with a vegetable and tofu soup?" Jeremy walked over to the peppers and pulled a few bright yellow and green ones off the vines. "These look great for dinner."

She nodded. "I'll bring out a block of tofu from the kitchen while you get set up." She left him in the garden to collect more ingredients while she headed inside. She tried to wipe away the small smile on her face. Having Jeremy around, having anyone around, was such a nice treat that she couldn't keep her happiness to herself. Even her father would be okay with having Jeremy around.

A small pang of sadness hit her as she thought about her parents, and she took a moment to look at the front window at their graves. She missed them, and nothing would ever replace them, but having company took some of the weight off her. She could get used to having a little less work to do and a lot more laughter in her life.

When she made her way back to the backyard, tofu in hand, Jeremy was slicing away at the peppers with a smile on his face. She watched him for a minute before placing the tofu next to him. "Do you need me to grab you anything or do anything?"

Jeremy shook his head. "I can do it. Let me help."

"Well, I'll be over here"—she pointed to the picnic table—"if you need anything."

Jeremy looked up at her, taking a break from slicing, and sighed. "It's okay to have help every once in a while. Who knows, you might actually enjoy relaxing."

"No one can relax in the after," she pointed out as she took a seat. She tried to ignore the fact that she was, in fact, relaxing as she said that. A small part of her itched to do something, to help in some way. She hadn't been able to relax, to not be the sole person doing all the work, since her parents passed away.

Dinner didn't take long. Soon enough, Jeremy was placing two large bowls of soup that smelled better than anything she had ever made. It smelled better than her memories of her parents' cooking. She looked down at the brown broth, eyeing the roughly cut pieces of onion and peppers with apprehension. It looked too good. "What's in it?"

Jeremy flashed her a big smile. "I made a stock with the skins of the onion and tops of the peppers. Then I stewed the onions, peppers, and tofu in that stock. Once it got boiling, I added some of the leftover salt from boiling the ocean water. Oh, I noticed that you had a thyme plant in the broken bed, so I added some of that."

"Wow," she said. "That is way more effort than I have ever put into dinner." She took a spoonful of the soup and slurped it up. It tasted way better than it sounded, and she quickly took another spoonful. Before long, she had finished the bowl and was planning on seconds.

"I guess you liked it?" Jeremy asked, before taking a hunk of pepper into his mouth.

"I think you'll be cooking from now on," she said.

Jeremy laughed. "I would be happy to."

Winona didn't want to admit it, but Jeremy was turning out to be much better than she originally planned. She didn't fully trust him yet, but she was surprised with how much she already trusted him. Out of the few people she had met in her years alone, Jeremy was the first person she could imagine keeping around for the long term. Not that she would tell him that, because she wouldn't. At least not until she was confident she could trust him. For now, she would just let him help her out, and she would see where it went.

# YEAR 5 AGC, DAY 263

## DEE

DEE WATCHED SILENTLY from behind as Rowan shoveled dirt into the shallow grave. It fell like a dusty blanket over the grayed skin of their parents. The air was still in the backyard of their home in Upstate New York. A tear slid down her face as she listened to Rowan's choked-back sobs. Dee swiped it away quickly before Rowan turned around. They had known for a while that they would have to say goodbye, and she'd known for even longer that she would be responsible for Rowan when they did. But she never expected goodbye to hurt so much. Her heart ached to hear her mother's soft words of wisdom and her dad's grunts of affirmation. Rowan spilled the last scoop of dirt onto the mound before dropping the shovel onto the ground. He heaved a heavy sigh.

"I'm not ready to do this without them," he said, turning around to look at his sister. His frown was deeper than she'd ever seen it. His eyes bore into her with ferocity. She twisted her lips, taking in his angular jaw and smooth, dark skin. He looked so much like their father that she had to choke back another sob before pulling him into a tight hug. Her pale complexion contrasted with his as much as their personalities.

For everything that made him like their father, there was something that made her like their mother.

"Me either, but they wouldn't want us to stop living. They didn't fight to survive through the before so we could just give up. We need to stay strong." Dee bit her lip, frustrated with herself. Her mother had said to take care of him, not to mother him. Why couldn't she ever just let Rowan be?

"I'm not giving up." Rowan pushed her off him. "I am strong. I just want time to reflect." He made a clicking sound. "Do we not get time to grieve, *sister*?"

The words stabbed at her, red hot and angry. It was like she never learned to just keep her mouth shut. "No one is saying you can't grieve." She sighed. "But…"

"There is no but right now, Dee. There's just us and the grief we both feel."

She ignored him. "But we need to start figuring out the next steps."

Rowan shot her a warning look. Regret filled her. Dee was always the calloused one compared to sweet, loving Rowan. Her mother had sat her down more times than she could count to chastise her for being so harsh, to remind her that Rowan was a different person than she was. And here she was, throwing their mother's words of warning out the door. Would she ever learn?

They were burying their parents in the backyard of their home at the ripe old age of seventeen, and all she could think to speak about was how they were going to manage without them. The rational part of her knew that learning to manage without them was a priority. That was the part she had been taught to listen to, not the part of her that felt like it was crumbling apart. She was supposed to pretend that part didn't exist.

"Do you even care that our parents are gone?" Rowan kicked some loose dirt in annoyance.

Of course she cared. But she had to push that aside to take care of Rowan. She had promised their mom that she would.

Promised for as long as she lived that he would have a supportive partner in her. However long they managed to survive. Their mother had always prided Dee on her ability to put her personal feelings aside for the betterment of the group. It had made Dee feel good to be able to do that. After she had learned to ignore her own emotions. Rowan and their dad had never understood.

If only their mom was here now. Dee ignored the hurt building in her chest and crossed her arms. "Of course I care, Rowan. How could I not care? But someone needs to take charge, and that responsibility falls to me. Like always."

Rowan threw up his hands. "There you go again. The Wondrous Dee, Martyr of the Great Failed State of New York, Apple of our mother's eye. I shouldn't have expected anything else from you." Rowan stomped away from her, his fist clenched at his side. She listened to him walk away until he reached a stop at the back door. "You're not the only one who is capable of taking care of us."

The words stung, and she sucked in a breath. When she heard the familiar smack of their back screen door, Dee kneeled in the dirt next to the freshly packed soil. The musty smell of the dirt filled her nose and helped calm her mind.

"I'll do better, Mama." She fingered the dirt, careful not to disturb the mound Rowan had created, and let a few errant tears drop. She couldn't give in to the pain until she fixed whatever she could with Rowan. "I don't know how yet, but I'll fix this. Nothing is going to stop me from fulfilling my promise to you."

She closed her eyes and thought of all the things her mother would say. All the words of encouragement she needed to hear. She let them soak in, but it all fell flat without her mom's comforting hug or a cup of her famous herbal tea. Dee had always wondered how her parents had managed to have polar-opposite twins in every way, but whenever she asked, her mom tapped her little blue book.

"One day, when we're gone, find this little blue book. It'll help you understand the past and build a future for yourselves," her mom had said. Dee had begged to look at it, but their mother never let it out of her sight. Rowan had shrugged as if it didn't matter when she brought it up. It was like they were on two different planets some days.

Sweet Rowan was always spun up with frantic energy, and Dee was weighed down by the weight of their world. How would they ever make it without their parents' guidance?

Drawing herself up and off the ground, she squared her shoulders. She would find the notebook and start there. Just like her parents found a way, she would take their past and build a way. They had survived, survived and provided for them. She could too.

Dee made her way into the house, walking past Rowan's angry lump on the couch, and headed into her parents' room. She pictured the stained blue notebook in her mind, trying to remember the last time she saw it. She pulled apart drawers, listening to them squeal with her angry tugs.

"What are you doing?" Rowan asked, leaning against the doorframe.

She stopped, removing her hand from the drawer she was touching. "Looking for Mom's journal."

"They've been gone for less than a day. Can't this wait?" Rowan ran a hand through his hair and took a deep breath. "What's wrong with you, Dee?"

She sighed and pushed the bedside drawer shut. Rowan was probably right. It could wait. But Dee couldn't stop thinking about the journal. It held all of Mom's deepest thoughts. Held all the before and everything her mom thought would help. "She told me to find it. Does it make a difference if I find it today or a week from now?"

Rowan just shrugged. He was used to her moods.

"Let me know when you find it," he added hastily over his shoulder, before leaving her to the mess she created. Dee surveyed the pile of stuff she'd strewn about the room in her search. For a second, she thought her parents might come marching in to scream at her. But they weren't coming back. They had died, their hearts giving out within hours of each other. Her mother had gone first, and the loss seemed to be too much for their father to handle.

They weren't coming back. She repeated the thought, forcing her mind to understand her new reality, as she folded everything and placed it gently back into the drawers.

"This is useless," she mumbled to herself. Mom's journal would still exist in a few days. She shouldn't be worrying about these things when Rowan was obviously upset. He should be her priority. He was always their parents; he was the priority their mother wanted her to have.

"Rowan," she called, stepping out into their living room. It was spotless except for the blanket Rowan had thrown off the couch. She walked over to it and silently folded it. The soft fabric felt good in her hands. "Rowan," she repeated.

"What? What are you going to ruin now, Dee?" Rowan snapped from the hallway.

She deserved that. But she shouldn't have let it get like that. She needed to salvage it. She could salvage this. "Would you like to play Mom's favorite game?"

Rowan watched her carefully. "Maybe."

It wasn't a great response, but at least he responded. "Come on. We can do it in memory of her. In memory of both of them." He just watched her. "Please grab the game board. I'll go get some water from the well. We can play all night if you want. We can play until we're zombies."

He didn't answer, frowning at her. They stayed locked like that for a few seconds, and she held her breath. She needed him to accept this peace offering. She needed Rowan. She couldn't do this without him, and she didn't think he could do it without her.

"Fine. Go get Dad's bottle of gin. If we are doing it in memory of both of them, we're going to need it."

Dee gulped. Dad was always willing to share his gin with Rowan but not with her. Gin was for the men to bond over. Not something Dee was allowed to take part in. She and her mother had other things. Other things usually meant books and heartfelt conversation. She wasn't sure she was ready for the gin. It didn't matter if she was. Rowan was willing to take her peace offering, so she had to. She nodded before turning to the liquor cabinet.

After grabbing the open bottle, she carried it into the dining room, where Rowan was already setting up the board. She sat down and gave him the bottle. He took a long sip. She watched him.

He locked eyes with her as he lifted it to her lips. "Drink."

"Rowan, do you think this is a good idea?" she mumbled against the edge of the bottle. She wanted to make him happy, but this made her uncomfortable. Dad wouldn't like her drinking.

"It's just us now, Dee. You wanted to pay respects. This is how I want to do it." Dee dropped her shoulders in defeat before grabbing the bottle and taking a small sip. It burned her throat, made her eyes water, and made her stomach feel like lava. She plastered on a smile. "Delicious."

Rowan grabbed the bottle out of her hands. "You're such a wimp. It's not that bad."

"It tastes like battery acid."

"Have you ever had battery acid?" Rowan cocked an eyebrow at her. "It was Dad's favorite."

She didn't respond, choosing to reach over to grab a handful of squares from the pile and stack them up. Rowan followed her, placing his on the board first before shoving the bottle back at her. She took another small sip, the harsh liquid going down a little smoother, before placing her tiles down. They continued in silence, alternating placing tiles and taking sips of the gin until they were out of tiles and Dee's head was fuzzy.

She felt lighter than she had in a while—the stress and pain of their parents' death had slid off her shoulders with each drop of gin in her stomach. She didn't even care that her head felt airy and attached to her like a balloon instead of firmly on her shoulders. It was a magical solution. She lifted the bottle up in the candlelight and watched it glint. It was beautiful.

"Feeling better?" Rowan slurred.

She nodded.

Rowan smiled, baring his teeth. "Good, it's time to start bonding."

"I thought we were already doing that," she said, giving him a look.

Rowan pushed himself back in his chair and crossed his legs. She watched as he uncrossed them and leaned against the table. "No. We need to share secrets. Do you have a secret you want to tell me?"

Dee tilted her head. Secrets? What secrets? They told each other everything. "Mama asked me to take care of you," she blurted out. Her cheeks burned as her face flushed. She rubbed a cool hand against it, marveling at this new sensation. Putting her hands on the table, she tried to focus her mind. She shouldn't have said anything. She looked up at Rowan. He didn't look surprised when his eyes landed on hers. The brown depths were troubled but not surprised.

"That's not a secret, Dee. You've always been the responsible one—Mom would never ask that of me."

"Well," she pouted. "Do you have something better?"

Rowan crossed his legs again. "I might."

"Are you going to tell me?" Dee was getting tired and just

wanted him to say it already. Say whatever it was he was holding back right then. She looked down at the board game they had forgotten about sometime after the first third of the gin bottle and noticed "secret" spelled out. It taunted her. She hated secrets.

Rowan took another swig of the gin and frowned. "This was a bad idea. I shouldn't have said anything."

"That's not fair," Dee pouted. "You can't just jerk me around like that. I already told you mine."

Rowan tapped his chin. "Fine. I'll give you a secret equal to your secret." She waited while he took a long pause, one long enough to make her squirm in her seat. Then he leaned forward so she could smell the alcohol on his breath. "Dad liked me better."

She shoved him away from her. "What the hell?"

"Well, it's true," Rowan mumbled.

Dee stood up, the room spinning around her, and walked toward the back door. "You don't say shit like that. It's just mean." She pressed a hand against the door to steady herself. "It's not my fault I was born a girl."

He sighed. "It's not that."

"Then what is it?" she asked, turning her head toward him slowly. The room was still swimming around her, and moving too fast wasn't a great idea. When Rowan didn't speak, she rolled her eyes. "Dad never liked me the way he liked you, and we all knew it. That was a shitty secret. You should have kept that to yourself."

"You're right." Rowan stood up from his chair, his body weaving slightly. "I've had too much to drink. Why don't we just sleep this off?"

She nodded. "Maybe you'll be less shitty in the morning."

## WINONA

WINONA SAT on the hard ground, fingers stretched into the patch of dying grass in front of her house and tilted her head to watch Jeremy. He was climbing the rusty ladder they had found in the garage to the roof. A bucket full of supplies she didn't even know they had dangled from one hand. He reached the top, placed the bucket on the roof, and then turned his face toward her.

"I need you to hand me the piece of plywood I cut," he said.

Winona bit her lip, her arms already trembling. She pressed her hands harder into the soil to stop it. "I'm not a huge fan of heights. Can you just come get it?"

Jeremy looked at his bucket, already starting to slip down the slope of the roof. He softened his voice. "Not really. I promise it'll be fine. I'll make sure you're okay."

She frowned at him but pushed herself to her feet and started walking toward the garage. The plywood Jeremy had explained to her would be the foundation he needed to fix the roof while cutting it was still on the workbench. She didn't even know they had a workbench until Jeremy had found his way into the garage.

The garage had always been her father's area. As much as she learned and helped her father, she wasn't allowed in the garage with him. Her mother said it was because Dad needed a place to sit in silence. It was something Winona had held a grudge against since she was able to walk.

After he passed, she locked the door that went from their house into the garage and never looked back. She didn't have the heart to go through his things. If she went through their stuff, it would make them being gone all the more real. Seeing Jeremy standing there, saw in hand, made her heart ache. Something about his wide-open smile, his clothing covered in sawdust, and his body poised over the bench opened a part of her she had shoved away. The part of her that welcomed the love and appreciation her parents had given her.

It wasn't the same, the feeling she felt toward Jeremy as she felt toward her parents. But it had shocked her so much. She had lost her voice and just stared at him dumbfounded. When she had pulled herself together, Jeremy had packed the bucket and was headed to the ladder. She didn't even have time to process it before she was watching from the ground.

Winona shook her thoughts off and grabbed the plywood roughly. The plywood splintered into her hand, making her yelp.

"You okay?" Jeremy called.

"Fine!" she yelled back. She bit her lip, picked up the piece, and made her way back to the front of the house. Her hand pulsed with pain.

"Why do you look like you're about to cry?"

"I don't know what you're talking about," she snapped. Guilt flooded in immediately.

Refusing to look up at Jeremy, she started to climb the ladder. She was too harsh on Jeremy, and he really wasn't asking a big favor. It wasn't until she made it halfway up that her fear of heights made her stomach roll. Pulling the ladder close, she tried to take a deep breath.

"Nona?" Jeremy said, his voice soft and caring. She cursed the nickname he had given her. The butterflies in her stomach were not helping the situation.

When she didn't respond, her nausea warring inside her, she felt the ladder shift with Jeremy's weight. The movement made her head spin, and she whispered, "Stop."

The ladder stopped moving quickly enough to make bile rise in her throat.

"What's wrong? Are you okay?"

She squeezed her eyes shut and croaked out, "Heights."

"Oh, Nona. I didn't realize it was that bad. Stay right there. I'll be right there."

She felt the ladder move, her body rejecting the movement, and she had to take several deep breaths to keep herself from puking. Winona could hear Jeremy moving things around, the roof creaking with his movement, and she wanted to tell him she'd be okay. She just needed a few minutes. Some days, Jeremy was too kind of a soul for her to accept that he wanted to stick with her grouchy self.

The sound of Jeremy moving around disappeared under the sound of her heart pounding in her ears, and the panic set in. He had just left her there. Jeremy had just left her floating over fifteen feet in the air. The idea that Jeremy was a kind soul became laughable. She wanted to open her eyes, scream, anything to see or find Jeremy, but she couldn't push past the panic. She was sure her knuckles had turned white from her vicelike grip.

Then the ladder started to shake, and she could hear a whining sound that, somewhere in her mind, she knew was coming from her. With every harsh movement, the sound got louder. She was losing it.

"You're okay. You're okay," Jeremy whispered, his arms

wrapping securely around her. He pulled the plywood from her grip and dropped it on the ground. The sound of it hitting the dirt made her jump, but Jeremy just kept whispering in her ear, holding her tightly to his chest until she could breathe again. He smelled like pine and freshly cut wood. The sharpness helped to clear her mind just long enough to move her hands from the ladder to Jeremy's neck. A soft hiss told her she had dug her nails into him, but she couldn't release her fingers.

She opened her eyes, the height making her stomach roll again. But the warmth and comfort of Jeremy's arms slowed her heart enough that she could function. It helped that Jeremy was actively making it hard for her to see past him.

She leaned her head against Jeremy's and whispered, "Thank you."

"Look around you," he said. "There is nothing to fear."

She lifted her head and looked at the space between herself and the ground. The panic was still there, but the comfort of Jeremy holding her helped keep it at bay. She shoved the implications of that as far back as she could. Once her feet touched the ground, she could deal with her very mixed emotions. "Can we just get down?"

Jeremy nodded before lifting her off the ladder, cradling her to his chest, and bringing her down to the ground. Placing her down to stand on her own, her legs instantly gave out. She landed on her ass and hissed. She put her hands down against the grass and yelped. Her palm radiated pain. The splinter she gave herself.

"What? What's wrong?" Jeremy kneeled down next to her.

She lifted her hand, looking at the angry chunk of plywood embedded in it. A red ring circled it. "It's nothing. I can take it out inside."

Jeremy gave her a look, concern blooming across his face. "If you say so."

The concern she kept seeing was starting to eat at the

tenuous relationship they were starting to build. Smacking it off his face crossed her mind briefly. He stood up and helped her to her feet. She gave him a meek smile before heading inside to find the tweezers in her bathroom. Once she had pulled them out of a drawer and started working at the splinter, she heard the banging of Jeremy working on the roof alone. She pushed away the guilt of forcing him to do it by himself. Nothing could be done until she got the splinter out.

* * *

ONCE THE ROOF WAS COMPLETE, the splinter had been removed, and dinner had been made, Winona served them each a bowl of the fish stew Jeremy made. It was more salty than usual since they had salted the fish earlier in the week to help keep it as long as possible. To even catch a fish in the ocean was a feat, and she considered them a lucky pairing for doing so. Today was the last day before it was too old to eat, and Jeremy had gone all out to make the spicy fish stew steaming in front of her.

"I think this may be my best dish so far," Jeremy said, giving her his classic wide smile.

She nodded, watching the light in his eyes dim. Grabbing her spoon, she took a sip of the soup and sighed. It was his best. Though, that wasn't saying much since every meal he made was better than the last. Even with the salted fish, it tasted better than anything she could produce. She gave him a weak smile.

He frowned, poking his spoon at her bowl. "Is it not good?"

"No, no. It's really good."

"Then spit it out. What's bothering you?" Jeremy waved his spoon at her. She watched little drops of soup fly across the table.

She looked down at the worn wooden table and pushed some of the fish around in her soup. "It's nothing."

"It's not nothing, Nona."

"Can you stop fucking calling me that?" she snapped. He shut down, sputtering apologies.

She closed her eyes and tried to center herself. "I'm sorry. Today has been rough."

"Are you upset I had to come get you?" he asked tentatively.

She mulled over his words. That wasn't it. There was something about him saving her that just didn't sit right. She had been raised to be independent, and it embarrassed her that should needed saving. She looked up at him, his eyes watching her carefully. He had put his spoon down and folded his hands in front of him. The set of his mouth was so steady she thought he might be made of wax. He was the calmest she'd ever seen him. It was probably the only time she'd seen him sit still for longer than a minute. Jeremy never let go of his puppylike traits, and she'd grown to like them. The bounce his personality brought to the house was the highlight of most of her days. His lack of movement made her shiver.

"I'm sorry I couldn't help today. I didn't hold up my end of our deal. I should have been able to do it." She felt her eyes burn with tears that wouldn't fall. "I understand if you want to move on. To keep looking for a place to settle."

The silence made her ears ring. Then the bench squeaked, and she felt Jeremy at her side. He wrapped an arm around her shoulders and pulled her close to him. "I don't plan on going anywhere. It's not your fault you have a fear of heights. We're a partnership. Each with our own set of skills the other doesn't have. If we're both good at the same things, how would we deal with problems?"

She laughed, a strangled sound pulled through the thickness in her throat. She rubbed at her face, and her hand came back wet. "When did you become the insightful one?"

"I have my days." Jeremy chuckled, pulling them both to their feet. "You laughed. That's it. You can't be sad anymore." He picked her up, lifting her off the ground, and spun her until she was laughing so hard she couldn't breathe. He placed her down, her mind still spinning. Then he said, "It's a house rule. Already set in stone."

*He definitely had more than his share of days*, Winona thought. There was no doubt that taking in Jeremy had been one of the best choices she'd made since her parents passed away. All his weird quirks made every day a little more bearable than it had been before him. At this point, she woke up in the morning excited for whatever task they were going to accomplish together that day.

"My dad would have loved you," she murmured to herself as they sat back down. She peeked up at him as she took a spoonful of the stew. The small smile on Jeremy's face made it clear he'd heard her. She hid her own with another sip of dinner.

# YEAR 4 DGC, DAY 1

## FROM THE DESK OF PRESIDENT
## AMELIA SHAW

MY FELLOW AMERICANS,

I have recently met with Dr. Diego Rivera, the Office of Climate Affairs, Representatives from Canada, and the Environmental Protection Agency (EPA) Administrator to discuss the recent environmental developments. It has come to our attention that our efforts to combat the flooding of coastal territories have yielded minimal progress. The White House is recommending all Americans who currently reside in the afflicted areas relocate to protected zones. By my order, the National Guard has been deployed to assist in relocation efforts and will be available on a state-by-state basis.

In addition, due to saline influences from rising sea levels, several states are at risk for further action. These states have been placed under a boil water advisory on a county-by-county basis, effective immediately. Surface waters in listed states do not meet minimum standards for drinking. A significant portion of underground water resources are in review to determine saline influences and should be boiled prior to consumption until further notice.

Finally, it has been recommended to my administration that

Americans currently residing in Washington, Oregon, and California immediately relocate to the above-mentioned zones. The United States Army Corps of Engineers has been unsuccessful in implementing plans to slow and/or stop the spreading of wildfires in these areas. As a result, these states are now considered unlivable, and evacuation efforts have begun with support from the United States Air Force.

At this time, my office has heeded warnings from top scientists to prevent continued deterioration of the situation. It is our belief that these warnings have been provided, in effect, too late to be properly managed by my administration. My administration is unable to reverse the effects of climate change and, in agreement with Canadian Officials, has created a safe zone that spans from Colorado into Canada's Alberta province. My press secretary will disseminate a list of afflicted states to local news outlets.

Every state has been categorized into safety tiers. States designated as Black level have already fallen victim to climate-induced disasters and are no longer sustainable. According to our reconnaissance team, these states have effectively ceased to exist. States marked as Red level are presently grappling with climate-related disasters and should be regarded as uninhabitable. Orange level states are anticipated to experience disasters in the near future and should be evacuated.

Several states are still under review at this time and have been placed in the associated safety level. Do not assume this means you are currently living in a safe location. It is my belief these states will be placed in the red level in the near future, and plans to relocate should be immediately considered.

Effective immediately, my office will be relocating to the protected zones. Once relocated, additional memos will be released in accordance with policy for situations outlined in the UN Climate Agreement.

. . .

With Care,
   Amelia Shaw


<u>Afflicted States</u>

Orange Level States: Illinois, Indiana, Iowa, Kansas, Michigan, Minnesota, Wisconsin


Red Level States: Alabama, Arizona, Arkansas, California, Connecticut, Delaware, Georgia, Kentucky, Maine, Maryland, Massachusetts, Nevada, New Hampshire, New Jersey, New Mexico, New York, North Carolina, Ohio, Oklahoma, Oregon, Pennsylvania, South Carolina, Tennessee, Vermont, Virginia, Washington, West Virginia


Black Level States: Hawaii, Florida, Louisiana, Missouri, Rhode Island, Texas

# YEAR 8 DGC, DAY 205

## DIEGO

Diego stared at the amber liquid in his chipped glass and wondered, not for the first time, why no one had listened to him. Years. He had spent years on the research, and yet he was practically the only one left working at the facility. The LED bulbs above him flickered as the generator caught, and he swigged back the bitter whiskey. It settled into his stomach with a comfortable warmth, and he sighed. If only people had understood the magnitude of the crisis before the economy started to collapse. Before nature started to revolt. Why did they let it get this bad?

There was no turning back now.

"You know it's only two p.m., right?" Mia pointed out from the doorway. Diego shot her a look before pouring himself another shot.

"Have you looked outside? Time doesn't matter anymore." He didn't look up to meet her eyes. There weren't windows in the lab, but the sound of the news broadcast, the only station still running, echoed in his head all these hours later. "Climate crisis leads to another billion dead and counting this year." It wouldn't have been this bad. He had tried—with his research, with his speeches—but it was all useless. The world had carried on without the "Great Dr. Diego Rivera," and they both knew it. He didn't need her pity any more than he needed the world. If only the world had listened.

"And yet here you are trying to prove the nutritional content of alcohol. Just go home and drink your sorrows from the comfort of your couch." Mia flipped her brown curls over her shoulder and spun around. She took a step into the hallway before looking back at him with pity. "Good luck out there. Things aren't pretty."

"Will you be back tomorrow?" he called.

"There's nothing here for us anymore. I need to keep moving." When he didn't answer, she kept walking. He listened to her retreating footsteps before taking another hit of the whiskey. Mia was the last to leave. His faithful assistant and best friend for the last five years, and he couldn't even get her to stick it out. She had been there when his family passed away from the virus a few years prior. She had been there from the very start—cheering him on and sassing him into laughter fits when his experiments fell apart. She was the only one who got him. He stood up, determined to keep her around, to stop her, but his legs buckled under his weight, and he collapsed back into his chair. His glass went tumbling from his grasp before shattering against the tiled laboratory floor.

"Well...I guess it's just you and me," Diego mumbled as he grabbed the half-full whiskey bottle and flung it back. The bitter taste was comforting on his lips. At least he could always trust his whiskey. He slammed the bottle down, disgusted with himself. When did he become this person? He was Diego Rivera, chemist extraordinaire and environmentalist. He was better than this. He was more than this. He couldn't let Mia go—he needed her, needed her more than ever now that they were both alone. Needed her to remind him that he wasn't just a drunk when he couldn't see past the despair.

"Mia!" he screamed, the sound of his weak voice echoing in the empty room. "Mia—wait!" Diego pushed himself out of his chair and smashed into the counter, knocking over the bottle of whiskey. He watched in horror as it poured out over the keyboard and down the sides to the electrical outlets. He caught the flash of light as it sparked before flinging himself across the room.

At the door, he stood, mouth agape, as the spark lit up the stacks of laboratory notebooks that had been left haphazardly behind by careless lab assistants. He had meant to clean this up. But so much about the lab wasn't up to code anymore—he never knew where to start and ended up only making the place worse. The notebooks tumbled across the floor and smacked into one of the hoods. The fire licked up, and it hit half-empty leftover experiments.

Diego looked up at the broken fire sprinkles, another code violation, and cursed his lack of funding. If the government had backed his research... Well...it didn't matter anymore. What mattered was the heat of the fire. He could feel it from twenty feet away. He barely turned his head back down when glass shattered, the sound pinging around the room as shards flew. Diego rubbed a rough hand over his face. All this research. Years of studying ways for humanity to survive this. Gone. He choked back a sob before reaching for the door and heading out into the hallway in a rush. He looked behind him briefly to see smoke obscuring the flashes of light. Warning bells rang in his head, echoing the fire alarm, as he contemplated his options. He wanted to laugh at the irony of the situation, but he had more pressing concerns. Had Mia made it out?

Diego pushed past his addled brain as he coughed and stumbled down the hallway. Mia would have had to go this way.

He swiveled his head around, searching the empty offices for her, but when he didn't find anyone, he kept going. He needed to get out of there soon, or he would be blown to shreds. Without the sprinklers, the chemical fire would overheat the gas cylinders. They were old and unstable, well past their prime. Nothing like chemicals and gas to destroy what little he had left. It was only appropriate.

What about Mia?

"Mia!" he called again, his voice trembling. He stuck his head in a few doors, stumbling against frames and tripping over his own feet. Where was she?

"Mia," he cried. She's not going to be able to hear him over the sound of the laboratory starting to spark. The sound of the metal squealing under the pressure of the fire in the lab ricocheted through his head as he collapsed to the ground. Diego cried out as his face cracked against the linoleum. Why did he always need to drink when he was upset?

He was useless, and he knew it.

"This is what I get for being a drunk," he muttered into the floor. This was it—he didn't want to live anymore without his family. Without Mia around. This was his opportunity to leave behind all the misery and failed work. He listened to the sounds of the lab exploding behind him and closed his eyes. At least he died trying. Or having tried? He wasn't sure anymore.

"This is what you get for being a drunk," a voice grumbled. Diego looked up to see Mia standing over him. Her brown ringlets swung back and forth as she stood with a hand on her hip. The other reached down for him. He couldn't tell for certain, but it looked like she was shaking, a sweat breaking out over her forehead. The fire licked at the doors behind them and cast an oppressive blue glare. In the light, Mia's face was lit up a sickly blue. Yet somehow, she looked like an angel. His angel. God, he was so pathetic.

"Get up, you pain in my ass."

Okay, maybe she wasn't an angel, but she was definitely his savior.

"No, I don't want to. Let me fucking die."

"I'm not going to let you die." Mia grabbed his arm and pulled, but Diego held himself firmly against the ground. He didn't want to be this pathetic mess.

"Let me die," Diego slurred out as he hit his fist against the floor like a child. Mia shook her head at him before grabbing his hands and pulling him up with a grunt. She got him sitting before dropping his arm.

"Diego Emmanuel Rivera. Get off the floor before this building blows, or I swear I will not drink at your funeral," Mia scolded. The words cut through Diego's fog like a sharpened blade, and he relented. Not drink at his funeral? How dare she. The only way he wanted to be honored was with an old-fashioned. Anything less than that would be offensive.

"You drive a hard bargain." Diego lifted himself off the ground, staggering back into the wall, before Mia put herself under his shoulder.

"Sucker. I just know you better than you think." He gave her a sidelong glance as he pushed himself out from under her. Only Mia would put up with this ugly side of him. He wasn't always this pathetic—had pulled Mia off many sticky floors in their years of friendship. They were two sides of the same coin. Today, Mia was the better half of this coin. He linked their arms and did his best to keep pace as they dragged themselves out of the main lobby and into the open-air parking lot. They fell to the pavement, Diego half on top of Mia, and watched the building burn.

"There goes a good bottle of whiskey," Diego said, letting out a soft sigh.

"And five years of research."

"Research? No one cares about research. Haven't you

learned, Mia? Everything we were working toward means nothing now." Diego coughed up blackened mucus into hand, which he rubbed off onto the pavement. "You were right—there's nothing left for us here. The world doesn't care about us anymore."

Mia sighed as she wrapped an arm around his tender shoulders. "At least we have each other." Diego nodded as he pushed himself off the pavement and plodded over to his car. He rooted around for his keys before the lid popped on his trunk. He grabbed an unopened bottled of whiskey and slammed the trunk closed. Tapping the bottle against the metal, he motioned for Mia to join him as he got situated. Diego cracked the bottle open and lifted it to the burning building. "To the next chapter in our lives."

He took a swig and pushed it into her hand. Mia eyed the bottle and bit her lip for a few seconds before mimicking him. "To surviving the end and building a new world." She took a hefty sip of the amber liquid before scrunching up her nose and handing it back.

"Do you really think we'll make it?"

"You would be doing a disservice to the world if you didn't continue on." Mia elbowed him softly.

Diego smiled at his friend. It didn't matter how many times he had taken the blame when Mia screwed one of his experiments up, he never felt he deserved to have such a loyal friend. Mia was a blessing he didn't believe he deserved.

"Then I guess we better get going before the fire hits the gas tanks in the basement."

He handed her his keys. "I don't think open-container rules apply anymore, but you better drive regardless." Diego laughed before sliding off the car. The whiskey sloshed in the bottle, and he swayed with the motion before plopping into the passenger seat.

Mia got into the driver's seat, buckled them both up when Diego didn't try to, and started the engine. "What's next, boss?"

With a sudden surge of determination, Diego pointed down the street. "First—supplies. Then—we start working on solutions. We have a long road ahead of us."

# YEAR 5 AGC, DAY 270

## WINONA

"I don't understand," Jeremy said. Pulling the book out of Winona's hand, he lifted it to point at the image. It was a picture of what used to be the Amazon rainforest. She'd seen it many times, had been told about it over and over again, but it didn't change how the photo made her feel. Her stomach twisted as she stared down at the half-cut forest, large machines ripping away habitats, the smoke of the fossil fuels. The part that got her, that made her jaw ache from anger, was the jaguar in the corner of the photo. Most people would miss it, but it was the first thing her eyes focused on. It was caught between what was and what wasn't. How anyone could do that, she never understood.

"What don't you understand?" she asked, gently taking the book back and shutting it. She couldn't keep looking at that photo, or she would need to punch something.

"What was even the point of fossil fuels?"

Winona laughed, a harsh unwelcoming sound in the quiet of the living room. The living room, where they ended up spending their free time, had been dusted and furnished with what they could find or build. Jeremy had made a couch out of some wood and an old mattress. She covered it in a pair of mostly clean sheets. That was where they had been curled up near each other, talking about their pasts, when she grabbed the ecology book her parents had kept from the before. She ran her finger over the cover of the book before looking up at him, her face serious and focused. "There wasn't a point, Jeremy. People got greedy, people got lazy, and that was the end result. The destruction of the things the world needed to survive."

"But it was damaging the world. Why keep cutting down forests, spilling oil into the ocean, making plastics? I just…" Jeremy trailed off. He looked flustered, and she didn't blame him. If she could take away the history of their ancestors, she would have already done it.

She sighed. She wished she wasn't the one who had to show him this, but when she found out his family had left him in the dark, she couldn't leave it like that. Like her mother always said, if you don't know of the past, how do you protect the future?

Winona stood up, feeling the sudden loss of Jeremy pressed against her on the small couch, and placed the book on a table Jeremy had also built. It wasn't the nicest table she'd ever seen, but it was stable, and Jeremy was so proud of it. It was the first thing he did after she had run out of broken things to fix. He had smiled for hours after revealing it to her. She turned and held out her hand. "Come."

He grabbed her hand, stood up, and let her pull him out of the house. She twined their fingers, the warmth of his hand in hers releasing the anger she felt about the past, and gave his hand a squeeze. He squeezed hers back. She dropped his hand and let the sudden emptiness sting.

"Where are we going?" he finally asked when the house had turned to blur.

They had made it halfway back to the cliff where they had

first met. The sun shining past the thin tree trunks created long shadows that ran from them like rivers that no longer existed. She made a noise and kept walking. Jeremy kept pace, trying to twine their fingers together despite seeing her annoyance build with his repeated question.

"Do you think you could just walk in silence?" she said, shooting him a sidelong glance.

"No. You would hate that. Imagine how silent and boring that would be." Jeremy knocked his hip into her and stuck out his tongue. "Imagine how much better your life is now that I'm here."

She laughed despite herself. "You know, it was quite enjoyable before I had to start listening to you talk. And sing. And hum. And—"

He cut her off. "Okay. Fine. I like to talk, but you're not so quiet yourself. You haven't shut up in three weeks."

She rolled her eyes. The cliffside was quickly approaching, and she stopped them a few feet before. She let go of his hand and sat on the edge of the cliff, careful to keep her eyes trained on the crest of the ocean against the sky. He joined her, wrapping an arm around her shoulders. She leaned into it. For a second, she thought about rolling him off her, but the weight made her feel just a little bit less anxious.

"Why are we here?" he asked.

She pointed out toward the water. "Do you see that dark spot out there?"

He looked around for a minute. "The one glistening in the sun?"

"Yes," she said. The spot had been there her entire life. Her father had been the first to show her back when she was a little kid. It was smaller then, barely the size of her tiny palm if she held it out in front of her. Now it was twice the size of her palm. Before, it didn't glisten, but now it shined in the sun like a beacon. Not in the way the ocean did. It didn't reflect the sun, didn't flow the way the water did. It reminded her that there was a reason people didn't survive the before, and maybe that wasn't always a bad thing.

"What is it?"

"That," she said, "is an oil slick. Not long before society started to collapse, a small tanker capsized out there. It was old, rusted out, and took on water. No one alive now saw it happen, but the story got passed down. When the tanker went down, it was too close to the ocean floor, and it cracked the tanks holding the oil."

She watched Jeremy's face as he stared out at the ever-growing spot. His eyes had never been so wide, so haunted. His normally cheerful expression had soured and hardened. The boy sitting next to her no longer felt like Jeremy, and she wished, again, that it wasn't her words causing it. "It's been leaking out, slowly but surely, over the last couple of decades. It hasn't hit the shore yet, but it's been killing the wildlife. Sometimes I'll find a fish floating, covered in slick, hitting the rocky cliffside. None of them are alive by the time I see them."

Jeremy sighed, letting out a long breath. "Did they not have other solutions to get around besides oil? Why was it so fucking special?"

Winona slumped her shoulders so she could snuggle into Jeremy's side. A tiny alarm went off in her brain, but she ignored it. They had built a relationship where this was commonplace, and she didn't want to think twice about it. "My dad had a book about something called sustainable resources. I really haven't read much about it, but you might like it. I'll find it for you."

"That would be cool." Jeremy squeezed her closer to him and placed his chin on her head.

She watched the sun slowly crawling across the sky, painting stripes of vibrant red and orange, before focusing on the reality of what the oil spill really meant. There was nothing she wanted more than to enjoy this moment, but it was impossible when the past was glaring at her. "One day, it'll get in the water supply, and we'll have to find a new water source."

Jeremy frowned. "You know, that's just another reason we should think about moving."

She ripped herself away from him faster than he could turn his head and stood up. The pounding of her heart gave away her fear. She wasn't ready to leave her home. She frowned, arms crossed in front of her. "We're not moving," she snapped.

He started to make a noise, but she was already walking away. Calling over her shoulder, she said, "It's time to get dinner started. I'll meet you back at the house." She didn't wait for his response.

* * *

OVER DINNER, Jeremy asked her question after question until her mouth was dry from speaking. He wanted to hear all her stories, all the stories he didn't get from his family that she held close to her heart as her most vivid memories of her parents. Bedtime was never complete without a story of the past, a lesson to learn and dream about. When his questions had finally ceased, she took the opportunity to ask him some questions. Specifically, one she had wanted to know since they met, since she had told him all about her past. She moved her empty bowl of tofu and vegetables to the side of her and linked her fingers under her chin.

"Since I've answered all your questions, do you mind answering mine?"

Jeremy smiled at her. "Anything. What do you want to know?"

"Well, I've told you what happened to my parents, but you've never said anything about your family. I want to know about them." She pouted at him. "Please."

Jeremy had a pained look on his face. She forced her hands to stay put, to not reach out and comfort him, but it hurt her. Almost as much as it hurt to not be able to save her parents. His face made her heart ache, and she softly added, "You don't need to."

Jeremy sighed, smoothing his face out as he focused his attention on her. "No. I do. You've been honest with me. It's just…" He frowned. Jeremy suddenly looked twenty years older, the weight of his story crushing him. "It was my fault."

She stared at him, her mouth slightly agape. "There's no way. I don't fucking believe that for a minute."

"You know how I'm able to drink anything?" He paused but didn't give her a second to answer. "When I was younger, no one realized the implications of that. They just thought I was lucky. But as I got older and went out hunting with my brothers, things became more complicated. It was fine when I brought home a deer or a duck, but when I gathered mushrooms? A lot of times, I would try them, not get sick, and bring them home to get everyone else sick."

She frowned at him, continuing the fight to keep her hands to herself. Winona stood up and started to kill the dying fire in the firepit. Jeremy was so focused on the table she wanted to let him have his space to talk. Jeremy didn't look up, using one hand to pick at the splinting wood of the table. It was hard to tell by the firelight, but she was confident he was holding back tears.

"Well, they sent me to get water at the creek near the house. I didn't know. I couldn't have. But the water had been contaminated from leftover waste at an old engineering plant a few miles north. It had leaked, but the water didn't look dirty. I swear. I only know where the contamination came from because I passed it when I left." He turned to look at her with pleading eyes. "I swear I didn't know."

She watched him carefully, her face firmly set into a concerned frown. "How would you?"

"Exactly!" He turned back to frown at the table as his foot started to bounce under the table. "I should have checked, should have asked someone to test it, but we thought it was clean. We all drank it. Everyone else started throwing up after a day, but I was still fine..."

He hiccuped as tears started to spill. "When everyone else started to get sick, I thought I was helping, since I wasn't, so I brought home fresh food and water every day. I thought..."

"That's not your fault," Winona said, walking over to him. Ignoring all her reservations, she wrapped her arms around him, leaning her forehead against his shoulder as he shook with tears.

"I should have known something was wrong." The pain in his voice was raw. She'd never seen him so broken. Her urge to comfort him grew, but she held back. She felt so horrible for him. She couldn't imagine feeling the weight of what he felt. Even if she didn't blame him, she knew he blamed himself, and that was worse than anything she could imagine.

"How would you?" she echoed. The words were useless, and they both knew it.

Jeremy leaned back to look at her. "I've never told anyone before." He sniffled. "Am I a bad person?"

She gave him an incredulous look. "Bad person? Because you didn't know the water was contaminated? Absolutely not. It's not your fault. There is not a way in hell any of this is your fault, Jeremy."

His lip trembled, but he nodded before collapsing into her arms. They stayed there, Winona holding Jeremy up as he processed his grief that had been sitting on his chest for far too long until the candles they lit died, and the whole area was drenched in the yellow moonlight. She didn't care if they stayed until sunrise. Jeremy deserved to know he couldn't keep blaming himself for the problems the before created for the people of the after.

It wasn't his fault, and she would remind him every day of his life if he needed it.

# YEAR 5 AGC, DAY 269

## DEE

EVERY DAY since their parents had passed away had been the same as the day before. In the morning, Dee would wake with the sunrise and head downstairs to make coffee while Rowan slept in. By the time he woke up, Dee would be tending to the household chores—pumping water from the well for them to drink, tending to the minuscule garden, cleaning up any messes left out from the day before. Rowan would spend the morning staring at old photos of their parents and sighing.

Every afternoon, Rowan would head out into the woods to look for food while Dee tried to discreetly search for the blue notebook. When he made it home, she would do her best to pretend she hadn't been turning the house upside down in a wasteful pursuit of nothing. Every day, when he came home with nothing, he would look at her with the same distaste she felt in herself. She would pretend she didn't see it and suggest they play in memory of their parents. Rowan would agree, he always agreed, but they only spent the game time in silence as they passed a new bottle of gin between them. Their dad had bottled a surprising amount of bathtub gin before he passed. It seemed to never run out.

It had been several days since their parents had been buried, but Dee wasn't any closer to finding the blue notebook her mom had left for her. She wasn't any closer to knowing what she was supposed to do. She definitely wasn't any closer to finding out whatever Rowan was hiding from her. She couldn't decide which was worse, but no matter what, she felt like she'd been dealt a pretty crappy hand. She needed something to budge before she just gave up and gave into their circumstances.

She took a deep breath and centered herself. Tonight would be different. Tonight she would get somewhere with something. She plastered a smile on her face and walked through the front door and into the living room. Rowan was where he sat every day after a useless forage. His body was sprawled out on the couch, eyes shut. She envied how relaxed he was, envied how relaxed he could be while she only stressed out further.

"Are you up for another game tonight?" she asked, her smile faltering a little. Rowan opened one eye and smiled at her lazily. She bit back her annoyance. It must be nice to be the relaxed twin.

"Not getting tired of it yet? We've played every day for almost a week."

She was exhausted of playing the same game, but she kept hoping to get another result. Game plus alcohol had to eventually equal secret. She had a sneaking suspicion that Rowan also knew where the notebook was, but she couldn't confirm it. She was determined to get somewhere, and if that meant living in the same cycle until something new happened, she would do it.

"It makes me feel closer to them," she lied. The game and the alcohol only made her head and stomach hurt, but she wasn't willing to give up until she knew whatever it was that he did. Maybe this secret would help uncover what she was supposed to do next. Solve two problems at once.

Rowan frowned, opening his eyes completely to watch her. "I miss them."

His words were soft and fragile. She let them linger in the air between them before responding. "Do you wonder if they wanted us to do more than wallow in sorrow and play board games?"

Rowan huffed, his face scrunching up. "You can never just leave anything alone, can you?" He stood up, anger blowing off him in waves, and went to get the game off the shelf she had placed it on earlier. He shook it in her direction. "Are you going to get the gin?"

"Mom and Dad would have wanted us to keep living," she said softly, hoping that by lowering her voice he would be less angry with her. It was a wasted effort; they had the same argument every night, and every night, they just played games until they were too drunk to talk to each other. It was a vicious cycle she kept hoping to break. All she wanted was answers, guidance on how to lead them into this future without their parents.

"You sound like a broken record. It's barely been a week. Can't you just miss them for a little while longer?" He was sitting at their dining room table, the board spread out in front of him. He shook the bag of tiles. "Maybe tonight you'll get to go first."

"Do you think I don't miss them? Because I do. I wish they were here to give us the guidance I so desperately want. But they aren't here anymore, and someone needs to pick up the pieces…" She trailed off. This line of thinking wouldn't work with Rowan. He didn't care, he just missed their parents and wanted to wallow in it. She could see it in his face. Dee placed the bottle of gin on the table next to them and stuck her hand in the bag. She pulled out an "A" tile and smiled genuinely. "Look at that."

"Maybe your luck is about to change, sister. Might even win tonight."

She narrowed her eyes. "I'll make you a deal," she started. "If I win tonight, you finally tell me whatever secret you are holding on to."

Rowan stuck out his hand confidently. "Shake on it." He laughed. "There's no way you're going to win tonight."

Looking down at her tiles, Dee took a deep breath. If she could just play her cards right, maybe she'd finally get somewhere. All the days of arguing back and forth might be worth it for whatever secret he had up his sleeve.

By the end of the game, Dee was fifty points ahead, and Rowan was sweating. She even managed to spell out "secret" at one point. "Give it up. I'm going to win."

Rowan fiddled with his last three tiles before placing "eat" on the board.

"See? I told you I would win." Dee couldn't control her excitement. She had finally won and was going to get everything she asked for. Answers, finally.

Rowan sputtered. "Well, you see, I don't know if you really want to know anything." Dee sighed. He didn't get like this often, but every once in a while, Rowan would get nervous and just start talking. "It's really not that big of a secret," he continued. Dee tuned him out as he continued to blabber about her not really wanting to know anything.

She let him go on in circles for a few minutes before cutting him off. "But I do want to know," she said sternly. "Are you going to tell me?"

Dee was getting tired, and she just wanted him to spit it out. It couldn't be that bad. She chewed on her lip as Rowan took another long drink of the almost-empty bottle. She could have sworn the bottle was mostly full when they started. Dee couldn't remember, but she didn't think they had that much to drink.

"Promise me you won't get upset," Rowan hedged.

Of course, she wanted to believe she wouldn't get upset, but she had no idea what he was going to say. Based on how long it took to get it out of him, she didn't think she was going to like whatever it was. In fact, she was confident she was going to hate it. It was better knowing than not, she reminded herself.

"I promise," Dee said. The lie fell out easily, slipping out as she reached for the bottle. She held it in her hand and contemplated if she really needed any more. But the gin wasn't nearly as harsh as it felt originally a few days ago, and they were finally getting somewhere. She took a sip. It was smooth going down her throat.

"Mom cheated on Dad before we were born." The words cut through the haze of alcohol. They forced Dee out of her seat and across the room. She shoved her face into Rowan's until their noses touched.

"Don't lie, Rowan. Not after all this." Dee searched his eyes for the truth.

"You promised not to get upset."

She blew out her hot breath into his face and watched him flinch at the sharp scent of alcohol.

Rowan frowned. "Please. There's more."

"There's more?" Dee backed up and pointed an angry finger at Rowan, stabbing him in the chest. "What more?"

"You're not Dad's." Rowan pinned her with sad eyes. The words hit her like a ton of bricks. She searched Rowan's face for signs he was lying, but all she found was honesty in his eyes. He was speaking the truth, and she knew it. Her mind spun, and she collapsed to the ground. Her head hit the wooden floor with a loud slam. The pain pushed the last of her alcohol haze away. How had everyone kept that from her? Why had they kept it from her? Dee's mind spun wildly with angry thoughts about betrayal and distaste. How could Mom have cheated? She closed her eyes.

"Are you okay?" Rowan asked.

Dee opened her eyes to see him leaning over her. "Of course I'm not okay, Rowan. I've been lied to my entire life, and you knew."

Dee just stared at him, recategorizing every little thing she had brushed off as a fluke into a list of why they weren't really twins. From their opposite personalities to the differences in her pale skin to his dark. She took in his face, the small dent right next to his left eye when he swung it into a counter as a kid. The way his lips created a straight line while hers lifted up like their mom's. The way his nose crinkled, just like their dad's, but hers never had. It was a wonder she believed them in the first place the more she thought about it.

What else had they kept from her?

## WINONA

WINONA WATCHED Jeremy artfully swish his net in the water. He wasn't wearing a shirt, and his tanned, scarred back made her spend more time than appropriate for friends staring. She'd gotten used to his goofy smile and slightly annoying shrug after the first night with him. After he fixed the stairs, he moved to the roof. Winona couldn't seem to kick him out—not when he was making himself so useful.

Winona didn't want to admit it, but she was starting to enjoy his company and didn't want to kick him out. She was getting more and more comfortable having him around. He was easygoing, helpful, and always there to hold her up when she needed him.

It wasn't lost on her that he was her only company. Or that this situation was originally supposed to be temporary.

"Empty," Jeremy called before throwing the net back in. They hadn't been able to catch a single fish since a few days after Jeremy had shown up. Perhaps the water was finally tired of feeding her. She threw her net after a shadow in the water. She knew it wasn't the water but the oil slick killing off the few fish left in the Pacific. When she pulled it back up, an empty plastic water bottle sparkled in the sunlight.

"We're not going to be able to survive like this," Jeremy pointed out as he plucked the bottle out of her grasp. He lifted it up and inspected it. "What was so important about these anyway? Were canteens not good enough?" He threw it to the ground angrily and pressed his foot into it. It made a satisfying crunching sound before the cap popped off, pinging off a jutted-out rock and landing in the salt water.

"I honestly don't know. I wasn't around in the before." She kneeled on the rocky gravel and stretched her arm into the water. It was warm, too warm, and made her arm tingle. Winona grasped the cap, pulled herself back up, and shook the wetness off her arm. Putting the cap back onto the bottle, she spun on her heel and handed it to Jeremy. Then she grabbed the water bucket to fill it. "My parents used to tell horror stories about the trash island in the sea. I can't imagine why anyone would care more about a plastic bottle than the world that cares for them, but throwing it back isn't fixing the issue."

Jeremy gripped the handle next to her hand, and she smiled at him as he took it from her. Jeremy dipped the bucket into the water as she shouldered the nets. "We don't get anywhere if we don't learn from our ancestor's mistakes," Winona added as they turned toward the burnt forest. "I swear my parents started every morning and ended every day reminding me of that."

The water splashed against the bucket as they began their uphill trek through the brittle forest. For a while, it was the only sound around them besides the crunching of the dead leaves. Animals didn't usually forage near here anymore. She couldn't remember the last time she'd seen a deer. They were lucky to find a mosquito. Nothing can kill a mosquito. No bugs made crops hard to cultivate. There was a limited number of plants that could grow without bugs, and her garden consisted of plants on that list. She was lucky the weather was so consistent that everything grew year-round. She was grateful she had such a beautiful garden. "Do you have anything in mind for dinner tonight? Peppers were looking healthy this morning. Maybe some vegetable stew?"

"Are you planning to cook? I'm not sure it'll be edible," he joked. She rolled her eyes at him but stayed silent. Jeremy's cooking continued to get better over the weeks. He could mix anything from the garden, and it tasted like heaven. She couldn't even come up with a measly complaint, especially after his vegetable stir-fry the other night. Her dry mouth filled with salvia just thinking about it. Jeremy poked her with his elbow. "I'll make spicy vegetable soup."

"Was it that hard to say without being snotty first?" she asked.

He stuck out his tongue. By the time they got back to the house, the sky was darkening to its usual deep red-orange. Winona was exhausted, less so than when she was alone, but hours in the sun tending to the garden while Jeremy fixed or built something and then fishing in the afternoon without shade was a lot, despite how tedious and repetitive it was.

"Do you think there are others?" Jeremy asked, chopping peppers on the patio table. His eyes were trained on the knife, and his movements were jerky.

Winona peered out into the deep-red sky, the product of years of abuse to the earth that had fostered generations of people before them. She knew what he was really getting at, but she ignored it. "I don't know, but I hope they understand the magnitude of our survival. The magnitude of work we need to accomplish. If we don't protect and nurture the one thing that cares for us, we'll turn out like every other generation before us."

"Do you always have to be such a downer, Winona?" Jeremy said, groaning.

"I wouldn't have to be if people learned from their own

mistakes," she snapped. "Besides, one of us has to keep a firm hold on reality." Winona pushed away from the table and plodded over to the fire to tend to it. Poking the flames, she took a steadying breath before looking up at Jeremy. "My mom, she loved to read, you know? She was a big history buff, and without anyone to keep me company…I relied on her books for company. Do you know how many times we've repeated our own history? How many genocides we've watched happen without stopping them? The earth is just another victim to our ancestors." Winona sighed before walking back to the table. She lay across the bench and stared up at the orange-tinged sky. "I'm sorry. I just don't want to treat the world or its people as objects the way our ancestors did."

Jeremy gave her a sad smile as he piled his chopped food into the metal pot. "I don't know that much about the before, but…" He bit his lip and walked silently to the fire. As he got the pot situated, Winona rolled off the bench to walk up to him.

"But what?"

Jeremy pushed the vegetables around for a few minutes as Winona fought herself. She wanted to press Jeremy to finish, to agree with her, but she knew that pushing him wasn't going to help the situation. She had had a lot of serious conversations with Jeremy over the last few weeks, and she trusted him to see her side. Jeremy cared about the world as much as she did. But a small part of her was on edge. She wasn't sure if she'd be able to continue this little back-and-forth if he couldn't see the importance of this conversation.

"I'm worried the others, if they exist, will not know the past as you do. I didn't know as much before I met you, and I'm sure there is much more to learn."

"What are you trying to say, Jeremy?" Winona cocked an eyebrow at him. She berated herself for believing she could avoid this subject. He gave her a sheepish smile before walking to grab the bucket full of water. She huffed but did her best to keep silent as she waited for him to return. She'd gotten better at keeping her mouth shut now that she was used to Jeremy, but sometimes it was impossible not to give her opinion.

"I just think…" They watched each other. "I think you need to share your knowledge," he finally finished, before tripping over a root sticking out of the ground.

Winona watched in slow motion as he smashed into the ground. His arm, weighed down with the water, smacked into the pot of food. Jeremy screeched as his hand seared against the hot metal, and the smell of burnt flesh filled the air. The smell made Winona gag as her mouth dropped open. The smell was quickly overpowered by the scent of burning earth. She felt rooted to the ground, watching Jeremy struggle to right himself, backdropped by her garden catching fire. When had it gotten so dry? Her mind tried to recall the last rainstorm, but it had been longer than she could even remember.

Winona stared, wide-eyed, at the dried-out trees and shed going up in the growing fire. A screeching sound, she quickly realized was coming from her, filled the air. Her throat stung as it filled with smoke.

Jeremy got to his feet, pulling himself from his shock faster than Winona could process, and started yelling, "Hurry. Get what you need. Now."

Jeremy gave her a shove, forcing her to move. "We need to go now, Nona. Right fucking now."

Winona struggled, her feet like lead, but managed to stumble into the house and up the stairs to her room. Acrid smoke had already taken hold in her home. She squinted her eyes as they started to burn. She didn't know what to take. She didn't know what to do. She couldn't leave her home.

"Nona! Hurry!" Jeremy's words slid through her brain like molasses—slow and bittersweet. He had to be close, but she couldn't see him anywhere in the smoke. It was horrifying how quickly the house caught fire. "Please, Nona."

His words were enough to kick-start her self-preservation skills, and she ran around the room to grab a few belongings and outfits. She ran out of the room, the heat starting to become oppressive, before stopping at her parents' door. A sweat broke out across her back. She hadn't been inside since they passed, but there was a family photo, and she needed something to keep the memory of her parents alive. She couldn't leave without it despite Jeremy's screams. She threw the door open, covering her face against the flames that overpowered one side of the room, and started searching the dresser.

The wooden frame that held the picture was burning hot, but the glass had managed to save the photo from catching fire. She smashed the heel of her hand into the glass and pulled the burnt photo out before turning and sprinting out of the house. Jeremy, watching her carefully, reached out to hug her as she collapsed into his arms and started to cough. She sniffled into his shirt as he rubbed her back.

"It'll be okay," he said. Winona shook her head before pushing him off her.

"No. No, it won't. This is all your fault. I should have never brought you in." Winona grabbed her belongings off the dirt before storming off into the forest. She didn't want to look back at her ruined home, didn't want to look at the hurt she knew would be on Jeremy's face. To say those words after the story he told her was cruel, but right now, she didn't care. Part of her thought she might never care again.

"Winona! Wait! Please," Jeremy called, racing after her. She focused on the sound of leaves crunching under their feet so she could ignore the cracking of her home as it started to collapse behind them.

"No. I should never have brought you into my fucking home." She sped up, heading away from the sea and toward whatever new future she had. A future she didn't want. A future Jeremy forced on her. "I knew I would regret this."

"I'm sorry, Winona," Jeremy whispered. She barely heard the words over the crackling fire and her own despair. She didn't respond. Didn't look behind her. Tried her best to ignore his footsteps behind her. She didn't need him, didn't need anyone. She was better off alone. Alone she still had her home. She still had her garden. Why did she let him stay?

"I didn't mean to," he pleaded. Winona ignored him—hatred and anger burning through her as the heat of the fire started to cool from the distance. The sudden change in the air made her back cold, and she shivered. She made it another hundred feet before she stopped.

A loud crash came from where her home most likely didn't stand anymore. She spun around to catch the last of it hit the ground. Jeremy moved into her, carrying his backpack and a canteen for them, shielding her from the blaze that was once her house. Furious anger and bittersweet appreciation for Jeremy's forethought warred.

Everything was wrong, and the panic in her chest was building faster than she could manage. She collapsed onto the soft dirt and cried. Her emotions battled—pulling her around like a turbine. The loss of her family, her home, her life rushed over her like a tidal wave. She couldn't breathe, the pain of everything so overwhelming that she started gasping. Jeremy kneeled in front of her and pulled her into his good arm. She fought him, doing her best to avoid his burnt hand, but he didn't let go. He just whispered "I'm sorry" over and over again.

Her tears were hot on her cheeks for barely a second before Jeremy wiped them away. Despite her anger, Winona gave into him and let herself be comforted by his presence and words. The fire inside her started withering away, covered by the darkness of hopelessness and the pain of loss. She didn't know how to feel about Jeremy at that moment, but he was the only thing left. Did she really have a choice?

"We'll get through this together," Jeremy said, kissing her head.

She could barely talk, her voice hoarse from crying, but she managed to whisper an apology for her harsh words. No matter the situation, they were too cruel for her to have even thought them. He nodded his head against her hair. She turned to stare at the ashes of her life that lay before her.

How would she survive this new world? How had her parents survived?

# YEAR 5 AGC, DAY 280

### DIEGO

DIEGO WATCHED Mia carefully clean out each of the glass vials. She checked every glass for cracks or debris by holding them up to the sunlight. She was so much more meticulous than he was. It was a wonder she tolerated living in the same house as him. He pulled his eyes from her cascading curls. They were swinging halfway down her back as she danced in front of the sink and turned to look at the pile of failed experiments Diego had left by the back door. It was a shame how far he had fallen.

Diego bit his lip as he turned to look down at the notebook he was holding open. It was empty. The page blank. Just like it had been for the last few days. He didn't know where to get started. He wanted to shake it like an Etch A Sketch, but instead of wiping away his words, it would write out his feelings for him. All he knew how to do was drink and write research papers. He didn't express words of affection. That wasn't who he was. How was he supposed to explain to his best friend, his confidante, that he had fallen for her so intensely he couldn't think straight?

He focused on Mia's happy form—now putting dishes away —he felt the familiar swell of happiness in his chest. The light

Mia brought to his life was the only one he felt nowadays. He used to be something, used to be someone, and now he was washed up and barely surviving.

"What are you doing?" she asked, turning her bright smile on him. Her smile didn't reach her eyes, and he frowned at the dark circles and disappointment that stared back at him.

"Nothing, nothing. Just thinking. Another useless exercise to fix this." He slammed the notebook closed as if she were going to read his unwritten feelings. Raking a hand through his hair, he stood up and grabbed the closest bottle of bathtub gin. It stung in ways that good whiskey never had, but he didn't have a choice. They learned fairly quickly they couldn't handle any of the processed foods they found in abandoned stores. Everything organic had died, withered away with the crisis, and Diego was incapable of growing anything new.

Just another failing to add to the list.

Dr. Raye's study had some nasty side effects. The vomiting, the pain, it didn't seem worth it. They were barely surviving, and he wasn't sure how much longer that would go on. Collectively, they had lost over sixty pounds, and it was obvious in the way their bones showed in their legs and rib cages.

Sure, they could eat the grass or the leaves around them, but they didn't provide anything. The alcohol gave them the bare minimum. They needed real food, or they would soon be too weak to manage. Diego knew they were lucky that the experiment worked well enough that they could survive on alcohol alone, but he didn't feel it.

"You can't just drink your days away, Diego," Mia said. She crossed her arms and leaned against the counter. He frowned as he took in her graying temples. Mia wasn't old enough to be graying. Her mom had never grayed. He was confident it was all the stress she held in. He wished he could lift it, but nothing was working.

"It's not like any of my experiments are helping us. What else is there to do?" Diego placed the bottle on the chipped counter and started pacing. "We're going to die in this fucking house. A house we stole."

Mia gave him an incredulous look. "Everyone dies, Diego, but that doesn't mean it's our time."

Diego stared ahead, keeping his eyes trained on the streaked windows and avoiding the desperate look he knew she was giving him. The dense trees that surrounded their borrowed home swayed in the evening breeze. It was serene and beautiful. Diego didn't want to leave it just yet. He wasn't ready to give up, but it felt like he already had.

Mia placed a soft hand on his shoulder. "Are you ready to say goodbye?"

Diego shook her off and walked to the creaky glass back door. He threw it open dramatically. He stepped out into the cooling evening air and took a deep breath. The smell of nature filled his lungs and brought a smile to his face. The air outside Denver was sweeter than anything they had in Florida. As the years passed in solitude, the scent only grew. "No, I don't think I'll ever be ready to say goodbye."

"Then we need to continue our fight." Mia quietly padded back into the kitchen and returned, holding the bottle of gin. "We will find a way. We've solved the world's most complex problems. The least we can do is solve our own." She took a sip of the liquid, her nose scrunching up, before taking a seat on the rotting wooden swing.

"What if there isn't a way?" Diego's shoulders slumped as he joined her on the swing. He was tired of feeling so hopeless.

"I've let you wallow in your self-pity for too long. It's time you step up. You are the great Dr. Diego Rivera. You are better than this. I've seen you do things no one else could. It's time to do that again."

"No, Mia. You are better than this. I'm just a drunkard." He grabbed the bottle out of her hand and finished it off before chucking it out into the wilderness. He tried to brush off the stupid gesture, but destroying nature was what got them here. The world had pushed back, and humanity had collapsed. He memorized where the bottle went. He would go get it later. "I'm just a drunk who managed to keep you around. I'm just a burden to you. Why do you stay around?"

Warmth burned in Diego's stomach and chest as he kept his eyes locked on Mia's shining blue eyes. Blue eyes like the ocean they left behind. The ocean was his home, just like Mia. Wonderful, caring Mia. He wished she felt the same, but he knew she didn't. Mia gave him a sad smile before placing a hand on his cheek.

"I stay around because I know you can do this. Even when you don't." Mia dropped her hand and stood up to grab the bottle. He wanted to tell her he shouldn't have thrown it, but the words died on his tongue. It didn't matter.

Diego couldn't pull his eyes away, watching her walk back carefully, holding the shattered bottle. She had always been too good for him. Mia frowned at it when she made it back to the porch.

"What if I can't?"

"You can. There's no doubt that you can." Mia watched him with earnest, and the heat in his gut burned sharply. "It's time to try again."

"It's time to die, Mia. We've already cheated death too many times." The words burned. He knew they were dumb, but he couldn't get himself to take them back.

Mia huffed. Her sweet, loving demeanor melted off her, replaced by hot waves of annoyance. Diego smiled at the ceiling of the patio. This was the Mia he loved the most. His little spitfire. No one will ever be able to temper the flames that burned within Mia, not even him.

"Diego. I swear, if you don't get over yourself, I'm going to…" She trailed off. Diego looked down to see her standing, her shoulders squared. Her hair was blowing in the wind, reminding him of a Greek goddess.

"Going to what, Mia? What are you going to do?" Diego snapped. He meant it as a joke, but the anger rolling off Mia turned sharp.

"I'm going to leave you behind." And just like that, Diego's burning turned to ice. He shivered in the breeze as a frown drew his mouth down. Mia had never threatened to leave before. She couldn't. She was his rock. She was his person. If she left, what did Diego have left to live for?

"Mia," he strangled out.

"No. Don't 'Mia' me. Get off your ass and do something." She turned and marched into the house. Reaching to close the door behind her, she added, "I'm not dying here."

Diego couldn't pull his eyes from the spot she had left. The image of her telling him she would leave burned in his brain. He had no choice. He needed to get up and prove to her that he could do it. He could save them. He pushed himself up, forcing his weak legs to carry him, and walked out into the grass. It was soft against his bare feet.

He kneeled down and ran the grass through his fingers before ripping it out. He pulled furiously, chunks of dirt flying behind him. They thudded against the patio. He dug and dug until his fingers were sore and ragged. Leaning back, he stared at the hole in the dirt.

"You're going to be a garden one day," he huffed, his breath coming in quick pants. "Even if it's the last thing I do."

Diego looked up and out into the trees. His breath caught in his throat as he took in the sight. A beautiful, brownish-gray baby wolf sat with its head tilted, watching him, curious. But it wasn't the wolf that forced him to his feet slowly, hands raised in front of him. It was the naked girl. She stood next to the wolf, mirroring its pose, with her long blond hair cascading like streams down her front side. Leaves were trapped in the tresses as if she had rummaged through the bushes before popping out to watch him. Her body was thin but muscular—like the wolf at her side. Diego pulled his eyes back to the creature, and with a squint, he amended his assumption. It wasn't a wolf. It couldn't be—they were extinct. It was a coyote.

Diego took a small step toward the girl, his body trembling. Whether it was from the alcohol, the exhaustion, or the sheer terror of the coyote's newly barred teeth, he wasn't sure. All he knew was that he felt compelled to offer the girl help. She may not want it, but he had to at least try.

"Hello," he called out, taking another terrifying step. They were maybe fifty feet apart, and he could just make out her murky blue eyes framed by her sun-kissed skin. The setting sun was just enough light to give him a vague idea of her features.

"Mine," the girl's voice sounded off, almost like a growl, as she raised a hand and pointed behind him. He turned around and looked at the house.

"The house?"

She nodded, baring her teeth. The coyote stood up and leaned toward him. He let out a soft growl that made Diego shiver.

"You live here?" Diego took a step back as he gestured toward their temporary home. The girl nodded again.

"Mine. Soon." The girl gave Diego one more withering look before backing out of sight. The coyote waited, watching him carefully, before trailing behind her. With them out of sight, Diego let out the breath he'd been holding back and ran into the house. He locked the door and closed the curtains before screaming Mia's name, his voice strained. What the hell did he just see?

"What? What's going on?" Mia asked as she strolled into the room. She had a towel wrapped around her head and some pajamas on. She must have taken a quick bath while he was outside. She didn't look as mad as before, but he knew she would hold on to that fire for a long time.

"There's someone living in the forest," Diego sputtered.

Mia stared at him for a minute, and he watched her process what he said. "That's it. You've drunk too much." She shook her head and grabbed the half-empty bottle off the counter. "If you don't control yourself, you're going to lose every viable brain cell you have in that noggin of yours. I'm starting to think you've already lost most of them."

"No. Mia. Really. There's someone out there. I saw her." Mia paused, her arm stretched to place the bottle above the fridge.

"What do you mean 'you saw her'?" She cradled the bottle, no doubt wondering if it was a good time to start drinking. Whether it was because she thought Diego was finally losing it —he wasn't so sure she was wrong about that nowadays—or if she was concerned about this person looming outside, he didn't know. What he did know was that they were going to have to cut their drinking down if they were going to make it out of this situation.

"Put the bottle away, Mia. We have to be clearheaded if we want to deal with this."

Mia laughed but shelved the bottle. "You? Clearheaded? That's like asking the sun to not shine. You haven't been all there since I pulled you out of the lab you burned down." Her bitter tone cut, but he admitted, if only to himself, that he deserved that.

"I've fucked up a lot lately. Maybe more than just lately. I get it. But I'm serious. We need to help her. I think she's living with coyotes—like full-on Tarzan of Colorado." Diego sat down on one of the stools that flanked the bar top and patted the seat next to him. Mia twisted her lips in thought before reluctantly taking a seat next to him. He looked at her concerned eyes. "I need to do something good. I need to contribute again, and she felt like a sign."

"A sign you need to get off your ass?" Mia barked out a dry laugh before shaking her head. "Why do I always let you talk me into the craziest ideas?"

"Because I am salt to your margarita." Diego plastered on a smile and watched Mia's face twitch as she tried not to laugh. At least he could still make her laugh.

"One of us is definitely salty." Mia cocked an eyebrow.

"That doesn't sound like a no. Wonderful. I'm just going to take some clothing and leave it out for her." Mis sighed but kept her opinions to herself as Diego stood up and pranced to the bedrooms.

"One of these days, Diego…," Mia called as he passed by with a stack of folded clothing he thought would fit the girl. He gingerly opened the back door and placed it on the glass patio table. He paused to look into the forest. Was she willing to let him help?

# YEAR 6 DGC, DAY 155

## ELIZABETH

"When are you going out for supplies?" Elizabeth asked, poking her head out of her bedroom doorway. She looked down the hall, but no one was upstairs with her. Shrugging, she made her way downstairs and out the back door. Her parents were staring at each other with a look she couldn't comprehend. Someone was mad, but Elizabeth wasn't sure who or why.

"Mom? Dad?" Her voice was soft, but both of their eyes flicked to her. Her mom smoothed her hair, placing the mug she was holding down, and gave her a weak smile. "Are you guys fighting?"

Her dad frowned. "Of course not, honey. We're just having some discussions about next steps."

Elizabeth sat down on the grass and squinted up at them. "Why are you lying to me?"

"Liz!" her mom reprimanded. "Do not call us liars. It's inappropriate."

She sighed. "I asked you to stop calling me that. I don't like that name."

Her mom stood up, grabbed her coffee mug, and stormed back into the house. She wanted to follow her, but it was useless. Her mom would never understand why she felt that way. It was probably why her parents were fighting again. Elizabeth looked up to her dad. "Are you going to tell me what you were arguing about now that Mom is gone?"

Her dad patted the place where her mom was sitting. Clambering to her feet, she put her elbows on her thighs as she leaned toward her dad. He took a sip of his coffee. "Your mom is just struggling with this whole name change. She doesn't understand."

"It's not that hard," Elizabeth said.

"I know you think that," he said, leaning back as he looked out at the forest before continuing, "but you've been her baby girl for as long as you've been alive. She needs more time to process this."

"I don't see your point. It's been a year now. What difference does it make to anyone if I go by Elizabeth or not?" Waving her hands in a wide arc, she gestured to the empty town they lived in. "It's only the three of us now."

Her dad reached out and squeezed her shoulder. "Your mom and I need to go on a supply run. I'll make you a deal."

She lifted an eyebrow but didn't say anything.

"Since you're twelve now, you can definitely take care of yourself and then some. If you promise to back off your mother for the next few weeks, I will do my best to get her on the same page as you. How does that sound?" Her dad gave her a hopeful smile, but it didn't stop the twinge in her heart. It was breaking her that she couldn't be herself with her mom. That she couldn't explore who that person was.

"I..." Her voice cracked. "Okay. I'll give you ten days, and you have to promise to help her see who I really am. Who I want to be instead of who she wants."

His smile was weak, but he held out his hand for her to shake. "It's a deal."

With the deal made, her father headed inside to get changed.

He emerged a few minutes later, her mom in tow. She watched them tie their shoes in silence. Her mom stood up and faced her. Her graying hair was tied back with a piece of fabric, highlighting the crow's feet that flanked her eyes. She looked tired, and Elizabeth knew it was her fault, but she couldn't keep pretending.

"I'll see you soon," Elizabeth said. Her parents nodded, whispered I love yous, and started out into the forest. She watched them fade into the greenery as the sun turned into shadows through the thick forest branches. From the way her father's shoulder's slumped, it was obvious they were already arguing. She just hoped they were coming to an agreement that respected who she was; she wasn't willing to pretend for the sake of her mother's feelings much longer.

* * *

When the sun had set, and her parents were still gone, Elizabeth began to worry. Her parents were always home before sunset, especially when they left her home alone, which wasn't often because they were still cautious of the coyotes in the woods. She had started pacing the length of their kitchen when she saw the deep reds and yellows of sunset, but when the sky turned dark purple, she knew she had to do something.

Her boots, caked in mud from their last hunting trip, were still lined up at the back door. She slid them on and tied them as quickly as possible. Her heart was hammering in her chest with every fear her mother instilled in her. Would they even be alive when she found them?

By the time she reached to open the back door, her palms were slick with sweat, and it took a few tries to get the door open. In the dark of night, it was hard to see past their backdoor light. Elizabeth flicked it off. When her eyes adjusted, she could make out the edge of the forest but nothing more. The forest wasn't what drew her attention, though.

Somewhere in the distance, she could hear a crunching sound that made her heart squeeze and her stomach roll. It was the same sound she'd heard during hunting season when a coyote caught a rare rabbit. She blanched; her whole body was shaking, but she forced herself to walk toward the noise. It was a horrible idea, and she knew it. She knew she should let it go, but if something happened, her parents deserved better.

Death was a reality she was used to. It was how she'd lost most of her neighbors, but it didn't make it any less scary.

She peered into the darkness before her and gulped. No matter how confident she felt in her ability to survive, she didn't want to survive without her parents. She didn't want to find out what that looked like.

The darkness of the forest wasn't nearly as hard to see through as she expected. The dark-gray shadows were easy to work around with her familiarity of the area. She made her way over and under downed trees the best she could. A few branches scraped at her bare skin and pulled on her clothing as she clamored through the woods toward the sounds. The closer, the louder, the more nauseating the whole thing became. When the sounds were loud enough to make her chest vibrate, she could smell the tang of blood mixed with the distinct hint of vanilla her mom always wore.

Elizabeth froze, her body poised for the next terrifying step, and then she stifled a cry the best she could. Her chest hurt, and she moved her hand to rub the spot, but it didn't help. Her eyes burned from the tears she was trying to hold back. Her body hiccuped, and she lost control of the emotions she was trying so hard to control. Her world started crashing down around her. She didn't need to see them to know everything, just mere feet from her. Her body heaved with tears. A wailing sound echoed through the trees so loudly it covered the sound of crunching.

Once she realized how out of control she'd gotten, the wailing cut off, and the sound of leaves crunching in her direction started.

Her head shot up in time to see the glowing eyes of two coyotes approaching. Her breathing stopped as they made contact. Her body tried to freeze in place, but she was raised to know better than that, and her parents had taught her to stand her ground against coyotes. They were supposed to be more afraid of her than she was of them. She reached out a shaking hand, palm out to them, and called out, "Stop."

They moved another inch toward her. She took a deep breath, pulling on her years of training with her parents, and lifted her other hand so both palms were facing the coyotes. Her voice cracked as she demanded a second time, "Stop."

This time the coyotes froze a couple of hundred feet from her. When they did, she forced the shock away as she stood up and growled. Her face was still slick with tears, but her body was filling with anger. She was furious with the giant creatures standing in front of her. She balled her fists at her side. "How fucking dare you…" The fear she felt disappeared as pure rage replaced every thought in her head. How dare they take her parents? How was she supposed to live without them? She was too young to be without her parents. There wasn't anyone else she could rely on, and these beasts were the reason she had to figure out a brand-new world. A world without her parents.

"Who the fuck do you think you are?" she roared. Her body reverberated with her anger. How was she supposed to do this without them? She took a deep breath, pulling in the cool night air, and tried to calm herself down. "What is wrong with you?" she asked, her voice full of venom but at a normal volume this time.

The coyotes stared at her for a moment, their glowing eyes locked on her. She stared back, using her anger to keep her standing firm as she watched the two coyotes shake out their fur before slowly taking a seat in front of her. Their eyes turned cautious as one of them whined. She waved a hand at it, and it bowed its head at her.

"You. Had. No. Right." Her voice came out stronger than she felt as she stalked toward them. "You had no fucking right." She stopped right in front of them. She could feel their hot breath on her skin, and she waited for the fear to come back. But she wasn't scared of them, she was just angry and sad. The emotions didn't leave room for anger. She reached out and flicked their noses as she had seen her parents do with her old dog. They whined back at her.

"What am I supposed to do now?" The anger was making her face flush. She was losing control again, and these giant coyotes were just staring at her. She didn't know it then, didn't realize until a few minutes later when she collapsed in front of them, but she was hoping they would kill her so she could be with her parents instead of in this horrible nightmare she was gliding through. Instead, they were respecting her; they were listening to her tone and actions as if she controlled them. It was as if she was commanding them. How? She didn't know, and right now, it didn't matter. What mattered was the girl she was didn't exist anymore.

Elizabeth covered her face with her hands. "What am I supposed to do?" she whispered, her voice mumbled against her palms. The soft fur of the coyotes rubbed against her, and she flinched. But soon the soft fur and her cry started to soothe her as she lay against the hard ground. When the tears had finally stopped, the sun was rising in the east, and she was still just as parentless as she was the night before.

Rays slid through the forest cover and stung her eyes. The beasts were still cradling her like a child, and somehow, it was comforting in a way she didn't feel with her mom for the last few months. She wasn't ready to process that thought, but she couldn't deny how nice it felt to feel comforted. She still felt the pang of sadness and pull of anger she warred with the night before, but another part of her, one that was growing steadily, recognized that those emotions would not get her through the future, and she needed to focus on the future.

She stood up, the coyotes following a few seconds later, and turned back toward her home. She could see it in the daylight. It was tarnished by the memory of parents who didn't love her for who she was and who would never be given the chance to do so. Her heart ached, her mind was numb, but her body knew she needed to push through. Ignoring everything but that, she let herself forget who she was, who she hated, and reached out a hand to touch the coyotes.

They whined, nipping softly at her hand, and started to drag her into the forest. She didn't know where they were going, and she didn't care. The only thing she cared about right now was running away from everything that hurt. She didn't want to hurt anymore.

# YEAR 5 AGC, DAY 283

## DEE

"How long do you plan on ignoring me?" Rowan asked, his voice echoing in the silent forest. The thrumming of his horse's hooves grew louder as he tried to catch up with her. Dee squared her shoulders, making sure to keep her face pinned forward, and clicked her heels against her horse so it would speed up. It went from walking to trotting instantaneously, and she scratched behind its ears affectionately. The house was the only thing in her life that apparently didn't lie to her.

"Will you at least tell me where we're going?" His voice was an octave higher than usual as he whined from behind her.

Dee sighed heavily. Rowan had caught up to her a few days prior when she took an extra day at the stream for her horse to relax. She didn't have a plan, didn't have a direction. She couldn't answer his questions. She didn't even have answers to her own questions. All she knew was that she needed to get away. Away from the lies and betrayal of their home. From the facts she didn't want to deal with just yet.

She wanted to tell Rowan she didn't want to be near him either, but the idea of living on this godforsaken planet without any company pained her. No matter the lies he kept, she knew he only did it for their parents. It wasn't his fault this happened. Her heart squeezed in her chest.

She didn't want to be alone—no matter how many lies circled her.

"Away," she said over her shoulder. There—she had given him something. The words felt odd in her mouth despite having known for two weeks that was where she was going. It was the first time she'd spoken to him since he told her, and she had run to hide in her room. How else was she supposed to act when she found out her entire life was a lie?

She didn't even tell him she was leaving. She waited until he went into his room, and she could hear his soft snores. Rowan had always been a snorer. After a few minutes, she just stood up, her body still weak from the gin, and grabbed her belongings. She was out the door before she could second-guess herself. She saddled up her horse, the one she'd had since she was a child, and headed into the dark forest with nothing more. Anything to get away from the death and lies.

So many lies plagued her in her nightmares. Little reminders that she had trusted people who didn't trust her with the truth.

"She speaks!" Rowan pushed his horse next to hers, and he gave her a smile. She frowned back at him briefly before focusing on the road ahead with annoyance. It was as if he didn't care about the lies. Must be nice to have had time to ask questions. Well, she certainly cared. She wanted answers she would never get. In her rush out of the house, she'd forgotten to find the journal. Any hope for an answer was days behind her.

"Wipe that smile off your face. You're lucky I haven't left you behind." Dee gave him a cutting look before squeezing her thighs into her horse. It started to run, its long mane bouncing with its steps, and she held on to the reins. She breathed in the swift air, the smell of moss filling her lungs, and tried to clear her thoughts. The crisp scent of pine hit her next, cutting her straight to the heart, and she took a second to close her eyes, to focus on just that and nothing else. To let the clarity give her a moment of centering.

She needed to get a grip on her emotions, or she'd spend the rest of her life in silence, her only companion the wind around them. The rational part of her mind knew it wasn't Rowan's fault, knew that he was all she had left and that she needed to make an effort not to lose him. The problem was that her rational part was getting beaten to a pulp by the irrational little girl hurt by her family's lies.

"Come on. You can't stay silent forever. Please. Don't you want the truth?" Rowan asked, his voice pleading.

Dee pulled her horse to a sudden stop, gripping the reins until her knuckles turned white, and turned to stare at her twin. *Half brother*, she corrected herself angrily. Running her hand through the horse's mane, smoothing it against its side, she tried to pull in her emotions before responding. "Of course, I want the truth. But how do I know you'll actually give it to me? You've already proven you can keep important things from me."

"I have no reason to lie. Not anymore." Rowan shrugged, giving her a half smile.

"Does that mean you had a reason to lie to me for our whole lives?" Dee asked, her voice dripping with venom. Her anger flared up again as Rowan gave her a wan smile. Their mother would be rolling in her grave if she knew how harsh Dee was acting. She had been taught better than that, taught to shove all those feelings deep down to protect Rowan. But their mom wasn't there anymore, and she knew there was more to the story. Being soft and careful around Rowan wouldn't get her past the anger. There was so much anger and hurt she thought it might swallow her alive. She needed to let it out.

"I didn't have a choice, Dee."

Dee growled under her breath. "You always have a choice, Rowan. We were always given choices. It was always going to be us against the world."

"It's not that simple, Dee." Rowan smacked his hand against his thigh. "You don't understand," he whispered, taking a deep breath. He watched her cautiously, picking at his nail beds. Dee recognized the action. Rowan didn't like fighting, didn't like getting angry. A small confrontation, a little hiccup, those didn't bother him. But long, drawn-out battles, ones that Dee specialized in, drove him crazy. Got under his skin, destroyed him from the inside out, and she knew it. She could just let him fester, and she would get anything she wanted. It was within her grasp, but it wasn't fair. Rowan wouldn't do that to her.

"You know what, Rowan? You're right. I don't understand. I don't, for the life of me, understand why you would keep something so huge from me. What else did you keep from me? What else did they keep from us?" Dee's face felt hot as a blush crept across her neck and up to her cheeks. Her eyes burned, and she swatted at them. She hated that her emotions always brought tears. With the sting, she could hear their mom telling her to hide her emotions. To put her feelings aside to protect the men. For once, she wanted to get mad without being undermined by waterworks or the lasting taste of her mom's words.

"Can you at least let me explain?" Rowan turned his eyes to his ripped-up fingers, then peeked over at Dee. When he saw her watching him, he flicked his eyes back to his hands. She didn't open her mouth, forcing herself to stay silent. She wasn't willing to tell him no, but she wasn't willing to say yes either.

"I found out when we were eleven." Rowan blew out a long breath, running his ragged fingers through his long dreads. "I was in the library and found Mom's journal. I thought it was just another book for me to read. I didn't know it was meant to be for you." Rowan paused, looking to Dee for confirmation to keep going. She didn't move, her body stiff as she listened to his words. When she didn't shake her head, he continued. "I spent the whole day reading it. Her anger at Dad, the straw that made her look elsewhere, their decision to raise us together. Their choice to lie to us. I was so angry that I confronted them."

Dee made a noise at the back of her throat. She couldn't imagine Rowan confronting anyone, let alone their parents.

Rowan shrugged. "At first, they lied. So straight-faced, I almost believed them. Until I threw Mom's journal down on the table. They sputtered for a little while until they finally confessed. They begged me to keep it to myself. When I disagreed, they threatened to separate us. They swore it would destroy our relationship if I told you, and I just believed them. Maybe they were right."

"Maybe they were right," Dee mocked. She made a face at him before hopping off her horse and standing next to Rowan. "How could you say that? How could you defend lying to me? I'm your sister. Whether it be by blood or not, we are family. You don't lie to family." She stabbed a finger into his chest. "We were raised not to lie to each other. Raised to be us against the fucking world, and you picked our parents. You picked them over us. How could you?"

Dee pivoted on her heel and climbed back onto her horse. She was willing to hear him out, but she wasn't willing to forgive him—at least, not yet. "How could you pick them over me? Over your sister after every time that I defended you against them? After all the times I protected you?"

Dee flicked him off. She wasn't ready to deal with him yet. Once she got situated on her saddle, she pressed her thighs together. The horse began trotting. She could hear Rowan's horse behind her. Dee knew he wouldn't stay behind, and she didn't plan to make him. Anger might still be burning through her like wildfire, but that didn't mean she hated him. In fact, she wished he would give her a good reason for lying to her so she could forgive him and move on. She didn't want to hold on to this anger.

Dee took a shaky breath and listened to the sound of hooves

crunching leaves. It echoed in her mind as she took note of the setting sun. The red-orange painted the dying leaves vibrant shades of yellow-orange and deep, fiery red. The colors swirled as she blew past them. The wind picked up her long curls, and they bounced against her back. She closed her eyes, letting the sensations wash away her frustration.

It helped—if only a little. When she opened them again, Rowan was trotting next to her. He held out a small blue notebook. Mom's journal. "I brought it for you. I found it before I headed out to follow you and brought it for you. I thought you should hear it all from her."

Dee held out her hand wordlessly for Rowan to drop the notebook into it. It landed in her hand with a heft she didn't expect. She clasped it to her chest. The weight of it warmed her insides. No matter what lies existed, her mom had made this notebook for her to read. Just because Rowan got it first didn't mean she didn't need to read it. She gave Rowan a weak smile.

One small step to forgiveness, one giant leap into the rabbit hole.

## WINONA

"We've been walking for days," Jeremy whined. Coming to a halt, he made a face at her before leaning against a rock.

Winona sighed, dropping her items and leaning next to Jeremy. Their arms were barely brushing, but she could feel the heat of his skin on hers as if he were a fire. Adding that to the list of things she didn't have the energy to deal with, she inched a step away from him. They had passed through a handful of state signs and landed somewhere in Idaho, or what used to be Idaho, without passing anyone. It wasn't a shock to her as most of their travels had been within the forest, but she had held out a small hope they would find others, find someplace to build roots to replace her home. Without a map, she was relying on her memory of the states and highways her father pushed on her for just this scenario. She could picture it in her mind just as easily as she heard him chastise her for once again thinking it was a good idea to meet with strangers.

"I know you're tired, but we need to keep going," she said. She reached out to rub his arm but hesitated in the air. Before she could react, Jeremy grabbed her hand, twined his fingers through hers, and gave them a squeeze. She pulled her hand away, avoiding the hurt that was probably in his eyes. She managed to forgive him for burning down her house, but the idea that they could be more than that right now was too much for Winona to handle. They were barely surviving. It didn't matter how much she appreciated his easygoing mentality. She couldn't get herself past everything going on around them.

A small part of her reminded her how comfortable she got with him before the accident. She knew her reaction was cruel, but she didn't have words to apologize for how overwhelmed she felt. Hopefully, he would understand without them. "There's nothing here for us."

Jeremy turned away from her, but not before she got a glimpse at the hurt on his face. She liked Jeremy a lot. She really did. But life was too much. It was all too much for her. Her brain was in a constant state of buzzing so loud that she almost didn't hear their approach.

The sound of twigs snapping in the distance filled the air. Winona's head snapped toward the direction it came from just in time to get a blurry glimpse of two figures in the distance. Wide-eyed and unarmed, Winona got to her feet and jumped behind the row of bushes rounding the curve in the trail. She dragged Jeremy with her and covered his mouth with her hand. "Shush. Something's coming."

"I don't hear anything," he mumbled against her hand, covering it in saliva. She pulled it off and wiped it on her jeans in disgust. She was so close to him that she could hear his soft breathing. His woodsy smell was stronger than the fresh scent of the forest. It was one of her favorite scents, but right now, it was distracting her from focusing.

"Just shut up, Jeremy." The bushes didn't give much in the way of viewing the path, but it was enough to see two figures wearing tattered shorts and baggy shirts. She couldn't see their faces but got a few glimpses of their matted waist-length hair. A redhead and a brunette. Winona wasn't sure, but she thought they slowed down—moving to a crawl in front of their bush. Winona contemplated whether or not they should stand up and introduce themselves as Jeremy leaned toward her.

"We should say hi," Jeremy whispered, his mouth dangerously close to her ear. Winona shivered involuntarily but clenched her fist before pushing Jeremy away. Why did he always make her feel that way? She tried to ignore her warring emotions as he fell over from his precarious position, balanced on the balls of his feet, and tumbled into the bushes. Lost again in her ever-present battle over what to do about her growing affection for Jeremy, the image snapped her thoughts back into place. Winona watched in horror as the bushes shook under his sudden movement. Twigs crunched under his weight, and the two figures stopped.

"Hello?" a gravelly voice called out. It sounded feminine but hoarse—like she hadn't spoken much in a few days while severely dehydrated. It sounded how she imagined her own voice did when she told Jeremy to stop whistling for the hundredth time that morning. "Is there someone there?"

"Hi!" Jeremy called out, pulling himself from the bushes and jumping up. Winona watched him from the ground, her mouth agape. Was she really wondering about her affections when this idiot was constantly putting them in dangerous situations? If only he wasn't so darn good-looking. Or happy. Or caring. Winona growled as she pushed the thoughts from her mind. Goddamn puppy dog of a boy.

"Jeremy," she hissed, pulling on the hem of his shorts. Jeremy smiled down at her, showing off his cracked tooth. Stupid, annoyingly lovable boy. He gripped her hand and pulled her up unwillingly. Pain shot through her arm. "Stop, Jeremy!"

"You gave me a chance," he said under his breath.

She rolled her eyes, and muttered, "Look where that fucking got us."

Jeremy ignored her to turn his bright smile on the two girls in front of them. She eyed the pair warily, not nearly as happy as Jeremy looked. Both girls had clean faces despite their ragged clothing. They were skinny in a way that looked healthy, not in the way Jeremy looked when she found him. The redhead, who was watching the two of them cautiously, had her hazel eyes flicking between them. Her gaze, calculating and cold, landed on specific locations. Hips, ankles, hands. Winona recognized the action as one she saw on her dad when inspecting passersby for weapons. One she never used despite his constant reminders.

Perhaps she could be helpful. She couldn't say the same for the brunette who was ogling Jeremy like a piece of meat. Winona ground her teeth together in annoyance.

"We're unarmed," Winona offered, patting the places the girl had looked at. The redhead relaxed and put a soft hand on the brunette as she leaned over to whisper something. The brunette nodded, her blue eyes looking Jeremy over before biting her lip. The redhead rolled her eyes.

The brunette, who was starting off on a very bad foot, slid a smile onto her face, and something in Winona cringed. Jeremy was not a plaything for this succubus. Winona blew out a soft breath and tried to collect herself. She needed to do a better job of keeping her emotions in check. Ever since she lost her house, she had been a Ping-Pong ball filled with emotion. She was the one who was pushing him away, remember? She literally did it less than five minutes ago.

"I'm Maeve," the brunette offered. "This is my sister Jenna." Winona narrowed her eyes in disbelief—sure, they had the same pinkish skin tone and build, but she just couldn't see the family resemblance. There was no way they were sisters—maybe cousins at best. Winona tacked one red *X* in the con column for Maeve.

One pro and two cons.

That didn't move her decision in either direction. Jeremy

was right. She gave him a chance and look where it landed her. Homeless. She promised herself she wouldn't make the same mistake, and so she created her new pro/con list. After twenty days of walking, she thought she had a pretty good idea of what reg flags would constitute a con, and none of them included hitting on Jeremy. And yet she couldn't remove the con, no matter how much she knew it was wrong.

"Jeremy. That's Winona. We've been traveling together for about a month now." Jeremy reached out a hand to them, and Maeve met him with a wider grin that showed off her perfect teeth. Winona's face turned scarlet. Toeing the dirt uncomfortably, she averted her eyes from the scene. Why was this bothering her so much?

"Where are you two headed?" Jeremy added, shaking Jenna's hand.

"We're looking for a place to settle down." Jenna offered her hand to Winona next, but she brushed it off. She already had to take care of Jeremy. She didn't need anyone else. She hadn't made up her mind about them, but Maeve's predatory gaze ate at the pit in her stomach. Winona didn't need that every day. She couldn't even make up her mind about Jeremy. Screw weighing the fact—they weren't picking up strays. Especially not two very attractive strays.

"That's great! So are we—lost our place back in Washington. Haven't taken a break in days." She stifled a laugh at his use of *our* before pinching Jeremy's arm. "Ouch. Jeez. What?"

She stopped herself from pinching him a little harder. Why couldn't he just learn to stay silent?

"Shut up." She pivoted so she could keep an eye on the girls while giving Jeremy the glare of death. He shrugged it off, building on her annoyance. Some days, she wasn't sure which of them was the stubborn one.

"Winona, you're being dramatic. We haven't seen anyone this entire trip. Give them a chance." Jeremy turned pointedly back to the two women. "I'm sorry. My friend here doesn't like new people."

Friend hurt more than she wanted to acknowledge.

"The last new person I met burned down my house," Winona snapped as she focused her glare on the girls. "I don't need any more trouble."

"I thought we were past that." Jeremy touched her forearm softly, and she felt some of the anger wash away. Not all of it, but enough for her to think a little more clearly.

"That doesn't mean I'm ready to take on new people. I'm sorry, you both seem"—she paused, eyeing them—"nice. But Jeremy here gives me enough trouble. I hope you understand." She tried to plaster on a more neutral face, but based on the looks the sisters gave her, she didn't think it was very good.

"What she means to say is that we're headed up the mountains to Denver. Hoping to find something more habitable based on Winona's history books. Did you guys want to join us?" Jeremy squeezed her wrist, begging her to agree, but she just couldn't. She couldn't get past this weird wave of jealousy or the feeling that Maeve was not going to be a good addition to their hiking group.

"That is not what I said. I said thanks, but no thank you."

"Winona," Jeremy snapped, moving his hand down to link their fingers. The push kick-started the logical part of her brain. Softer, he asked, "What is wrong with you?"

What was wrong with her was right. Sure, she didn't need more trouble, but these girls were just staring at them like they were crazy. Correction, like she was crazy. Was she being crazy or just crazy protective? Why did she feel the need to protect Jeremy in the first place? He was just some guy she found in the woods. He wasn't anything more than a helping hand. That was all.

"I... I... I'm sorry," Winona stammered out, running her free hand through her knotted waves. "Jeremy is right. We're headed to Denver. You're welcome to join us, but we have ground rules." Jeremy squeezed her hand, and she turned to see him smirking at her. He mouthed something that looked like "thank you." *Thank you for what? Potentially allowing more puppies to follow me around? Why was it so hard to say no to Jeremy?*

"Ground rules?" Maeve asked, looking between them. Her eyes narrowed in on their hands before winking at Jeremy. "Are you guys into some freaky stuff?"

Winona felt her eye twitch, the scarlet in her face hotter than before. She took a deep breath. "No. We just expect everyone to pull their weight. If you're unwilling to help out, we're unwilling to help you." Winona cocked an eyebrow at the girls. Neither of them balked, and she put another *X* in the pro column as Jeremy let go of her hand to wrap an arm around her. The sudden weight and warmth made her shiver, but she managed not to pull away in front of the girls. Her body rooted her in place despite the part that screamed she was giving Jeremy the wrong idea. The exact thing she was trying to avoid when she couldn't give him a fair chance.

"Jenna's a good tracker—she's been finding our dinner every night. And I can hunt. Does that work?"

Their breakfast of berries sloshed in her stomach. They were sorely lacking food and hadn't stayed anywhere long enough to plant the jar of seeds she had brought from the house. The jar of seeds Jeremy had managed to pull from the shed for them, she corrected. She placed a protective hand on the strap of her bag and pulled it over her shoulder as she stepped out from under Jeremy's arm.

"That's perfect! We've only had vegetables and berries we've been able to find on the road. I could go for some rabbit or deer. What have you guys managed to catch?" Jeremy started grinning like a fool. He was always so naïve. She wanted to punch him into a neutral face but clenched her fists at her sides. She tuned out the conversation about possible food sources farther east and what skill sets the two of them offered the group as she contemplated their future. The future of this weakly connected group of people. It pained her to admit that having the two girls tag along was probably a good choice if a foolish one. The idea of a meal with meat in it made her mouth salivate.

"We'll lead the way," Jeremy said, wrapping his arm back around Winona. She shook her head as he pulled her ahead of the two women. "Oh, Winona. This is great. I'll finally be able to make you deer stew. You're going to love it!"

She gave him a wan smile as she felt their eyes on them. *What are you getting us into, Jeremy?*

# YEAR 10 DGC, DAY 75

## DIEGO

Diego clenched a fist around the wheel of his barely functioning car before blowing out an angry breath. "What do you mean…we should stay in Florida?" He narrowed his eyes at the empty road ahead of them. In the distance, a sign welcoming them to Georgia loomed. "Don't you think we're a little far to be having second thoughts?"

He gestured angrily at the sign.

"I didn't say we should stay. I said I didn't think our hunk of junk would get us much farther." As if agreeing with Mia, the car made a squealing noise Diego recognized as the fan belt slipping. He pulled the car over and sighed.

"What are we supposed to do?" Diego whacked his hands against the wheel as he eyed the fuel gauge. Half a tank. They'd be lucky to make it to Jacksonville with that. He didn't want to admit it, but Mia was probably right. They hadn't seen a working gas station in hours.

"We need a vehicle that doesn't run on fossil fuels. It's not practical." Mia was right, of course. They had tried to fill the tank up about an hour ago and found the station out of fuel and unattended. They hadn't seen another car running for days. The world was far quieter than he was expecting this fast. "There's a facility nearby that I think we could get something."

"What does that even mean?" Diego raked his finger through his short spikes. They were uneven from Mia's last scissor trim, but at least it wasn't falling into his face. He hated having to brush it away. "Are you telling me you want to steal a car?"

"No! That's outrageous. We won't be stealing anything. We're just going to repurpose a vehicle that's been left to rot." Mia made an exaggerated face of innocence.

"So you want to steal it?" Diego threw the door of his weathered sedan open, hefting himself out of the vehicle, and stomped to the trunk. It popped open, bouncing on the hinges, to reveal their measly belongings and several unopened bottles of alcohol. He rooted around for the last bottle he'd opened and pulled it out. Uncapping it, he took a long sip while listening to Mia get out and circle the vehicle.

"You can't always drink away your problems," Mia remarked, pulling the bottle from his hands and holding it up. It glittered in the midday sun as she lifted it to her own lips and swallowed the bitter liquid.

"Pot," he said, gesturing at her, "meet kettle." He reached for the bottle.

Mia rolled her eyes before shoving the bottle back into Diego's hand and getting into the passenger seat. Diego contemplated returning the bottle to the trunk but thought better of it; if they were going to "repurpose" a car, he needed liquid courage—even in today's society. Just because there were no societal standards didn't mean they weren't ingrained in him.

"I'm going to regret this," he added, slamming the trunk shut.

Bottle in hand, Diego walked up to the passenger seat and gestured at Mia. The car roared to life with an angry growl as Mia squeezed into the driver's seat and restarted the engine. He dropped himself into the seat. Diego squinted at her, watching her brush stray hair away from her face before roughly grabbing the seat belt. It clicked into place, and she grimaced before easing onto the gas. Even annoyed, Mia had a certain quality about her that made him...made him uncomfortable. Uncomfortable in a way he'd never felt before. He shoved that thought aside with a hearty swig of whiskey. Now wasn't the time for him to process his unrequited emotions.

The whiskey settled in his stomach warmly and forced a smile on his lips before melting away as it dawned on him how long they had gone without food. He placed a hand on his stomach, but he didn't feel the usual pangs of hunger. He tilted his head and paused, searching his mind for the last time he'd been hungry but came up empty. "Mia?"

"Hmmm?" she practically hummed over the sound of the engine. He turned in his seat to look at her.

"When did we eat last?"

Mia laughed.

"What?" Diego frowned at her.

"Diego...don't you remember?" When he didn't respond, she placed a soft hand on his thigh. "I guess we never had a chance to see if it worked until now. I thought you would remember..." She squeezed his leg before focusing on the road again.

"Remember what?" Diego pressed. He knew the alcohol was mottling his brain, but he couldn't figure out what Mia was getting at. What did she know that he didn't?

"We agreed to take part in Dr. Raye's study..." Mia trailed off, biting her lip. Diego waded through his memories of Bryan for a few moments before something clicked in his brain. Bryan's study on creating humans who could process alcohol as nutrition. They couldn't find any participants, so he had agreed to get the implant. No one had wanted to replace their stomach with a mechanical version. How could he have forgotten?

Diego ran a rough hand up his shirt and across the scar. It was a smooth but uneven line where his stomach was supposed to be. His stomach that was crafted in a laboratory—not the one he had been born with. He looked at Mia and said, "I forgot."

"I couldn't." Mia lifted her shirt to reveal a matching scar. Diego looked at the pale line against her tan skin with regret. "I'm impossible to forget."

"You shouldn't have agreed. He only needed one person to prove it worked."

"If I hadn't, I don't think I would have survived this long. We haven't eaten in days. If it wasn't for this modification, I probably would have killed you from lack of food." Mia shot him a look that he chose to ignore.

"I'm lucky you haven't killed me for lack of usefulness," Diego quipped. Mia gave him a wry smile as she dropped her shirt back down. Once again, Diego was left feeling like a burden that weighed Mia down. She had been nothing but a resourceful companion while he'd just drunk. He was just a washed-up scientist with a mechanical stomach.

What good was he to Mia?

* * *

"You want to steal a top-of-the-line electric SUV?" Diego huffed, breaking the long silence of their drive. The idea of stealing anything still upset him, let alone the idea of stealing something from a company hell-bent on destroying anything in its way.

"Do you have any better options?" Mia cocked an eyebrow at him while he opened and shut his mouth a few times. "That's what I thought. Now get out of this piece of shit and help me break open this door. I'm sure one of these batteries will still have juice in it. It looks like they just shut down a few weeks ago, and some of these are still plugged in."

Diego stared up at the building with its bright-red sign and panel glass walls with a mixture of regret and excitement. He'd always dreamed of having an electric car, especially something as glamorous as what they were looking at, but taking care of his ailing parents and lack of funding had drained his resources to the same fire red as the sign. In the before, he would have given anything to have one of these sitting in his driveway. He contemplated another gulp of whiskey before shaking his head and dragging himself out of the car and next to Mia.

"Fine, but I want that one." Diego pointed to a gray SUV that had the least amount of bird shit on it. Not waiting for a response, he whipped off his blue college-branded shirt, wrapped it around his hand, and smashed it against the door of the building. A small crack appeared, but the glass remained firm. He tried a few more times without success before gesturing for Mia to combine her weight with his. With a coordinated effort, they slammed their shoulders into the door, and it crumpled, dropping them onto the floor into a heap of shards.

They cried out, small gashes covering their sides. He felt every pinprick from the glass digging into the thin skin between his bones and the floor. When they had collected themselves, Diego paused to note that the alarm hadn't gone off as expected. He silently thanked the powers that be before getting to his feet and brushing the glass off him. He went to reach for Mia, but she was already standing a few feet away and digging through drawers. Not for the first time, Diego was mystified by everything that was Mia. She was really something.

"Aha!" she exclaimed, holding a small car-shaped object. She clicked it, and a beep went off. "Perfect." Mia turned to eye Diego's bleeding side with a shrug. "You'll heal."

"Ouch," he mocked, feigning offense as he spun to look for the flashing lights of the car. "You know, you should be nicer to me. I'm your boss."

Mia laughed harshly as she brushed past him. "You haven't been my boss in years. At this point, you're closer to an annoying brother than a boss. At best, you're a constant pain in my ass that I tolerate."

"I resent that!" he called, jogging behind her in swift moments toward a small white car. Diego ignored the tightness in his chest and the sudden pain in his heart. He added to the list of things to deal with later. Mia clicked the remote, and it beeped. "Great...you couldn't have gotten the keys for that one?" Diego eyed the gray SUV longingly as Mia got into the driver's seat. The lights turned on, and she flashed them before rolling down the window.

"Get in, loser. We're going out." She snorted. "God, I have always wanted to say that!" She patted the seat when he didn't move. "Really...get in. It looks like a hurricane is blowing in."

Diego looked over the building where she was pointing to see a line of angry clouds rushing over the empty landscape. The air around them was still, stagnant almost. The sky was darkening quicker than he could process. Storms were different in the after—faster, stronger, angrier. It was like they took direction from his mother when Diego tried to sneak out as a kid.

"Fine, but I get to decide where we're going." Mia nodded before reaching over to pop his door open. He got in, and she inched the car up to their old, rotted sedan. She got out of the car and transferred over their belongings. Before he could even open the door, she was done. Mia was back in the car, handing him his precious bottle before he could come up with a destination. Where would they want to go? Where had he never been?

He shook those thoughts away. They weren't important. He needed to decide where would be the most stable place to get situated. Had he not spent so many years studying the environment, he wouldn't have understood how special some parts of the US could be. There was one city, one mountainous region that would fare better than the rest. He smiled as he settled on his decision.

Mia pulled out onto the street with a giddy smile before slamming on the accelerator. The car jolted forward, and his stomach lurched. The sudden movement made him nauseous. He was going to throw up all this alcohol if she kept driving like this. He mulled over how to tell Mia his decision as she got settled with the new vehicle.

"Well?" she asked, turning the car onto the freeway that led out of state.

"Denver."

"Denver? You're literally the most tropical person in the world." Mia snickered to herself. "To quote yourself, the last time we went to a conference in Boston, 'I'm too tropical for this snow. Get me the fuck out.'"

"It's not as cold as it used to be," he defended. "Besides, wildlife is traveling farther north. It'll be a good location to set roots. Actually. I don't think anywhere besides Denver will be livable soon."

"I want to tell you that Denver is a bad idea, but I really have no arguments. It's hard to argue when you've spent the last decade studying just how viable Denver is."

"Mia Cruz without an argument." Diego laughed. "Hell has really frozen over."

Mia waved a hand at the dying landscape around them. "Pigs are going to start flying soon, Diego. Hell freezing over is the least of our concerns."

# YEAR 6 DGC, DAY 125

## OFFICIAL NOTICE – TO BE POSTED ON ALL AVAILABLE SOURCES

It is our deepest regret to inform the people of the United States that President Amelia Shaw passed away last night due to severe complications from a coyote attack. At 5:03 p.m. last night, President Shaw left presidential housing in Boise, Idaho, for a walk with her two kids. Despite being trailed by several secret service agents, the group was attacked under the cover of night by a group of five coyotes.

All efforts from our in-camp medics and our secret service agents were made to save the president. However, President Shaw and her children passed away at 11:15 p.m. Due to current circumstances, without a named vice president or representatives from Congress, the Secretary of Defense has been declared temporary Head of State. Interim President Steven Verde will be releasing a statement in the near future regarding the state of the union.

Please be on the lookout for missionaries directed by the press secretary from the Idaho colony to disseminate further information.

# YEAR 5 AGC, DAY 287

## WINONA

DEER STEW WAS as gross as she imagined. It took significant effort for her to choke it down with a smile on her face. She'd grown up on fish only, and the grisly meat didn't sit well in her stomach. She had to sneak away, claiming a bathroom break, to throw it up in private. She didn't want to hurt Jeremy's feelings since he'd tried so hard. His eyes lit up when she said it was delicious, and she wasn't willing to take that away.

It was clear Jeremy and the sisters were getting along. Maeve looked particularly happy as Jeremy fawned over her shot that landed them this unappetizing dinner. After so much time with him, she knew Jeremy was just interested in the bow she used. It was something novel to him. Winona wanted to believe that she just didn't like the deer, not that Maeve's giggle as Jeremy cracked jokes next to her on the log wasn't making her queasy. Not the fear that maybe she didn't know Jeremy as well as she thought.

"Where are you both from?" Jenna asked, giving her a tentative smile. It was a kind gesture, trying to inject in the increasingly flirty comments between Jeremy and Maeve. Winona studied the discomfort in her eyes, adding it to the list of things that didn't add up about the pair. Something to figure out another day.

"I grew up outside of what used to be Seattle. This is the first time I've ever left the state." She peeked to see if Jeremy was going to respond, but he was whispering in Maeve's ear. She sighed before looking back at Jenna with a resigned smile. "Jeremy was raised in Southern California. Traveled north for food and crossed paths with some errant rocks I was kicking about on a hike. What about you?"

"We grew up in New Jersey. When my mom"—Jenna coughed—"when our mom died, we decided to just travel the country. It's been almost three years. We've met some interesting people along the way but never found any to really hold us down." She eyed Maeve. Her use of my instead of ours was added to Winona's growing list of concerns about the girls' relationship. She still wasn't sure if they were actually related. "Maybe that's going to change. You both are extremely talented; your knowledge of the area is so extensive."

Winona shrugged. It hurt, but there was nothing tying Jeremy to her, and he looked happy. Happy in a way he wasn't before. She swirled the soup in her bowl. It was a wooden one that Jeremy had carved as they walked and was slightly lopsided. "My dad wanted me to be okay when he passed away. For a long time, it was quiet without them around. It would be nice to have some company," she added, looking up at Jenna's curious face.

Jeremy erupted in laughter as he stood and plopped next to Winona. His shoulder brushed hers in the casual way they were developing. It made her stomach flip-flop. "Nona! You will not believe the things Maeve and Jenna have been up to."

She bit her lip. "Like what?" She tried to sound casual, but her voice cracked.

He held out his hand and ticked off his fingers. "Hiked Mt. Rushmore. Walked the Appalachian chain. Seen what used to be

New Orleans. Did you know it's completely underwater now? Visited the beaches in California. I didn't even know if most of those things were real." He shouldered her. "Do you think we could do some of that?"

She laughed and shook her head. "Why don't we start with Denver?" She looked at Jenna. "Have you ever been?"

"No, but that was our next stop," Jenna said.

Jeremy's eyes lit up, and he wrapped an arm around Winona. "Thank you," he whispered in her ear, his lips just barely brushing her ear. His hot breath made her shiver.

Her eyes connected with Maeve, and she bit her tongue from commenting on the annoyance there. She looked over her head to see the slight darkening of the sky. Sliding away from Jeremy, she started to get their makeshift tent out of the bag. "We should start getting ready for dark."

Jeremy had managed to find the carcass of a tent while they were walking, but since it didn't have the poles, they had to prop it up using branches from the surrounding area. It wasn't perfect, but it had more than enough room to keep the two of them dry. The fact that they needed to lie so close that she could barely move without touching him had its positives too.

*  *  *

IT WASN'T until the fire had died down and the two pairs were curled up in their own tents that Winona built up the courage to say what was on her mind. She had spent the whole night distracted by the constant running thoughts. "If you like Maeve, you should go for it."

It came out as barely a whisper, but Jeremy stirred in his spot next to her. He rolled his head to the side. She couldn't see his face in the dark but could feel his confusion. "What are you talking about?"

"I…" She cleared her throat. "It just seems…Well…I just don't want to hold you back."

"Hold me back?" He laughed, rolling to look up at the ceiling of their tent. "Nona. You're the only reason I've survived this long."

She bit her lip. "I'm serious, Jer. You guys seem to really get along."

He reached out to squeeze her hand, linking their fingers. "I'm good."

"You're good?" She cleared her throat. "What is that supposed to mean?"

What she didn't ask but wanted to lingered in the air. Was she good enough? Was she not in the way? Did he want her? Was she sure she wanted to open this issue up right now? Her hands ached to reach out, to grab him and shake a better answer out of him. But instead, she watched Jeremy yawn in the shadows.

"Let's talk about this in the morning," he mumbled.

Her nails bit into her palm as she nodded, sliding her hand out of his and rolling away from him. It wasn't easy, but she created a gap between them. It felt like a chasm. It took everything in her not to let out the sob building in her chest. It wrecked her chest until it became hard to breathe. She shouldn't be this upset about anything. It's not like Jeremy said he wanted Maeve. Right?

"I'm going to get some air," she said, pushing herself off the floor and slipping out of the tent. The cool night air hit the tears that were streaming down her face. Her chest ached, her heart beating double time as she tried to process Jeremy's words. Of course, he didn't want her. There was no way she was even in his way of getting with Maeve. Maeve was talented in all the ways she wasn't. She wasn't anything special. The only thing she was capable of was taking care of Jeremy and growing food. She was more like a big sister than…

She didn't know how to finish that sentence. She wasn't even sure what she wanted from Jeremy. How could she be so upset when she was so lost? She walked into the woods, pacing around the camp in larger and larger circles until she couldn't see the tents anymore. Closing her eyes briefly, she took stock of the situation and let out a long breath.

The decision whacked her in the chest, and she struggled to breathe as she snuck back into their tent and grabbed the few things she owned. Holding them close to her chest, she leaned down next to Jeremy's ear. She closed her eyes and listened to the sound of his soft snoring, before whispering, "Goodbye."

Before she could second-guess herself, she started the trek down the hill to the nearest highway. Far enough away that they wouldn't run into her from their position on the trail. She had been using the highway to guide their path to Denver anyway.

It took a few hours, but by the time the sun started to break through the horizon, Winona was on the highway and headed toward Denver. She was exhausted. Her muscles ached from trying to safely trapeze herself down the hill, her eyes felt like sand from lack of sleep, and her throat was raw. She hadn't taken the canteen since they were sharing one. She would just need to find a freshwater source and hope it wasn't contaminated. The prospect of those stars aligning was dismal at best, but it was better than leaving Jeremy without water.

Exhausted was better than crushed. It was the fear of being crushed by Jeremy that propelled her forward until her legs were ready to give out. They shook more with each step. She didn't want to find out what he meant. She didn't want to watch something she kept telling herself she didn't want crumble. She just wanted to transport herself back to the empty house where she didn't know anything about the world. She just wanted to go home and have her parents be there to make everything all right again.

But that wasn't how the world worked, and she needed to keep moving.

The "Welcome to Utah" sign caught her attention as she marched her way down the highway. She had gotten farther than they had originally planned for that day. If she got just a little farther, she would be a whole day ahead of them. That should be more than enough to make sure they didn't find her.

She made it another hour before she felt confident they wouldn't run into her. She untied her jacket from her waist and strung the heavy fabric between two trees. It was a small hammock, just enough for her to sit in, but she squeezed herself into a ball and tried to get comfortable. The hammock had no give, and when she tried to turn to get more comfortable, the fabric bit into her sides. She huffed in frustration. She just wanted to get some sleep.

She tossed and turned for an hour before she dragged herself out of the hammock. With squinted eyes, she untied the jacket from the trees and rolled it into a ball, shoving it against the trunk of one of the trees. The ground was hard on her back, but the makeshift pillow made it a little more tolerable, and she was able to get relatively comfortable.

As she lay there trying to fall asleep, her mind wandered to Jeremy and the girls. She hated that she let the girls win. She didn't want to give up what she had with Jeremy. She wanted to find out what it was. That thought pulled Winona out of her stupor, and she berated herself. She didn't want to find anything out. She wanted to go back to her solo life in her empty house. At least that was what she tried to convince herself.

Her emotions and thoughts warred against themselves for a while longer before her body started to drift off. Neither side won, her heart and her head at ends, but she fell asleep thinking about Jeremy.

# YEAR 5 AGC, DAY 288

## JEREMY

JEREMY WOKE up to the sound of birds, something so foreign along the barren, burnt West Coast that it forced his eyes open. The sun, shining through the open tent flap, kept them open. The empty spot next to him pushed him out of bed faster than he had moved in a long time. He emerged from the tent in a blur, the world spinning around. When he steadied, he took in the gamey smell of the deer stew and turned toward it. Maeve and Jenna were surrounding a fire, cooking some leftover deer. He swiveled his head around, looking for Winona, spinning in a full circle, but she wasn't anywhere he could see.

He tried to ignore the sudden fear that she had left him just like his family did, the sudden squeeze of his chest. He shoved away the fear that she had disappeared into the forest. He just couldn't take finding another loved one's bones chewed so furiously he could see how starved the animal was. The bones of his brother still haunted him, the deep crevices filled with dark-brown dirt that covered them circling his dreams.

"Good morning," Maeve called with a smile.

He bit his lip and shrugged. It wasn't starting out to be a good morning. "Morning. Have you guys seen Winona?"

"No, I figured she was still asleep," Maeve said, giving him the briefest of looks and a simple shrug before going back to watching the fire. Jeremy bristled. He wanted to scream—how dare she care so little! Did this drive Winona as nuts as it did him when he shrugged carelessly? That's probably why she left. She was tired of him. It was why she was pushing him away last night too. Telling him to get with Maeve. She knew how he felt, and she didn't feel the same way.

A small part of him wondered if she did know. If she understood how warm and comforting it felt to be near her, no matter what their relationship looked like. How despite the toughness she presented, she was caring and kind to a fault. If she knew how many times he had wanted to shake her into reality when she downplayed how little she cared about anything. He pushed that out of his mind. He could worry about this when she was safe. When she was next to him again. Right now, it didn't matter. Only finding her again mattered.

Jeremy took a deep breath and tried to focus on having one tree standing in front of him instead of the three he saw. When the extra trees disappeared, he rolled his shoulders and focused back on the girls.

"She's not in the tent," he finally said. "Are you sure you haven't seen her?"

Jenna frowned. "Do you want me to track her?"

"Can you?" he asked, his optimism seeping out with the rise in his voice. He knew Winona would chastise him for being so positive, but she wasn't there. She was somewhere in the woods, and if his positivity brought her back, he would be as optimistic as he could.

"I can try. I've never had to track a person before. But I smelled her when I came out...thought maybe she went to the bathroom in the middle of the night."

"She did say she wanted to get some air. Do you think something happened?" Jeremy asked. It was hard not to let the panic take hold. He could feel it rising back up like a pot boiling over. He felt it trying to take hold and bit his nails into his palm in hopes of stopping it. Based on the look the sisters were giving him, he wasn't doing a very good job hiding it.

Based on the way his throat felt like it was closing, he wasn't doing a good job stopping it. He didn't really care, though. Winona was the only reason he was alive. She took him in when he had nothing else. She was the only thing he had that was actually good in his life. He wasn't going to leave her out in the woods alone. He wasn't going to leave her to do it alone like she had before. They both deserved better than the world they faced right now.

Even if she didn't want to be with him, he could still watch out for her. Like a brother. He scratched his neck so hard he came back with blood. He looked at it wildly. He felt the panic rise again, biting at his hopes and dragging them away to leave him with only despair. Why did it hurt so much to think she didn't care about him the same way? He was just a friend for so long. It shouldn't be so painful. Yet, his heart squeezed in disagreement.

"We can look for her after breakfast," one of them said. But Jeremy had already spun on his heel and was marching back to his tent. He could feel all the questions pinging in his head as if acorns were dropping and smacking him. Did something happen, or did she leave? Did he really mess up this badly? He couldn't get over the idea that she left him behind, and the reality that she did was the only one that he wanted to feel real. If she left, at least she was alive. At least he had the possibility of seeing her again.

He ripped the tent flap back and searched through their belongings. It was easy for him to see that it was just his belongings left. Winona's clothing and the photo she carried with her of her family had disappeared from where she had placed it when they got camp set up. He kneeled next to the spot and pictured the younger version of Winona. The image was gritty and yellowed, something she had claimed came with the dark-room technique her father used. The smile on her face, something he had only caught a few times over their time together, made his heart tighten painfully and his stomach drop.

His stomach rolled, and he leaned out of the tent to throw up. It burned, making his eyes water, and he rubbed his face roughly.

"You okay?" Jenna asked, her shadow filling up the ground in front of him.

"I'll be fine." The words felt thick on his tongue, heavy with the weight of his lie. He hated lying, but he didn't need their pity. He'd already seen it and hated it. What he needed was Winona back safely. He wouldn't let her do this alone, no matter what. He was okay without her loving him back, right?

"You know, she's probably fine. You shouldn't worry so much," Maeve quipped.

He looked up sharply. "The problem is that I know she's fine. She's always been fine, and she's never needed my help. She didn't need me. She'll never need me." He waved an angry hand in front of his face. He replayed the words a few times until what he said finally sunk in. "I failed. This is my fault."

"This isn't your fault," Jenna said. There was no strength behind her words. They were hollow to Jeremy's ears—providing little comfort and much more annoyance than he had ever felt.

"You don't know that. You can't know that." Jeremy blew out a long breath. "Can you just leave me to pack, please?"

Jenna nodded silently, and she turned around to walk toward Maeve. He watched her for a second, feeling guilty as leaves crunched under her feet, but feeling guilty for snapping wasn't going to bring Winona back. Nothing would bring her back. He was being ridiculous for trying to go look for her.

Shaking his head clear, he turned back to packing up what was left.

* * *

WHEN THE TENT-TURNED-BACKPACK was cleaned up, Jeremy finally sat down and ate something. The deer should have tasted as good as it did last night. Winona had been so excited when she found a small bunch of rosemary to help flavor the meat along with the salt she'd boiled out of the saltwater stream they had passed on their way out of Washington. But the deer was tasteless, just leaving a bitter feeling with the weight of her disappearance.

"If you want to find her, you're going to need to eat more. I started to follow the trail, and it headed down toward the highway. If she made it to the highway, she's farther than I expected."

Jenna's words were enough to force the stew down his throat. When he had cleaned the bowl, he held it close to himself. It was made from a downed tree not far from her house, and he had carved her name into it along with the image of the cliff they met at. He had carved it for Winona, and she didn't care enough to take it with her. She didn't care about them. He swallowed down the hurt.

"Are you two packed and ready to move?" Jeremy heard the way his voice sounded bitter and angry, but he swallowed it away. He had every right to feel that way.

The two girls stood in front of him carrying their own backpacks. "Ready when you are," Jenna said. She pointed down the cliff. "She headed that way."

"She climbed down a cliff," he muttered. She hated him enough to climb down a cliff in the dark. Did she even make it safely?

"It's not a cliff. It's a steep hillside. Perfectly walkable," Maeve said, rolling her eyes.

Jeremy bit back a comment as Jenna jabbed her with an elbow. "Shut up," she hissed.

Jeremy waved a hand, brushing off the comment, and followed as the sisters headed down the hill. He focused on the silence of the forest under their voices as they rambled about memories they shared. They had traveled the country and didn't have much to talk about besides the different places they had been. Jeremy didn't mind. It was easier to listen to than deal with the panic and anger that simmered under the surface.

"Are you even listening, Jeremy?" one of the girls said.

Jeremy snapped his head up. "I'm sorry, I must have spaced out. Can you repeat it?"

Maeve huffed. "I was just telling you about how I almost drowned in the ocean."

"Really? That's wild," he said. He felt numb, and he couldn't push past it enough to care, but he tried. The enthusiasm sounded fake to him, but Maeve smiled wide enough to show her teeth.

"Yeah. It was. There I was, just floating in the water, and all of a sudden, I was pulled under. It was like the ocean sucked me down. Everything was dark. I had salt water in my nose. It was horrific."

"How'd you survive?" He didn't really care, but he didn't want the girls to leave him behind too. He'd never find Winona without them.

"Lia over here pulled me out. Did you know her mom was a nurse during the fall? She taught her all kinds of things."

Jeremy squinted at them. "Don't you mean your mom?"

"No, of course not. My mom..." She trailed off. "Shit."

"Life would be a lot easier if you learned to keep your mouth shut," Jenna said. She rubbed a hand over her face. "I guess the secret is out."

"Secret?" Jeremy wanted to scream as his fears dug into him. Winona had said something was off, and she was right. She was always right. He should have just listened. He wouldn't be in this position if he had. He sighed to himself. Just another reason for her to leave him behind.

## YEAR 5 AGC, DAY 290

### WINONA

WINONA COULDN'T STOP THINKING about Jeremy as she leaned heavily against the tree trunk and listened for the sound of running water. It had been a couple of days since she left him, and still, the decision weighed heavily on her. Even the distant sounds of a stream only gave her temporary joy. She was getting closer to fresh water and hopefully some kind of food. It had been two full days of walking without either, and she was starting to feel faint. Her body was starting to fail her the longer she went, and she knew she didn't have much time left. Why did those two women have to ruin the good thing she and Jeremy had going?

Every time she paused against a tree, it was harder and harder to push herself off and keep going. Her body was exhausted, and she missed Jeremy. It was a horrible combination that left her feeling disoriented and angry.

She cursed Jeremy for what felt like the hundredth time that day. She had gotten comfortable and happy with having him around, and he had to go and fuck it up. First with her house, then with Maeve. She wondered, not for the first time since she'd left, if he was even worried about her or if he had moved on to Maeve. Winona sighed, her body and mind at war over the loss of Jeremy. Her mind constantly strayed to him, but what did that matter?

With a deep breath and more energy than it should have taken, she pushed herself off the tree and started trekking toward the bubbling of water. She refused to keep battling with her mind about Jeremy and forced her thoughts to focus on the sounds of the forest. She wasn't willing to admit that if she did a pro-and-con list for Jeremy, he would have way more in the pro column than in the con. That reality was too painful for her to acknowledge.

She wished there was something to distract her, but in the after, forests were eerily quiet, leaving her to her thoughts alone. The muffled sounds of crunching leaves under her shoes and the soft bubbling from the stream weren't enough to keep her mind at ease. She missed the sound of Jeremy rambling next to her. She had less room to stew in her own misery when he was around. She berated herself for once again not being able to think about anything other than stupid Jeremy.

It didn't take long for the stream to appear in the distance, and once she saw it, Winona was jogging to close the distance. Thoughts of Jeremy vanished as her body reacted to the presence of salvation. Her body collapsed along the side of the river, and she breathed in the musty smell of the waterlogged plants. It was comforting. She paused to appreciate that she was going to make it another few days. Maybe to see Jeremy again. She brushed away the errant thought angrily before cupping her hands together to gather water. She filled them with the cool water and savored the feeling. It had been a long time since she was able to get fresh, cool water. Taking a long sip, she let the liquid fill her belly.

She smiled briefly at the clear water before taking in her reflection. Her brown hair was slicked down against her scalp and knotted behind her back. Her eyes were surrounded by dark circles from lack of sleep, and the frown on her face was deep and worrisome. She looked horrible. She looked sickly. Had she looked this bad before leaving the camp? Did Jeremy hate her reflection as much as she did?

She never looked this sickly and miserable at home. The mirrors in the house, at least once Jeremy showed up, made her look happy. Maybe it was Jeremy that made her look so happy, and this was what she looked like without him? She mentally added this to the growing list of pros Jeremy had. The pros most definitely outweighed the cons, and she knew it. It was a painful reminder that she didn't even give him a chance to defend himself.

She shooed that thought away as her stomach growled. She needed to focus. She had gotten water but nothing to eat. Winona looked around the stream for anything of color. She couldn't find any berries, not that she was surprised about that. Without pollinators to help berries grow, they were scarce at best. Her parents had told her that berries could only exist if they were pollinated, and that required flowers with pollen. In the early days, her mom had cross-pollinated the plants in their garden, but eventually, that didn't work either. She was confident that berries were a thing of the before and would never return.

She had almost given up when she noticed a lump of something underneath a healthy-looking green plant. She crawled over to it and plucked what looked to be a cucumber from the ground. She rinsed it off in the water before taking a bite out of it. It was underripe, but she didn't care. It was the first food she'd found since she left, and she was grateful it was there in the first place.

Once she had finished the cucumber, she spent another few minutes picking the three other mostly ripe cucumbers off the plant and stuck them into her bag. It wasn't much, but it would last her a few days at the least. Enough time to try to find more food along the way. She smiled, proud that she was still able to do this alone. She turned back to the water to see her reflection. The smile made her look happy, but when she looked into her own eyes, the smile didn't reach there.

# YEAR 5 AGC, DAY 294

## WINONA

WINONA WOKE up to the sun blinding her and the sound of soft growling. The growling forced her awake. Catapulting off the ground, she spun to face whatever creature had found her. Once the stars disappeared from her vision, she caught two eyes watching her from behind a bush. A week without sufficient water or food made her brain foggy, distorting the image as it darkened on the edges of her vision. She cursed herself for choosing this path and the week of constant hunger pangs over sticking with the group. All she had done was walk and eat the few mushrooms she was able to find. It was miserable.

After blinking a few times, her vision cleared. She froze, eyes locked with the creature staring at her. Black pits drew her in so intensely that she could hear her heart hammering away in her chest. They didn't blink as they watched her.

It wasn't until the bushes started to part that Winona pulled herself out of the trance. The darkness was still there, but she felt in control of her movement. The beast, what looked to be a very large coyote, started toward her. As large as it was, it looked malnourished. Bones showed at its chest. There was no way this coyote wasn't starving.

It stalked slowly as if not to startle her. She scrambled up the closest tree, pulling at branches until she was halfway up the trunk. The swipe of its paws just missed her. The coyote continued to claw at the tree with no purchase.

She whispered a thank you to her father for teaching her that coyotes couldn't climb.

She watched the gray fur as it straddled her bag, just barely missing the jar-shaped object inside. Its slight outline was the one indication it hadn't broken. Focusing on the ground, the height sunk in, and she started to get dizzy with a strong roll of nausea. She uttered a curse.

The coyote growled again as it shook the tree. It forced her to try to think past the fear despite her increasing heart rate. The force of its claws made her grab the trunk to steady herself. Her nails ripped at the bark, and she threw it away. The beast turned its head to check out the movement it caused. She tried to keep herself planted despite the efforts of the coyote or her fear of heights playing with her head.

There was nothing in the tree to hit it with, and it clearly wasn't leaving without her. The bark had distracted it briefly, but it wasn't big enough to draw it away. She rubbed a rough hand against her face before studying the area. She needed to get out of the tree before she puked on top of this coyote, and it got angrier. Bile rose in her throat. Maybe the puking would gross it out, and it would leave her alone.

There were at least two trees within jumping distance if she got the right leverage. She pushed the fact that jumping at this height would most definitely force her to throw up. One of the trees was just as bare as hers. The other had a pine cone nestled a few feet higher up the tree. Her stomach rolled with the idea of going higher, but she gauged the distance anyway. She was at least twelve feet in the air, and if the roof incident was any indication, any higher would not be kind to her. She wished

Jeremy was there. Not having his comfort stung, and her eyes burned.

"It's not that far. You can make it," she said out loud, trying to psych herself up.

The beast growled, digging its claws into the bark and lifting itself into the air. It couldn't hold on, but the jump was enough to push past her fears. She stood up on the branch and bounced. The branch bounced with her. It would be enough to help throw herself across the gap in the trees. She had no doubt this stunt of sheer stupidity would lead to her death, or at least to her puking all over the coyote and her stuff.

Winona bent down, her hands firmly planted on the branch. With her palms flat, the right one stung from where the splinter had ripped into her and never fully healed. She used the pain to keep herself focused on anything but the ground. She pulled her weight down, aiming toward the other tree, and launched herself up and out, her hands giving her the last push before she was flying.

For a moment, she was weightless and breathed out a light laugh. It was so much less scary than staring at the ground from so far in the air. It felt like she was floating, and she never wanted to come down. The tree was within distance, and she was going to make it.

Before she could rejoice, the distance between herself and the tree was closing way too fast. She couldn't slow herself down. She smashed face-first into the rough, unforgiving bark. Her face bloomed with pain as she tasted blood in the back of her throat. Gagging, she held back the throw-up as she began free-falling down to her death.

The pain mixed with fear drew Jeremy's face, smiling at her over a bowl of his famous vegetable soup, in her mind. Her heart ached. She didn't want this to be the end. Didn't want her disappearing into the night to be the last memory they shared.

She shouldn't have left in the first place. She should have fought for him the same way he fought to keep her safe.

A sharp pain in the middle of her back pulled her back to the present in time to grab hold of the branch that slowed her down. She moaned, her feet dangling a few feet above the coyote's snout. She hadn't fallen much, even though it felt like an eternity. She was still fairly high in the tree and was only a few branches below her target.

The beast snapped at her as she pulled herself up. Her arms, burning with the effort and lack of food, shook as she got herself onto the branch. It was thinner than the last, and she wasn't sure how it didn't crack off when she landed on it.

When she had caught her breath, she bent to look up the tree at the sole pine cone. Without looking down at the coyote, she could convince herself she wasn't as high as she was. The pine cone was her only salvage, and she needed to live long enough to apologize for deserting Jeremy. That was enough to push her up the tree toward the pine cone. She was grateful she hadn't knocked it down. But it was a good fifteen feet above her.

"Fucking shit," she muttered. She took a deep breath, using the sharp pine scent to center herself, and started to climb the tree.

"Just don't look down," she repeated as she climbed. Her arms protested, giving out multiple times as she climbed. The sudden dips made her heart flip-flop. She focused on the fire, the burning sensation in her arm and face, to push herself farther and farther.

When she reached the pine cone, slumping herself against the trunk of the tree, she pulled it off the tree and held it to her chest. It was a long shot to assume this beast would go for her pine cone versus her bleeding self right here, but she had to try.

Gently rubbing her hand against her bleeding nose, she covered the pine cone in blood and her scent. She winced as she ripped a chunk of bark off the tree and threw it to her left.

When the coyote turned its head, she chucked the pine cone to her right. It soared through the air before landing with a thunk that echoed inside the forest. She wanted to thank whoever was watching over her.

The coyote swung its head toward the sound and then back up to her. She watched the indecision as it looked between what she hoped sounded like easy prey to her in the tree. In what felt like hours, Winona waited with her nausea seeping back in like a cold river. Her body wavered as her mind spun, but she held on to the tree for her life. Dark spots blossomed in her vision.

When the coyote finally decided the pine cone was a better option, she let herself breathe in. Releasing her breath, she felt her heart start to slow. She couldn't get down yet, but the immediate threat was gone. Looking down, she took stock of her items, most of which weren't smashed, let alone touched. Her body fought her as she tried to recenter on the branch.

"Didn't I say I wouldn't look down?" she muttered.

Listening for the sound of rustling, Winona waited until the sun hit the top of the sky without any noise before clambering down the tree. As soon as she placed her feet on solid ground, they gave out on her, and she threw up into the brush. Her eyes stung with unshed tears. Grabbing her jacket, she cleaned her face before collecting her items as quickly as possible and then heading back toward the highway and away from the coyote.

When her feet finally landed on the pavement, she started down the cracked road. Her chest released all the tension as she looked up to the clouds and whispered repeated thank-yous. She was finally breathing normally and the closest to calm she had been since she lost her home. She had fallen much farther behind than she wanted. Without knowing if Jeremy was heading toward the highway or still parallel, she would need to keep going.

The eyes of the coyote still burned into her mind, Winona kicked herself for leaving Jeremy behind. She couldn't deny how distraught and lost she felt without him. She had been and always will be capable of doing this alone. But there was something about Jeremy's presence and helpful mentality that made everything just work out. Jeremy drove her nuts, and he fawned over Maeve so quickly she felt invisible, but he also made her smile. He made her laugh, took care of her even when she didn't know she needed it, and gave the warmest, most calming hugs she'd ever experienced.

Winona patted her bag, feeling to make sure everything was safe and secure, and then focused on heading toward Denver. If she was going to make her way back to Jeremy, her best bet was to get to Denver. Unless the girls convinced him otherwise, and she had to hope they didn't, he would show up at the college eventually.

She would be there, waiting to apologize.

She hoped that he would accept it.

# YEAR 5 AGC, DAY 297

## DEE

BY THE TIME they made it to Nebraska, Dee was willing to let Rowan ride next to her consistently. She hadn't forgiven him, hadn't really said much, but she also hadn't run ahead of him anymore. That meant something. At least, she wanted to believe it did. Every night, Rowan would sit next to her in silence while she read her mother's journal. She started with the entries from right before they passed away, traveling back through time. She was reaching their toddler days by their first night in the state. Her mother's warring emotions had started to bubble up in her cursive script, and Dee started to shake as she read it.

Their mom hadn't outright said what her father had done to push her over the edge, not yet at least, but Dee knew it was coming. She snapped the book shut, eyed her half brother, and got into her own hammock. Rowan muttered something under his breath, but she ignored it. With the long days of travel, she was exhausted, and she fell asleep immediately.

If only for her nightmares—images of her parents' graves and Rowan's face as he told her the truth—to force her eyes open.

When she woke with a start, she flipped out of her hammock

and smacked into the hard dirt. She winced but managed not to wake Rowan up. Even now, she was still protecting her despite her anger. Picking herself off the ground, she went to get a fire going. Rowan had left a pile of chopped wood in a pile next to the firepit she had created when they got there. They were a team, even without her having to say anything.

Once the flames started licking up at the sky, she started brewing some coffee for the two of them. At least, what she pretended was coffee. It was closer to black tea. She had picked up different herbs and plants on their way that, when boiled with water from the creeks they walked parallel to, vaguely tasted like the canned coffee her parents had stockpiled in the basement.

It was the best she could manage. Normally, she just made it for herself before she packed her horse up and started back on the trail. It was the first time she had made enough for both of them. It was the closest she would get to a peace offering with how angry she still felt. The journal had taught her so much, but the one thing it didn't do was make her feel any less angry.

Surprise flitted across Rowan's face as he stumbled out of his own hammock and over to her. "That smells good." He gave her a weak smile. "You made more than usual."

Dee nodded, pouring him a cup before perching on a nearby log. The dew soaked into her pants, and she sighed as she took a sip of the bitter liquid. "We're a couple days from Denver. There's a college there that Mom talks about in her journal. Supposedly Denver's ecology didn't collapse like the rest of the US. At least, according to the memos from the last president. I think we should search the area for supplies at the least."

Rowan smacked his chest with the first smile they shared in weeks. "She speaks. I didn't think your voice worked anymore. Does your throat hurt from lack of use?"

Dee picked up a stick and threw it at him. "Don't make me regret that, Rowan. You and I both know you can't find your ass from a hole in the ground." Despite the bite, they shared a second smile. It warmed her inside to have their usual banter back, if only tentatively. She wouldn't say it out loud, but she missed him. She missed him more than she missed their parents.

Rowan rolled his eyes but nodded solemnly. "You're right. But you also can't find water for shit. You'd never be able to make coffee without me. I don't think you'd be able to survive without it."

She scoffed. "I wish this was real coffee." She swirled the liquid in her metal cup. It had been years since the last fresh batch of coffee was used up in their house. According to their mom, they were lucky to even have coffee. "Tree bark and peppermint leaves just aren't the same."

"You could navigate us to Central America..." He waved in what she assumed he thought was south.

She didn't correct him that it was North. She wasn't kidding about Rowan's sense of direction. It was the exact opposite of hers. Dee understood direction in the ways Rowan understood water. It was like they were individually connected to their different affinities. They each had skills that helped them survive together. Something, according to her mom's journal, that started when they were barely three years old. "If it's this hot up here. I can't imagine what Mexico is like, let alone Guatemala."

"Maybe it would be better to burn." He snorted. Dropping the subject, he gave her an inquisitive look. "So where are we going after Denver?"

"Farther into the mountains, I think. See if we can find an abandoned cabin there. Restart in a cooler place." She sounded far more confident than she felt. It was the first time she even suggested a plan, let alone thought of one. For the longest time, she was just running. Today was the first day she thought about walking, maybe even stopping.

He nodded, easily accepting her half-assed plan. They sat in silence, sipping their coffees, until Rowan got up and headed into the forest. Dee watched him leave. A small part of her worried for a second before the rational part reminded her that he was probably getting more water.

When he was out of sight, she tended to their horses with the little bit of feed they had left and fresh water. She rubbed each of the horse's snouts, whispering soft words of affection. By the time she finished, Rowan was making his way back with a handful of mushrooms. He handed her some.

"We should get going," Dee said, shoving the mushrooms into a pouch before starting to pack up her hammock and saddling up onto her horse.

"We should eat first. You can't just feed the horses but not yourself." Rowan gave her a look that was a mirror of their father's.

She rolled her eyes at him but didn't fight him when he handed over a stick of roasted mushrooms. "How many of these did you pick?"

"Enough for two days. They're safe, I think." Rowan took a bite and smiled at her. She watched him. "Look, I didn't die. You'll be fine."

"That's a low bar." She took a tentative bite. They weren't the best meal she had, but it was her first meal since breakfast the day before. Her stomach rumbled, and she housed it down. With her mouth still full, she asked, "Can you find water before we keep going? I gave the rest to the horses."

Rowan nodded. "I'm not sure it's on the way, but it should be fresh."

"We're in no rush," she said, taking the journal from her things and holding it against her chest. "I have a lot left to read."

When they had finished their food, Rowan got onto his horse and guided them down the path until making a sharp right at the bottom of a slope. They trotted for another half an hour before they found a stream Rowan claimed was clean. She climbed down, taking both of their canteens to fill them, while Rowan led the horses to the water and filled their water pouches.

Working in silence, Dee felt herself slipping back into the comfortable twin relationship they used to have. It was hard to pull herself back out of it, but she managed to at least frown in his direction. Goddamn Rowan. She'd never been very good at staying mad at him. It was probably why their mother expected her to take care of him. Would they have lied to her if she wasn't responsible for him? Dee brushed the thoughts away. It didn't matter now.

"Are you ready?" she asked, walking to where he was brushing the horses. He didn't respond, just handed her the reins to her horse. They trotted off, Rowan following her lead as she wrapped her way around the mountains until they were back on a steady incline.

By the time they could see what looked like a city, the sun had started to set. Dee slowed down, pulling herself off to the side at a flat zone, and gestured to Rowan. "We can stay here for the night. I'd like to head through the city in daylight. We're not close enough for this to be Denver, so who knows what is going on there."

He didn't question her, just stopped to tie his horse to a tree and start unpacking.

Now that Dee had opened the floodgates, it bugged her that he was being so silent. It made her furious if she was being honest with herself. Angrier than when he lied to her. She tried to push it aside, if only to get herself unpacked, and managed to hold it off just long enough for the two of them to get the fire going. Their parents had taught them more than enough to take care of themselves, that was for sure.

She watched Rowan from the other side of the fire.

"What?" he asked, giving her a look.

"I'm sorry," she said, biting back the anger. Rowan's eyebrows lifted so high she thought they might merge with his hairline. "Don't be a little shit, and most definitely don't get used to it."

Rowan laughed with his whole body. Wiping his tears away, he looked at her soberly. "I shouldn't have lied to you."

Dee made an affirmative noise. "I'm not ready to deal with that yet. But I'm sorry for letting this pull us apart. We were raised to be a team, and no matter what, that's how we should be. It's just us now."

"Take all the time you need."

Dee nodded before reaching into her bag and pulling out the journal. By the light of the flames, Dee flipped back to when they were infants. Back to the days when their little family was established. Taking a deep breath, she prepared herself, making sure she wasn't facing Rowan in case she cried, and started to read.

# YEAR 5 AGC, DAY 297

## JEREMY

"ARE you sure that she would have headed this way?" Maeve said, her voice a little whinier than Jeremy could handle after so many days with only the three of them. Jeremy was confident that despite leaving him behind, Winona would still go to Denver, to the abandoned college. How many times had she told him the old fables about the city and how it still shined like an emerald? The idea that she would change course just to avoid him was too harsh to think about. He forced an easy grin on his face, shoving his hurt farther down, and looked at Maeve.

"I'm confident that she would go this way."

"I can't smell her here in the forest, but maybe she got onto the highway?" Jenna shrugged, giving him a pitying look.

He hated that they pitied him. Hated that he was stuck between the two girls who shared secret looks. Hated that Winona had walked away from him. Hated himself for not telling her how he really felt. Most of all, he hated that he was so filled with anger and hatred that he couldn't see straight.

"It can't be much farther. If she's not there, you two are welcome to keep moving." His voice was harsh, something he'd never associated with himself before. Without Winona, it felt like he was being dragged under the current with no chance of air. The darkness that edged his thoughts grew stronger with every thought spiral.

They didn't respond. He listened to their footsteps crunch through the dry underbrush of the Colorado forests. Despite the dead leaves, the forest looked every bit the emerald color Winona had shown him in her books. Not only could he hear the chirping of birds, but every once in a while, the bright yellow or blue of a larger bird caught his eye. He could smell the dewy moss on the trees, and he focused on that to keep his mind in the present. But it wasn't as easy as he'd like. It was like the area was under a protective bubble, and every minute he appreciated was a minute he hoped Winona was in the same bubble. Protected in the ways he had hoped to provide.

He closed his eyes, trying to pull her face from his memory, but all he got was the sound of her voice in the darkness of their tent, her last few words echoing in his head. He lost himself, replaying the conversation over and over again until he got the result he wanted. Until he woke up to her instead of an empty tent that felt like a black pit full of misery. It was hard to imagine the happiness he'd felt when she'd let him stay. It was even harder to imagine life before her in comparison to the current.

"Jeremy. You can't just stew. I can see the misery weighing you down, and it's definitely making this walk feel like a march of death," Maeve quipped, snapping him back to the present.

"I just…," he mumbled.

"You just shouldn't have said what you did. We know, and we're working on fixing that. But you need to focus on something else, or you're going to be crazy by the time we find her." Her words just echoed his fears. He still wasn't sure she even wanted him to find her. If they had switched places, would he have run too?

Jeremy chewed on her words before sighing loudly. "Fine. Why don't you tell me a story?"

Maeve gave him a blank look before elbowing Jenna. "She tells better stories, don't you, Lia?"

Jenna cleared her throat. "I guess I tell a better story than your disjointed mess of sentences you call a story."

Maeve laughed so hard that even Jeremy smiled. After they confessed to being a couple instead of sisters, the two girls relaxed. Jeremy was mad for a split second, frustrated with their lies and jealous of them, before settling into an understanding. Safe-guarding secrets was the only way to survive in this life. Besides, as much as the way they looked at each other stung him, it wasn't their fault he wasn't in the same place as them. Jeremy, no matter how miserable he felt, would never tell them they couldn't love each other. How could he when they so obviously fit together like a puzzle?

When Maeve could breathe again, she linked her arm through Jenna's, and said, "Why don't you tell him about how we met?"

Jeremy shrugged.

"I'll take that as a yes," she said. "It may not surprise you that I have always been the more cautious of the two of us. Part of which comes from my tracking nature, which requires steady movements as quietly as possible, or I would force whatever creature I was following to flee. The rest comes from my family. Maeve, on the other hand, is the reason we have to keep moving, as she has scared away many possible communities.

"When I was eighteen and still lived with my mom, I was in charge of tracking and capturing anything I could find for us to eat. I had spent the entire morning following the trail of what looked to be a family of deer. If you didn't know, deer scatter easily, or the buck will charge depending on how close you are. They were finally in sight from my perch in a tree, maybe a hundred feet away.

"The buck had separated from the group, so I started to set up the shot."

Maeve giggled. "This is my favorite part."

Jenna rolled her eyes. "If you interrupt me again, we won't ever get there."

Maeve mimed locking her mouth shut before sticking her tongue out at Jenna.

"As I was saying," Jenna said. "I had positioned myself against the branch and the trunk and started lining up the shot. Just as I started to pull back, there was this high-pitched screeching. It was so close and loud that I lost my footing. I tumbled out of the tree, barely having time to chuck my bow and arrow away from me, and landed on my back. I had to bite back my scream as I tilted my head toward the meadow in hopes the deer was still there.

"It wasn't, but suddenly a pair of brown boots filled my vision. I rolled my head to look up, and the happiest, most infuriating girl in the world was smiling at me so hard that there was no way her cheeks didn't hurt. She reached down to help me to my feet, and the rest is history."

Jeremy gave the couple a rare real smile. No matter his problems, Maeve and Jenna were a perfect match. "You're lucky to have each other."

Maeve frowned at him. "Don't be like that. Lia here ripped me a new one after that little stunt. I was confident she was going to hunt me next. Barely spoke to me, despite me following her around like a lost puppy for the first year. If it wasn't for her mom, we wouldn't have gotten this far."

Jeremy fought the urge to compare them to his situation. They had made it through, and every day he didn't find Winona, he was uncomfortably sure that they wouldn't.

Jenna nodded. "The point of the story is that just because you're having a rough patch, just because she's struggling right now, doesn't mean that you are done, or she doesn't care about you."

"You say that, but…" He couldn't finish. His words were strangled enough with thoughts of Winona, and he was tired of the pity he saw in their eyes. "Listen, I appreciate your help, but I just need to keep moving forward. If I spend all my time focused on why she left, I'll never be able to convince her not to leave again."

Jeremy shrugged before speeding up to walk in front of the girls. He was glad they had made it work, but every day he didn't see Winona was another day toward never seeing her again. He wasn't sure they would find her at all. He could still see the paling of Jenna's face when she picked the pine cone off the ground. She had stilled, holding it in front of her as if it was going to explode at any second. When he finally prodded her, she told him it was only a small amount of her blood. It was nothing to worry about. Her words felt as hollow then as they did ringing in his head.

He wasn't sure how long they had gone on like that until Jenna cleared her throat.

"You can't spend the next few weeks in this misery," Jenna finally said, cutting through his thoughts and forcing him to look at her. "Not only is it making this walk quite literally a march of death, but you're not going to win her back being"— she waved a hand at him—"whatever this is. From what you've told us and what we've seen, she needed your positivity. This is not the Jeremy she knows and adores."

Jeremy made a noise of annoyance. "She doesn't adore me."

"If that's what you think, you haven't been paying attention. In the short time we saw you two together, you are both just as fucking crazy about each other as the other one," Maeve said.

"Well, you don't know shit," Jeremy snapped. His vision turned red as he watched Maeve fall back. "Shit. I'm sorry." He took a deep breath, letting his anger and frustration melt away.

"I guess you're right. This is getting to me more than I'm willing to admit. I need to focus on the positive and stop taking it out on you two for helping me."

"Damn right," Maeve said. "Now, pick up the pace. We're days away from the college, and the faster you get there, the faster you stop being a pain in our butts."

He wanted to tell them that they should leave him to do this alone. No doubt he was more trouble than he was worth, but without them, Jeremy would be alone again. He would be that scared boy who traveled the coast alone for months before he found Winona. Winona who, despite her snark, made him feel like the confident man he wanted to be. The man that picked up the slack when Winona couldn't. The man who balanced so perfectly with Winona that he thought, at first, she was just pretending to need him. At the start, he was sure she was. It wasn't until the roof incident that he realized she might actually need him too. He could still feel the way she shook in his arms as he carried her down.

Hope bubbled up in his chest, but he popped it. Hope was great, but it wouldn't bring her back.

# YEAR 5 AGC, DAY 300

## THE FOREST PERSON

THEY HAD STUDIED the pair for a while before making it clear they were trespassing. Not that they or their family had lived in the house since the collapse. Not that their family existed anymore. All they had was the coyotes that showed up after their parents had disappeared in the woods. From the porch, all they saw was the flash of light when the coyotes looked down at them from the forest's edge. They had been scared, body trembling as the pack stalked over to her. When the largest, their alpha, stepped forward, their body stiffened, but when the cool, wet nose of the alpha pressed into their palm, calm swept over them.

Now the coyotes circled them, pushing them into the center of the pack protectively as they surveyed the house they grew up in. It had been almost fifteen years since they last stepped in its glass back door. It had come alive when the two adults showed up. The pair had cleaned up the overgrown plants, fixed the broken bits, and renewed the home to what it looked like when they were a kid. But tonight, it was quieter than usual. The sound of laughter that normally floated out was dead and replaced by the eerie echo of pure silence. It made them shiver.

They planned to check out the house while the couple was gone, but they never left. In the cover of darkness, they had hoped to sneak into the house, despite the coyotes trying to hold them at the top of the hill above the neighborhood.

"I'll be back," they growled. The pack gave them a knowing look. They had learned in the early days how to pitch their voice in the same range as the coyotes. It wasn't that the pack understood what they said. It was that they recognized their tone and posture.

The coyotes parted for her, the alpha pressing a snout into their thigh as they slid past the group. They wanted to turn, to scratch his chin and beg him to join them, but they held back with a stern look toward the house. They locked their eyes on the house and marched down the hill with a straight back and confidence they didn't feel.

When they got to the bottom, there was a flicker in the window. Nothing more than a breeze hitting the old curtains that still hung in what was her parents' room. They paused, studying the house, waiting for signs the couple was still awake.

Another flicker, a curtain pulled away from another window in the same room. This one on the side that faces where they stood. The scrape of the window opening gave her goose bumps as it echoed through the open expanse of field. They waited a few minutes, then shivered at the sound of another window opening, before heading back up the hill. They needed to wait.

* * *

BY THE TIME the moon hit the middle of the midnight sky, the orange globe bathing the meadow between the forest and house in golden light, there hadn't been any movement in the house since they retreated. The confidence they lacked earlier had built up in the time they watched from the trees. It was clear whoever had been awake was finally asleep.

With the pack of coyotes off to hunt by the moonlight, they were alone to search the home. The coyotes had made it clear they didn't want their help, that their roasting of the meat the pack or they brought home was disgusting, but they did their best to help anyway. They were indebted to the beasts that circled the woods.

Their stomach grumbled as they pushed the idea of meat aside. It had been several days since the last meal, but the pack was bound to find something without them tonight. That left them with just the house they once called home. They headed back toward the house.

* * *

THEY DIDN'T PLAN to break in, just collect the items on the porch and sneak a look or two. It hadn't been their house in such a long time it didn't feel like home anymore. Despite trying to scare off the couple, they didn't want the house back —they just didn't want anyone else replacing their family. But the man, the one who watched the forest for them, left clothing out. From the way it fit, it was clear it belonged to the woman. They would rather have something baggy, but they had run out of clothing that fit her, so they didn't have a choice in the matter. Without a way to raid any of the stores in town, it was the clothing left out for them or covering their body in leaves.

The pair had a car she'd never seen before. It didn't make noise how their parents had described it would, but somehow it still ran. One of them would go out during the day and return with random boxes or bags full of things they never saw after it was unloaded. Sometimes the woman would come back with piles of food in dusty boxes or a basket full of clothing. It helped ease her guilt about collecting the clothing left on the porch for them. The woman looked to have a never-ending supply of outfits from what they could see, though she didn't come out back very often, so it was hard to be sure.

Tonight was no different. They stepped onto the porch to find the man had left more than usual out for them. The stack had what looked to be undergarments, a pair of jeans cut a few inches above the ankle, and a shirt a size bigger than usual. It had a logo on it that she'd seen the man wear. Not that she recognized what it meant. The blue and red circle with curly writing on it wasn't something their parents had shown them.

It didn't matter. They'd wear anything, and the larger the shirt, the more comfortable they felt. Sleeping naked on the floor of the forest, regardless of the soft fur that surrounded them, wasn't nearly as comfortable as wearing something to protect their fragile skin from the rough leaves and dead branches. They weren't as rugged as the coyotes, despite the years in the wilderness.

Picking up the stack, they turned to stare into the living room that bordered the kitchen. The couch, a well-worn white monstrosity designed to hold more people than existed in the small world their parents had created, looked just as soft and comfortable as it was when they were young. A red knitted blanket, a family hand-me-down, was spread haphazardly over the back of the couch. Someone had thrown it there recently.

It perplexed them. They had never come at nighttime to see the living room not in perfect order. They reached for the doorknob, starting to turn it as concern mounted when a figure stepped off the bottom step of the stairs on the other side of the couch. Just because they didn't know each other didn't mean they didn't care about the couple that helped them survive.

Light filtered into the room just enough to make it clear it was the woman. She was looking down, focusing on the floor, as she padded over to the kitchen.

They pulled back, the clothing pile smooshed against their chest, and hid in the shadows of the house. They could still see the woman dig around for a glass. She pulled out a glass bottle with Snapple written across the side and poured a clear liquid from the bottle into a glass. She took a big gulp of the liquid, finishing it in one go, before dropping the glass in the sink.

The woman leaned against the counter, a hand on her forehead, and mumbled to herself. She couldn't hear her, but based on the movement of her lips, she wasn't speaking English. The only word she made out was Diego. It was the only word she recognized and assumed it was the man's name.

It wasn't long before she started toward the stairs. She made it into the carpeted area behind the couch before she started to waver. Her body weaved in the air before collapsing in a pile on the floor. Her eyes were shut, her mouth left wide open. The glass flew from her hand, spilling liquid across the floor as it bounced to a stop on the rug.

Dropping the pile of clothing on the porch, they turned the knob. It was unlocked and squeaked as it flung open. They cringed when it clattered against the wall. They paused for a second, but when the house stayed silent, they continued toward the woman. After years of living in the wilderness with the coyotes, there were some things that were unexpected benefits. They were strong, strong enough to lift the woman. She was lighter than even they expected, and placing her on the couch took minimal effort.

Her eyelids fluttered but didn't stay open.

The second benefit, one that helped more often than they wanted to admit, was their ability to hear and understand the body. To recognize signs that should concern someone. They placed an ear by her chest and listened to the steady beat of her heart. It was weak, much weaker than their own, but didn't appear to be under duress. It sounded as if it was too tired to work any harder. It sounded like they felt in the morning when they had to spend another day fighting for life.

They didn't know what that would mean for the woman

except that she would wake in the morning, and the man could help her out. There was nothing more they could do without jeopardizing the fragile balance that had developed. They laid the soft red blanket on her, covering her the best they could, before slipping back out of the house.

Once outside, they ran toward the forest in case the man woke up and stumbled downstairs. By the time they were obscured by the thick bushes on the edge of the forest, they realized they had left the clothing dropped across the back porch of the house. Looking back at the house and then up at the slow lightening of the sky, they sighed heavily.

Hopefully, the couple wouldn't believe they didn't appreciate their kindness because of such a small mistake. Hopefully, the couple would make it through whatever was wrong with the girl. They took one last lingering look at the quiet house before heading deep into the forest back to the pack's den. They would trek back at night after they got some rest.

## DEE

DEE SKIDDED her horse to a stop outside the large concrete building. The sound of its hooves scraping the concrete made goose bumps break out on her arms. She shivered and then looked up at the several-stories-tall building. It was covered in cracks, hundreds of vines were digging into the walls, and several large chunks of concrete had fallen off and left giant gaps in the structure. She studied the holes in the walls that let light filter through the building, a soft orange hue spewing out, and tried to determine what the building was originally used for.

"Do you plan on scaling the building to get away from me?" Rowan said, pulling his horse to a stop next to her. "I know you're tired of my jokes, but the last one wasn't that bad!"

"You mean you repeatedly saying Route 69 while giggling?" Dee snorted. "I'm not sure that is even considered a joke. I'm going to have to give your comedic skills a two out of ten at best and a zero at worst."

"That was at least a six," Rowan said, before calling out, "Sixty-nine."

The sound bounced off the building as if echoing the last

three hours with Rowan since they had passed the interstate. It dug into her sanity as another reminder that they had spent the last month just the two of them. They needed to eventually find more people, or she would lose her mind. The continual jokes, while cheesy and horrible, made the last half of the ride far more enjoyable than the first, at the very least. Dee would take the horrendous humor Rowan lived for to the painful ringing of silence.

The silence and pain they had barely left behind still lingered in the distance, close enough to still hurt but far enough to pretend it never existed. Pretending was an uncomfortable thing she didn't want to believe was needed. She couldn't imagine truly dealing with the unspoken words between them, so she refused to stop pretending. She brushed away her thoughts as just useless musing and turned to focus on Rowan. "I think this would be a good place for us to settle for the night."

Rowan scoffed, waving at the sun still high in the sky. "We have a few more hours. We could make it into the city to finally get that over with and move on."

Dee hesitated. The city felt wrong. Just thinking about the city made her skin crawl, and she shook out her curls as chills ran across her skin. She couldn't explain the twisting in her gut, but she hated the idea of finding out what it meant. If they went into the city and something happened to either of them, she'd never forgive herself.

She looked at him sternly. "We're going to stay here tonight."

Rowan snorted but jumped off his horse anyway. He grabbed the reins, walking him toward the giant concrete building and tying him against a thick trunk that was protruding from the sidewalk crack. He ran his fingers against the building. "It looks to be what Dad called an office building. Don't think we've seen one outside Mom's history books."

Dee bristled at Rowan's causal tone of voice talking about

their parents as if they hadn't done anything wrong. Having finished reading the journal and starting from the beginning, she knew that both of their parents were at fault for the cheating and the lies. It was silly for her to get annoyed about it, the situation, or Rowan's tone, but she hadn't forgiven the whole situation. She hadn't even gotten a chance to process the words she read, let alone her own feelings. She bit into her palm with her nails and took a deep breath.

Dee waved at the building. "You're probably right. Let's get to the second floor and find a good place to start a fire. I think it might rain tonight." They looked up at the sky. It was the bright yellowish-orange of the beginnings of dusk. To the south, a patch of dark clouds was emerging over the trees. She pointed it out for him. "If that's not a thunderstorm, and I bet it is, I will personally cook you breakfast."

Rowan held out his hand. "You have a deal. Can't wait for my roasted berries tomorrow!"

"No, no. Don't get your hopes up." A crack of thunder ripped through the air, and Dee laughed. "It's not looking good for you."

He flicked her off. "Whatever. Let's get the fuck inside this building. We'll have to get the horses set up inside with some cut grass."

"Don't be a sore loser," she said, handing the reins of her horse to him. "I'll get the grass. You can get the horses comfortable and start a fire."

Rowan took the reins and stalked off inside. She rolled her eyes at him, a small blossom of happiness building in her chest. They may be broken, they may be beaten, but they weren't beyond repair, and she was eternally grateful they could still care for each other despite the lies and hurt.

Once they were set up inside, Dee pulled out the notebook and placed it between them. She stared at the dirt stuck on the cover of the notebook and sighed. While the information in there had been enlightening, she didn't feel like it gave her the guidance she was looking for. It was lacking the steps needed for them to move forward in their lives. She should have known better than to expect a written plan for their future in the past, but she had still hoped.

Rowan reached for it and thumbed through the pages. She watched him from her spot around the fire that he had built. Maybe he had found more in there than she did. Maybe he had some insights.

"Did you finish it?" Rowan asked.

"I finished it last night," she replied.

She reached for the notebook, but Rowan pulled it away from her with a frown. "Do you want to talk about it?"

She nodded. "I don't know where to start."

"Mom and Dad were both wrong," Rowan said harshly, slamming the book into the concrete between them. "They were wrong in how they dealt with each other before we were born, and they were wrong to make me lie to you. They were just wrong."

She sighed, picking the notebook up and cradling it to her chest. "I understand that Mom felt Dad didn't appreciate her. I get that completely." She leveled a look at her brother. "But I don't think she should have stepped out of the marriage. It didn't even sound like the other guy was that great to her. He seemed worse than Dad in a lot of ways."

"He was an ass too," Rowan added. "I mean, he barely did anything to make her feel special. I don't understand why she would pick him over Dad."

"Do you wonder if it was stress? If the stress of living in the before was so heavy they didn't know what to do with themselves?" Dee flipped through the pages to an entry at the beginning.

She read off the page. *"John came home today with nothing again. He hasn't been able to catch anything to eat in three days. Our* *supplies are dwindling, and I'm worried we are going to run out of food soon. We only have so many canned goods in the basement. I brought it up to him over dinner, and he snapped at me <u>again</u>. As if it's my fault we are running out of food. I swear he doesn't appreciate all the effort I go through to make our rations last. As if I'm not caring for our child while he runs through the woods. He treats me like I'm a slave to this house.*"

Rowan cleared his throat. "Do you wish you had Dad's side?"

"I would give anything to hear the other side of the story," Dee said. She read the whole notebook, flagged different life lessons her mom had left for them, but she felt incomplete. She wanted to know what their father thought. If he had any guidance for their future. "Do you think Dad would have had better advice than Mom?"

Rowan shook his head. "All those nights, where Dad and I would sit together and drink, he gave me the same advice. 'Treat your sister right. At the end of the day, she's the one capable of doing what needs to be done.'"

"What does that even mean?"

Rowan waved his hands in the air. "Seriously?"

"What?"

"Look at what you've done for us since they passed? You're the reason we are still living. You managed everything back at the house, and now you are leading everything in our future. Without you, I would be wasting away on our couch. I would have no direction; I would have nothing. You're the one who has their shit together."

She laughed. "You think I have this down?" She laughed harder. "I'm just guessing. Hoping I get the right answer."

"That's better than no answer," Rowan countered.

She shrugged. Maybe he had a point. Maybe she was good for something. Maybe she didn't need this stupid notebook. She held the notebook out in front of her. "Do you think we need this thing?"

Rowan shook his head. "I think we're better off without it."

"Me too." Dee smiled at him before throwing it into the fire. A small part of her cringed as it caught quickly. The fire turned the pages dark brown before catching completely, a bright light where the notebook used to be. "Good riddance."

# YEAR 5 AGC, DAY 320

## WINONA

IN THE HOUR before she crossed into the deserted city, Winona stopped to listen to the sounds of the birds as if in a trance. She wasn't used to so much sound, her home having been devoid of most creatures, and she couldn't stop getting trapped in the songs echoing over the empty highway. It was something beautiful to break up the sound of her boots crunching the deteriorating highway. She wished the sweet songs could be bottled and kept with her for when she needed them most.

The only other sound was her mumbling to herself. After so many days alone, she needed some kind of companionship, even if it was her imagination.

She had never needed it before, having grown used to the emptiness of her home after her parents had passed, but Jeremy had changed that. He had cracked open her shell and exposed her to herself. He didn't make her feel insecure or weird; instead, he embraced her quirks and let her learn who she was beyond the girl who was just barely surviving alone. She liked the version of herself that accepted help from other people. That person was who her mother tried to raise her to be.

She tried to shut away the things he had pulled out of her,

but they weren't budging. Pushing back against it was like slamming into a mountain and thinking it would move. It was like trying to climb a cliff without a rope. No matter what she did, she slipped right back to the new Winona. After so many days, she was finally accepting that person as herself, but that just reminded her of Jeremy. Her heart ached to just get one more minute with him, even if all she got to do was apologize. The guilt of how she left things was eating her alive. She nibbled her lip in an effort to stop the tears from tumbling down her cheeks, but it was useless.

By the time she crossed the city line, she was full-on crying. The kind of ugly cry that made it so hard to breathe that she had to collapse on a concrete bench. The last time she cried this hard, she was mourning the death of her parents. The last time, she was swearing to her parents that she would make them proud. She would go beyond surviving. She would thrive.

How had she fucked up this badly?

Not only did she feel the disappointment her parents would have had if they saw her, but she had pushed Jeremy away. To lose the one person who constantly reminded her that she was more capable than she gave herself credit for, that she was what her parents thought she was. The person who listened to her tell stories about her parents as if they were still alive. She let out a moan, wiping furiously at the tears that weren't stopping. She could feel herself losing control of the situation as her brain flooded with memories of all she had lost. All the people she had pushed away or disappointed. Her parents who had left her alone in a house that reeked of loneliness. The only person who stopped long enough to learn about her and care about her. The house she had made her own after years of zombie-walking around it in hopes her parents would reappear.

It was all too much, and she couldn't push it away. Couldn't make it go back into the box she had been shoving it into for the last handful of years. Every thought, every emotion she had pushed away was flooding in. Her heart ached. Not because of all the things she lost. No. It was the stupid hope that man who should be sitting next to her comforting it away would show up right when she needed him to.

A hope that was being crushed with every minute she sat alone.

She didn't know how long she spent sitting there. Fighting to regain composure, she focused on centering her breath. The deep breathing was enough to stop the shaking, but she couldn't repack what she had opened up. All her emotions were right there, and she wasn't sure she was able to process them. It was shocking she had even acknowledged them. It was the first time she had dealt with anything since her parents died. She never learned how to.

When she could finally breathe normally and had waded through the pain of losing her parents, she looked up to see the sun setting. The orange light shined against the few leftover panes of glass in the office buildings and cast a sparkling show in the air as it reflected back through what she assumed to be cracks from old age. It was beautiful. She carefully surveyed the city and corrected herself. The whole place was beautiful. Jeremy would love it.

Her eyes tingled, the tears fighting to escape again, but she took a deep breath and pulled herself off the bench. She had processed enough for now. Without looking back, she started the march toward where she thought the college might be. She had it mapped in her head from all the years she had stared at her parents' old atlases, but that wasn't much help when she didn't have any landmarks to look for. Every building was the same concrete block covered in vines.

Eventually, it didn't matter if she had a map. There were old signs, the paint peeling away, that pointed her in the right way. While they didn't really have much paint left, the outline of where the word *college* was still imprinted on the map. She was so close she could taste it.

She was so close to finding Jeremy her breath hitched. She wanted to apologize, but more than that, she wanted to tell him that she had fallen for him. The thought brought her joy and propelled her faster through the city.

As the sky started to darken, she could barely make out a sign next to a small walkway, but it was different from the others. The sign was engraved stone instead of the reflective signs on the highway. Once the shadows made the words readable, she was sprinting. Her lungs fought her, crying for air, while she could feel the dehydration digging into every part of her body. But that didn't stop her. She wouldn't let it win. She was so close, just feet away.

Her hands grazed the rough stone. Falling to her knees painfully on the stone path, she wanted to sing out loud. She had made it. She was here. Every step had brought her closer to Jeremy, and now she was confident she was days away from reuniting. All she wanted was to curl into his arms, to feel his finger twine with hers. If only he was already here.

He wasn't. She knew it without having to look around. The air around the college smelled too strongly of nature. No one had been here in a while. The mere thought made her shoulders relax. She pulled herself off the ground using the sign to leverage her and looked out over it.

Taking in the college, there wasn't much she could see that wasn't deserted and covered in overgrowth from the weeds. The sight of all the plants growing wildly around her made her heart skip. She hadn't seen anything like it before. Her home had been bare everywhere but the garden. The trees were rotting from the inside out, having never recovered from the forest fires. She walked to the nearest building and petted the soft leaves of the vine. Their velvety texture made her smile. She could have sworn they reached back to her as she pulled her hand away.

"What a magical place," she whispered to the empty space in front of her. She evaluated the buildings before deciding on the only building still standing without any obvious signs of damage; it was as if the plants had circled the building protectively instead of claiming the building as an artifact of the past. She let herself amble across the large open space between buildings and breathed in the sweet smell of wildflowers that were growing in patches.

She reached down, plucked a small flower, and placed it over her ear before finally landing in front of the building's metal door. It was rusted, but with a good push, it flung open, and dust blew at her. She coughed, clearing her throat. The cloying feeling of dust made her throat feel tight. Scratching her neck, she pushed past it and headed toward the staircase. If she wanted to be safe, wanted to make sure her scent would waft in the area for Jenna to find her—because how else would they find her—she would need to make camp on the roof.

Because they were coming. She wouldn't let herself think anything else and focused on seeing them again to push her aching body up the never-ending stairs until she reached another metal door. Unlike the entrance, this one was half open, rusted in place. She carefully slid past it to the empty roof.

The floor was covered in small stones, but there was a medium-size box made out of metal. After a quick inspection, it looked to be stable and big enough to fit her. She placed her bag next to her and walked to the edge of the roof. She kept her eyes straight, looking over the campus, and did her best to swallow the nausea. The whole city, empty and overtaken, was such a sight that it was worth it to push herself.

She surveyed the area for people, her body weaving with exhaustion. Nausea made it hard to keep looking out, but no fear of heights would make her miss reuniting with Jeremy.

# YEAR 5 AGC, DAY 321

## JEREMY

AFTER WHAT FELT like years of walking along the highway, half hidden by the progressively more and more overgrown trees, Jeremy, Jenna, and Maeve made it. Denver was the densest city he'd ever been in, lush greens knitting together the trees like a soft quilt. He had gasped in awe when he'd seen the low-hanging branches. He touched them, letting the soft needles brush his palm. He wondered, not for the first time, if Winona had felt the same awe. Did she reach out to knit her fingers with the branches like she did in her garden? Did the forest feel homey to her?

When they had stepped out of the forest and scaled the closest concrete building, he was shocked by the view. If the forest felt dense, the city was crowded. The trees and animals had taken over the streets. He was surprised they could even see the college from their perch. It was pure luck the trees didn't obscure it. He tried to shove his hopes down. Just because the city, the college, felt right. Just because he could feel her presence, her warmth radiating in the city, didn't mean she was there. Jenna didn't get any indication that Winona had even made it when they crossed the city limits sign.

"I think we should circle the city," Jenna said. Jeremy followed her finger as it outlined the edge of the city. "If she made it, she could have entered in any direction."

"When she made it. She left ahead of us." Jeremy bit back any harsher words. Every day without Winona was painful, but he never expected to become so brash. He wasn't this kind of person, but he couldn't control it. He didn't need to be so worried. Winona had lived years alone without getting hurt. He didn't believe that she might have gotten hurt on the way here despite the evidence. She had to be fine, had to be okay, and that should have been enough to make him feel better. But even that didn't stop the concerns and fears that ate at his psyche.

A small part of him, made up mostly by the frowns Jenna and Maeve constantly gave him when they thought he wouldn't notice, didn't believe he would ever make it back to Winona. It was that tiny part, growing like the infections that killed the people he loved, that was eating him from the inside out. The first few weeks, he had been able to push it aside and keep a smile on his face. But as the weeks dragged on, as the girls continued to show no hope, he couldn't hold it back, and he was worried that finding her wouldn't fix it.

That it was a part of him now. Would she like the man he was becoming?

"Jeremy!" Maeve said, snapping her fingers in his face. "Wake up."

"Sorry. Are we ready to start looking for her?" Glancing at their faces, he saw their concern. Jenna lifted her chin at the sky. It had darkened in a way he'd never seen before. The sky was no longer the soft orange of dusk but burnt orange and covered with dark-gray clouds. The colors swirled in the distance, turning the world murky. "What is that?"

"That," Jenna started, "is a thunderstorm by the looks of it."

Jeremy paused. A thunderstorm? He'd never seen one. They didn't get rain where he grew up or at Winona's home. The rain had completely dried out before he was born. There was a discussion of them in one of the textbooks he found lying around the house, but he hadn't gotten the impression they were as bleak as the world looked right now. "Are you sure?"

She shrugged. "No. They aren't common on the West Coast, and it's been a long time since I've seen something like this on the East Coast."

Maeve laughed hauntingly, pointing out to the right of them. The sky had opened up, a sharp light snapped to the ground a few miles away, and then the area blurred. It was followed by the crack of a tree collapsing. The thud echoed across the area. A loud clap of thunder rumbled, vibrating inside of him, and he watched another streak of light shoot down. It was moving faster now, the wind picking up and blowing through the open cracks in the building. They didn't have a lot of time before it would make it to them.

"So we camp here?" Jeremy pointed down the hall. "I think I saw some couches that way."

The girls nodded, and Jenna motioned for him to lead. They stayed silent, the sound of approaching rain and claps of thunder so loud the windows shook was enough noise for any of them. Jeremy wasn't sure if he thought this storm would last that long or was enough to stop him from looking for her, but the girls made it clear they wouldn't go with him, so what could one night really hurt? It wasn't like he was any use finding her without Jenna.

When he had found the office, he saw two small couches pushed to the side of the room. They were a dusty green and smelled musty, but they were at least free of holes or critters. There wasn't anything else on that floor. It was gross couches or the hard tiled floors. "You both can take a couch and this room. I'll get myself set up right next door."

"Yep," Maeve snipped. He narrowed his eyes, trying to figure out why she suddenly seemed extra irritated, but decided against opening that can of worms. At least before they had dinner and beds set up. Maeve had made it clear over the last few weeks that she was tired of him and his search. He wasn't ready to deal with that.

* * *

By the time they could find a good place to sit for dinner, and Jenna had passed out some of the berries they found a few days back, Jeremy's stomach was growling. It echoed against the empty walls. Which made Jenna laugh so hard she couldn't untie her bag to pull out the dried deer they had.

"You know, laughing that hard isn't going to stop my stomach," Jeremy said, sticking his tongue out at her. He tried to contain the shock of how light his voice sounded. Which just made her laughing fit worse. Her laugh, so unlike her usually focused manner, was so infectious that soon Jeremy was laughing with her. The laughter felt like a good omen. Denver would be the place they found her. He knew it.

"Can you two stop and just hand out fucking dinner?" Maeve snapped, sobering up the room. Jenna looked down, focusing on her bag, as Jeremy turned to meet Maeve's hard gaze. He wanted to yell, to tell her to stop being so selfish. But he didn't know what to say to her. He barely knew how to talk to Winona when she was upset, and that had taken weeks of one-on-one time. He was confident any attempt would sour the night more.

"Sorry," he mumbled, dipping his head. She just looked away from him and snatched the jerky out of Jenna's hand. He caught the hurt in Jenna's eyes before she turned away from them. They ate in silence. He kept his eyes trained on the pile of dust he found on the floor. There wasn't anything he could do to fix whatever was bothering her. Hopefully, Jenna could.

When the sun had set, the storm started to peter out and

finally stopped in time for them to get into bed. Without a couch, Jeremy spread out the sleeping bag they found at an abandoned campsite and balled up his bag for a pillow like he had for the last couple of weeks since they had lost the house. It wasn't too uncomfortable, but it didn't make it easy to fall asleep with the flurry of thoughts fighting for his attention.

He was still awake when furious whispers next door floated into his room. The words were blocked by the walls between them, some words barely audible, but he had caught enough to know that Maeve had been so annoyed with him.

He didn't know what he would have done. It wasn't like he was that mean to them earlier. The Winona search was eating at everyone in the group, and it was clear the girls didn't think she was alive anymore, but it didn't feel that dire. It didn't feel like the ticking time bomb Maeve was. It was more of a steady flow of water filling the room until they drowned. He thought their heads were still firmly above water.

He stayed up, listening to them go back and forth for hours until they quieted down. They were still arguing when his body gave in to sleep.

* * *

WHEN HE WOKE UP, the girls were already sitting next to each other where they had dinner the night before. There were vivid dark-purple bags under each of their eyes, which he probably had too, and Maeve looked murderous. Her eyes cut through him. He inched his way toward them with a sheepish grin. When they didn't stop him, he grabbed the last portion of breakfast and sat down across from them.

They ate in silence, an echo of the night before until Jenna elbowed Maeve and whispered something into her ear.

"It's not worth it," Maeve said, heaving a sigh. The anger radiated off her.

"Having your opinion heard is always worth it." Jenna placed a hand on her leg. It looked tender, but Maeve brushed it off as if she were a fly.

Maeve took a deep breath before squaring her shoulders and capturing Jeremy in her gaze. "I think it's a waste of time to look for Winona. We haven't been able to track her for weeks. We haven't found any sign besides the blood—"

"Don't say that," he growled, cutting her off.

"Jeremy," Jenna warned.

Jeremy felt his heart seize, gripping him in a panic. He stuttered a few times but ended up just nodding at Maeve and admitting defeat. If they didn't want to do this, they were more than welcome to leave. It would be much harder on his own, but he wasn't willing to give up. Not when it felt like she was so close he could sense her presence.

"That's it? Just a nod?" Maeve's annoyance bubbled out. Her words ripped through his stomach.

He ignored his warring emotions and projected the calm person he always saw in Winona. It was hard to project that stability and strength, but he tried. "You both know how I feel. If you don't want to help, then that's up to you. I won't stop you."

Jenna bit her lip, leaning to get between them. "We're not going to leave you behind."

"The hell we aren't," Maeve said, leaning to shoot him a rude look and flip Jenna off.

"No," Jenna said, remaining the calm he had tried to hold on to it. "We won't."

Jeremy mouthed a thank you.

"Why would we stay?"

He studied the indecision on Jenna's face. "I woke up early this morning. The sun hadn't even risen. I was just going for a walk to clear my head." She gave Maeve a pointed look. "I walked farther than I planned, almost to the college, and I found…"

"What did you find?" Jeremy pressed.

"I think she might be there."

Jeremy tamped down his excitement. He couldn't get too excited. It would hurt too much if she wasn't. He didn't finish the thought, didn't want to imagine those possibilities.

"Maeve and I would like to head north into the mountains. We think there might be people there. BUT, we will help you search today. Help you follow the trail I found."

"I'm not leaving without her," Jeremy stated. Originally, he had just hoped to look, but the newfound hope made him confident.

Jenna drew her mouth into a line. "I'm not sure she's alive anymore. The last time we caught her scent, we found her blood splattered on the forest floor. Her scent feels uneasy. I can't describe it. Something is wrong."

Jeremy bristled. They had said she was probably okay. That she hadn't lost that much blood. Now Jenna thinks something is wrong, and they are just debating on looking for her? Why would they have let him stay hopeful if they thought she wasn't capable of taking care of herself? He knew she could. He'd seen it. He gritted his teeth and forced out, "Don't fucking say that. She's alive. She's okay."

The girls exchanged a look, and it was clear they were having a conversation he wasn't privy to. Finally, Jenna turned back to him with a pitying expression. His palm itched to smack it off. How dare they? Both of them would do the same for each other. He would never pity someone for having hope. Winona had never.

"Why don't we make a deal? We can spend today and tomorrow searching, following the trail. If we don't find her by sundown tomorrow, we need to make a plan to move on. You don't want to find her if she's not…" Jenna trailed off.

The unspoken words hung in the air. He blew out a frustrated breath as he ran his hands through his hair. Then he leaned over, taking Jenna's outstretched one, and shook it. "It's already midday, so we need to get up now and start."

The girls wordlessly stood, Jenna taking the lead, and they followed each other out of the building. He looked up at the sun, high in the sky, and for the first time in his life, prayed to whatever powers there were that today would be the day. There was no place in this shitty world that it wasn't.

## DIEGO

IT WASN'T that Diego didn't want to find a solution to their problem. He missed eating as much as Mia did, but it just wasn't in the cards. He had tried almost everything. No matter what he did, everything they ate made them sick. His stomach turned, just thinking about the last failed attempt.

Diego had one last idea but had yet to bring it up to Mia. It was far-fetched and likely to make their life infinitely worse. He had to at least tell her, even if they didn't try it.

"You know, if you stare long enough at the sun, you can add being blind to your building list of problems," Mia commented from her place, stacking clean dishes next to the sink.

"Being blind isn't so bad," Diego said, indignant. His mom had gone blind when he was a kid. She lived a great life after that. "It might not be as easy for us as it was for my mom."

"You're right. It's not. Your mom was a badass, but I can promise you that I won't be helping you clean yourself while you adjust. You'll have to wipe your ass all on your own."

He flicked his eyes in her direction and stuck out his tongue. "You're in a good mood today. Did you hit your head in the bath this morning?"

"That's because I managed to distill another thing of bathtub gin for us." She dried her hands on a red towel before folding it and placing it on the counter. Heaving a sigh, she leaned back against the white granite. "It would be nice to have a solution other than me trying and mostly failing to make gin."

"Speaking of that…," he hedged. Mia watched him carefully as he stepped away from the window and leaned against a barstool. "I don't have one yet, but I've been thinking. It might not be worth the trouble, but…we're not far from the university. Perhaps we could find some material in their food sciences department that could help with our problem. We might be able to track down some organic seeds or grow lights."

The only sign that Mia might agree was the slight jerk of her lip that hinted at a smile she was trying to contain. He watched her carefully as she mulled over his idea. Mia had always been very transparent with her thoughts, whether it was flat out telling him or the subtle changes in her face that gave her away. It was one of the things he loved about her. She was always open. It made him feel safe, as if he had someplace he could land if he failed. Mia sighed.

"I don't know, Diego. That's a lot of electricity. Besides, you remember last time we went that way."

"The car is charged. Our house is self-sustaining. I doubt that group of shitheads is still holed up off the highway. It's been years. They are probably dead."

Mia snorted. "Our? You mean the house we stole."

"Repurposed."

"Oh, that's better. I should have known you'd find a way to justify it." She rolled her eyes before giving him a small shove. She made a small growl in the back of her throat. "Okay, fine. Make sure to bring something we can use to protect ourselves if we run into them again."

"Really?" Diego was beaming. He didn't think she would agree so easily. Not that Mia was prone to big blowout fights, but he expected some push back. Especially with how poorly he had been acting lately. He was surprised she still trusted him.

"Don't make me regret this. Go get everything we need while I get ready. Make sure to bring some tools. Who knows what we're going to find out there."

Diego shot her a look but couldn't argue as he ran down the stairs into the basement to rummage through the tool chest. He pulled out an old backpack they had lying around and filled it with a crowbar, some bolt cutters, a few screwdrivers, and a mallet. It was a pretty sparse pile, but there wasn't much else that had been left in the house. Mia had been hesitant to steal things, never sure if the owners would come back, so by the time she got over her aversion, there was nothing left. They were lucky the house they found had anything at all lying around.

By the time he made it back upstairs, Mia had her hair pulled back by a rubber band into a messy bun and her work boots on. The brown boots were tattered from years of use, but somehow, they had held up enough for her to wear. With her dark jeans and black T-shirt, she looked much more like the badass he knew she was than the general sweet appearance she gave off. He shoved the sudden uptick in his heartbeat into the box of things he couldn't deal with right now and gave her a smile. "I see you've planned to be a ninja."

"At least my pants aren't ripped," she commented, looking at the rips at his knees from his gardening attempts. Unlike Mia's boots, Diego's clothing was slowly deteriorating, and he had started to steal from the men's clothing that was left there.

He pulled at the strings. What a fruitless effort. It didn't matter how much he worked at it. They were never going to get a garden going. He looked out the back window forlornly, the afternoon sun glinting against the glass. It shouldn't be so hard. There was no reason the soil shouldn't support plants. "Let's just get out of here. We're losing sunlight every minute we chitchat, and I don't want to be caught outside at night."

"It's barely noon, but I know what you mean." Mia eyed the sky seriously before swiping the keys from the counter and leading them outside to their vehicle. He let her drive. She was always better at it than him, plus he wanted to keep an eye out for any good places to look for supplies. He had never felt that he should be the one driving just because he was the man of the house. It would be stupid of him not to play to each of their strengths. Even if he was slowly running out of them.

There was something eerie about the emptiness of the streets in this new world. Rusting cars, overturned tractor trailers, forgotten luggage carcasses devoid of anything useful littered the streets. Diego eyed them, looking for anything they could scavenge, but sighed heavily when they pulled off toward what used to be Denver. "Nothing good from here on out. Hopefully, they aren't there anymore."

"You think they just moved on? Do you remember how built up their hideout was? We were lucky to only drive by," Mia said, giving him a side-eye glance.

"You don't know. Maybe they died. It's possible they found a better place to settle."

"They may have moved on," she echoed weakly, eyes glued to the road ahead of them. They sat in silence for another few minutes, and he listened to Mia tapping the wheel nervously. Instead of her normal quips, Mia's voice was subdued—soft and wispy in a way that was often carried away in the wind. Diego wanted to grab her hand, remind her that he was here to deal with this, but she never kept her hand down long enough for him to try. Not that she would even have an interest in that. She was tired of his inability to save them, not willing to let him wallow in what was objectively a shitty situation, and he didn't blame her for the resentment he saw in her eyes.

It wasn't until they rounded the last bend, pulling off the

highway, that the metal boxes—old steel shipping crates with large veins of rust like gutted geodes—lined up on the truck bed gave them pause. The image was almost the exact same as the last time they had gone out to look for more supplies, except the tires had lost all their air. Metal wheels flat against the gray asphalt glinted in the midday sun. He eyed the dark figures with long, sharp poles strapped to their backs.

"The shitheads haven't moved on." It fell flat in the cabin like a lead balloon.

Mia didn't meet his eyes as she bit her lip and eyed the road in front. "You don't think they have a trap set, do you?"

Diego looked at the empty stretch of road in front of them. There were no obvious signs of something to stop them, but out of the corner of his eye, he noticed a figure stepping out into the road, his spear pointed toward their slowly approaching vehicle. "I think we should stop."

Mia pressed the brake lightly, easing them to a rolling stop a couple of hundred feet from the guy. The man, close enough now that Diego could see his features, looked more horrendous than the dark shadows and spear that appeared.

"Roll down the window," he hissed as the guy started to circle the hood of the car. With a shag of gray hair and enough wrinkles to mimic a hydrogeologic map of the East Coast, the man had to be either in his late seventies or had been living in this compound since the collapse. He wouldn't be surprised if both were true. He limped slightly, using the flat end of his spear to propel him to the driver's side. When he peered into the window, his dark eyes flicked between Diego and Mia before landing on him with a sour look.

"What are you doing on my land?" he rasped.

Diego leaned over Mia, covering her protectively, before tipping his face up to the man. "We're just passing through to the college."

He could feel Mia's hand digging into his side, reminding

him that she was perfectly capable of taking care of herself. That she could have handled this man. Diego focused on the snarled lips of the older man. It didn't matter if she could do this without him. It only mattered that she was more important to him than anything else in this shitty new world they found themselves living in.

He held out his hand. "Pay up."

Mia cleared her throat before pushing Diego off her and slipping out of the vehicle. The old man scuffed as she slid around the vehicle and popped the trunk. Objects clanged around the inside of the trunk before the lid slammed shut. Mia marched to the front of the vehicle and shoved an orange-and-black drill into his hand. The old man spun it around.

"What am I supposed to do with this?" His disdain gave Diego chills. This wasn't going to save them. This was the end. Diego wished he had told Mia how he really felt. He didn't want to die without her knowing how amazing she truly was.

Mia waved at their compound. "Repair things. Build new things. Use the scrap pieces to engineer something. It's really better than it looks."

The old man nodded before narrowing his eyes. "I expect something better on your return trip."

Mia got back into the car, the old man tapped his spear on the hood, and then she pulled forward. Diego watched the old man grin as he inspected the drill when he thought they weren't watching anymore. Several of his teeth were missing, giving him a crooked smile that made Diego shiver. At least he was satisfied for now.

When they had made it out of view and near the college, Mia sighed. "We should have just gone the long way. This whole thing could have been avoided."

"We didn't know they would still be there. Besides, going that way will push the car's electric range. We might not make it home if we do that." Diego patted the car affectionately. It had survived and lasted longer than he ever expected, but the technology wasn't designed for the extreme variations in weather it went through. "We can take the long way home if there's enough power." He pointed out a mostly clear surface lot outside a building with half the sign missing. Dirt outlines from where it used to read "Cech School of Physical Sciences." "Park over there."

"This is too obvious. Everything is going to be pillaged in there. We should look for the agriculture building."

Diego leaned into the backseat, pulling out a hammer and their spare drill. "I'll go in here. I start searching for something to bring him on the way back in case we can't go the long way. I'll meet you in the plaza in two hours."

Mia huffed. "Do you think that's the best idea? Haven't you seen enough slasher films?"

"This isn't a slasher film. It's real life. What could possibly happen with so few people on the planet?" He waved at the building. "The place has been ransacked and is just another monument to the life before this. I doubt there is anyone else nearby besides those creepy old men."

"You know you're becoming a creepy old man." A deep frown set across her face, but she agreed to separate. He got out of the car, clipped his tools to his belt, and slammed the door shut. The campus, eerily quiet compared to the last time he walked the same paths, was overrun with grass and shrubs. The quiet sound of Mia's tires running over the gravel echoed as he waited for her to keep going. His heart ached, a tightening to remind him that they might never be reunited, and he still hadn't told her what she meant to him before he made his way to the heavy basement door of the building.

The gray paint was chipped along the edges, but the door looked untouched. He grabbed on and gave it a pull, but without solid food in his system, he was weak and useless. He pulled the drill from his belt and tightened the cobalt bit into place. It was a wonder the owner had such quality supplies but didn't survive. He always held the belief that they had moved on, maybe farther north, where the ground might have been more fertile with the stronger set of seasons. It was a dream he forced himself to hold on to instead of what reality probably held.

They, too, had fallen with the collapse of society.

The drill bit caught on the lock and, with a little pressure, ripped right through the mechanism with a resounding click. When he pulled the door this time, it gave way after a few good jerks. Flakes of metal and paint floated down as fresh air and light streamed into the musty hallway. It smelled like someone had left an open container of benzene in one of the labs. He didn't have a gas mask, so he pulled his shirt off, folded it over itself a few times, and then wrapped the layered cotton over his mouth and nose. He had no interest in dying like Kekulé did.

His shirt reeked of sweat and dirt from their useless garden, but he would take that over, fainting from benzene inhalation. The chemical-soaked air made his eyes sting as he made his way through the basement level and up the stairs in the middle of the hallway. In the enclosed stairwell, his eyes stopped burning, and the lack of tears made it easier for him to see the directory.

Brushing away the dirt and cobwebs, he scanned the different lab types until he found the chemistry floor. Housed on the top floor, he took a deep breath and prepared for the five-flight walk. Before this whole thing started to unravel the world, he used to be pretty athletic, and five flights wouldn't make him gasp for breath as lightheadedness made him sway, but once again, the surgery that kept him alive was doing so in the most underwhelming way possible.

It was a wonder they had made it this far.

# YEAR 5 AGC, DAY 322

## MIA

THE STILLNESS OF THE CAMPUS, coupled with the almost imperceptible quiet of the electric motor, made it impossible for Mia not to worry. She would give anything to have something to distract her from her concerns and fears. It wasn't that worrying was new for her. In the twenty years she had worked and lived side by side with Diego, she had spent the majority of them fretting over him. Whether it was his excessive drinking, his depression after the collapse, or his slowly degrading sanity as more and more time passed, she had thought about it and stared at her bedroom ceiling for hours, thinking about it in the dark.

All of that was nothing compared to her biggest fear. Her heart-stopping horror that one day he would find out her deepest, darkest secret. Not that she would even admit it to herself, so her worrying was, at best, useless and, at worst, draining on her energy reserves. Reserves she didn't have to spare.

Leaving Diego behind in the physical sciences building while she took their vehicle to the agriculture building was more than just a concern. Watching him in her rearview mirror hurt her more than she was willing to admit, the pain stabbing at her chest hot and sharp. She rubbed her chest and reminded herself that her feelings for Diego meant nothing if she couldn't get him to take care of himself. The heartache now was better than actually losing him.

By the time she parked the vehicle in an open spot of gravel beside the overgrown bushes that surrounded the whitewashed bricks, her chest felt like someone was sitting on the knife embedded in it. She tried to push past the pain, past the black stars blooming from her lack of food, and focus on the steps in front of her. She hiked up the stairs slowly, pausing every few steps to grab the dirty railing so she didn't fall.

When she made it a few flights up, she narrowed her eyes at the door. The dirty gray door was ajar, already pried open. She touched the handle softly and studied the marks. Someone had been here very recently. None of the marks had rust or dust lying on top of it in the way the world did now. Thin layers of dust covered most things, but these looked pristine. It made Mia shiver so harshly that her teeth clattered together.

There was a time when the dust made her shiver, made her uneasy, but that time didn't exist anymore. That world, so foreign when everything started, was now what she called home. She pulled a screwdriver from her belt and held it out in front of her.

She stuck it into the gap between the door and the frame. Giving it a tug, she pried the door open. When the dust had settled, revealing an empty hallway, she called out, "Hello?"

There was a sharp intake of breath farther down the hall but no response. The soft sound pinged in her head, and Mia gripped the screwdriver as she inched down the hall. As she drew closer, a soft rustling sound came from the last door on the right. She sucked in a large breath and held it as she edged the last few feet. Her soft steps were barely loud enough for her to hear, but as the door became within reach, the rustling stopped completely.

The door had a small sliver of light streaming out from the gap between it and the wall. It was the only door not firmly latched shut. Pressing into the wall next to it, she leaned over and peered right into the eyes of a tanned brunette. Hazel eyes studied her as she gasped and then choked on the air she was holding. Her eyes watered as she coughed violently.

The girl, she realized, continued to watch her, not moving anything but her eyes, until Mia got a hold of herself. She pulled her shoulders back, lifted the screwdriver in her hand to chest height, and locked her eyes on the girl. "Who are you?"

"Winona," she responded. Her voice was barely audible. Winona pointed to the screwdriver as she cleared her throat. Louder, she asked, "Any reason you're pointing that at me, or do you just stab strangers you happen upon?"

Mia huffed out a laugh. "I'd rather be the one pointing than being stabbed."

Winona shrugged, letting her neutral face slip slightly to show a grimace before opening the door. "Well, you might as well come in. I won't stab you if you tell me how you've managed to stay so clean."

Mia raised an eyebrow before looking down at her neat clothing and running a hand through her curls. She'd forgotten how lucky they were to have a house to live in.

"Have you been living in the woods?" she asked. With Diego waiting for her, she was more on guard than usual, less comfortable with small talk. Even with that, she couldn't help her concerns about this young girl. Winona had to be close to her age when she met Diego only a few years before the collapse began. Mia had felt so lost then. Winona was clearly on her own in this scary new world. She couldn't imagine how she felt.

Cataloging the twigs caught in the girl's brown tresses that hadn't been brushed in what looked like months, Mia decided she would convince Diego to let this kid be a part of their group. Winona had definitely slept in the woods for the last few days based on her smell alone. Mia felt bad for her. It was hard not to when she and Diego had snagged such a nice place to live in the new world. That she even had Diego to rely on, if some days only for conversation.

Winona paced around the dusty classroom. "My house burned down, so I've been looking for a new place to settle. I was walking with someone, but..." She kicked a desk, and it screeched, the echoing filling the silence. She looked up at her and swallowed hard. "He's better off now. Anyway, I've been looking for growing supplies."

Mia nodded. That's what she had been after as well. Grow lights and seeds. "You have seeds to grow?"

Winona narrowed her eyes. "What's it to you?"

Mia tried to hold back her frustration. There was no reason for her to be so hostile unless she had seeds. She cocked an eyebrow. The reasons to bring Winona back with her grew with every word she said. "We might have some common goals. I'm here for the same things, but I've been looking for seeds since we moved out here. I've never found anything."

"You have something to offer?"

Mia could have sworn that Winona would have pointed a knife at her if she had one. Since she hadn't, the rational part of her brain told her she probably didn't have any weapons. She added this to her list of pros. If she wanted to get anything from her or bring her back to help at home, she needed to put her screwdriver away and show some of her cards. This woman was too flighty to threaten. She put the screwdriver into the waist of her pants and held up her hands.

"Me and..." She paused. How did she explain Diego? She started over. "Diego, a friend of mine, and I live about half an hour south in a house with solar energy. We have room for another. We can't provide seeds, but we can provide power for some grow lights."

Winona ran her fingers through her hair, yanking at the knots, and started pacing on the far side of the room again. Based on her reaction alone, it was clear she was considering Mia's suggestion. Mia just hoped she didn't know how badly they needed new seeds. How badly they needed the grow lights and someone who could actually grow. She hoped Winona didn't realize how she was just as desperate as Winona looked. Diego wanted to solve their problems with experiments and chemicals, but something in Mia told her that wasn't the way.

The way was going back to nature. Winona felt like a sign Mia was on the right track. But Diego wanted to be the breadwinner, wanted to be the world-renowned scientist he used to be, and she couldn't take that from him. Diego, no matter how frustrated he was or how far he had fallen since the collapse, wanted nothing more than to provide for them the way he did at the very beginning. Before everything started to fall apart.

She could take it away with a snap of her fingers, but crushing him would mostly crush them both beyond repair. She wasn't willing to lose him, no matter how bad things got. They had too much history for that.

"Okay."

It was a whisper. So quiet that Mia had her repeat it three more times. When it settled in her chest that they might be saved, that someone might be able to help, she almost wrapped the stranger in a tight hug and cried. Instead, she nodded with a solemn expression. "I think the spare supplies might be in the basement. That's where we kept it when we were working in the research department at the University of Florida."

Winona gestured for her to lead but didn't turn with Mia. "What kind of scientists are you?"

"Chemists. Diego is a trained biochemist, and my degree is

in environmental chemistry, but I did all my postbac work under Diego. We were studying the effects of climate change on the human body and how to survive all this." She waved around them. "Let's walk and talk. Diego is waiting for me."

She didn't move. "I…"

"What's wrong?"

"The person I traveled with. He was supposed to be here too. I was…" Winona bit her lip. "I was hoping I could wait for him. I know he's better off, but I can't help but worry. If we could wait at least one more day?"

Mia studied her, the way Winona fidgeted, like when Mia was worried about Diego. Whoever she was waiting for, they meant a lot. If she had left Diego behind, he would have been fine without her. But she couldn't imagine actually doing it. "I'll make you a deal. Let's keep moving to find the supplies, and when we get back to Diego, we can figure out a solution."

Winona nodded as she waved for Mia to walk out of the room. Mia waited for her to start walking before taking the lead. They walked in silence, the sound of their shoes shuffling down the silty hallways for several minutes. Mia bit back any thoughts—it was clear Winona was going to be a tough nut to crack. Besides, she wanted to get to know the woman she had just welcomed into her home, but if she rushed it, she was confident she would be going home with just Diego. Everything about Winona made it clear she was holding a weight much more than she could bear. If Mia didn't give her a chance to open up instead of pushing her, they would get nowhere.

"What's college like?" Winona asked, fidgeting this the hem of her shirt.

Mia eyed her. "How young are you?"

"Seventeen."

It didn't shock her, but at forty-three with two degrees, Mia felt her heart squeeze for the memories this young woman missed out on. Memories she held fondly as the moments she knew Diego was someone she wanted in her life. Memories of late nights on the grass, watching the stars with her roommates. Her first real boyfriend. She sighed softly as they headed down the dark stairwell. "College is a very stressful but beautiful experience. Being a science major, a lot of my college was spent studying with a close group of friends. I like to think they all made it and are traveling the world."

"I hope they are as well."

Mia turned back to meet the young woman's smile, letting the moment sit between them before opening the door to the basement. Without windows, the room was pitch black. She pulled out her shake-to-charge flashlight, gave it a few good extra shakes, and flicked it on. The room flooded with light. Small dust particles glittered in the air. Mia tried to hold her breath but ended up taking a lungful of dust. She coughed into her elbow, her eyes stinging.

Through her blurry eyesight, she caught Winona searching the area where her flashlight was pointing despite the shaking it did with her coughs. By the time she had collected herself, Winona was holding up one large rectangle. The girl's smile was so wide it made Mia smile back.

"Do you know how this would plug in?" Winona held up the circular, industrial-sized plug in her other hand. "I've never seen a plug like this." She cleared her throat. "I've actually never seen anything electric work before."

"It might work in our basement outlet where the washer and dryer are. We probably should look for something like grow lightbulbs that we can put in our light fixtures." Mia frowned, realization dawning on her. "You've never seen electricity?"

Winona shook her head, walking a little farther down the row of shelves. She turned her head slightly to angle herself toward Mia, and said, "We've always lived by candlelight or daylight. My parents used to have it growing up, but it was dead by the time I was born. How is it that you have electricity? My parents said it wasn't possible anymore, not where we lived at least."

The raw wonder in her voice was unmistakable. It was the wonder Mia didn't feel anymore after the long years in the after. Winona's excitement brightened the room in a way she forgot was possible. What it must be like to see things, experience things, for the first time. To still feel the pull of joy that the world wasn't just a wasted version of the past. That mindset was something Diego and she needed desperately.

"Well, hopefully, it lives up to all your expectations," Mia finally said. She stopped walking, her light landing on a set of smaller grow lights with standard plugs and a set of planter trays. She grabbed it off the shelf. "Here. This is perfect."

The younger woman met her in the dusty corner and took several items off the top of her pile. "Where are we taking this?"

"My car is parked outside."

Winona's eyes widened. "Car?" She let the stack of lights and trays slip slightly as she gasped.

"Yes. We have an electric car." It struck Mia that this adult, fully formed and traveling on their own, had never seen things like a car moving or electricity. Another reminder that she was lucky to be bubbled up with Diego. The thought of it warmed her stomach like a good whiskey. The feeling was ripped away as memories of what alcohol had done to their lives. She bit her lip as her thoughts hurtled back to the misfortune that was their stomach surgery.

"I've never..." Winona's eyes lit up. "Will I be able to ride in it?"

Mia scoffed, giving the girl a smile. "How else will you come with us?"

She pitied the girl almost more than she pitied her current situation. Winona didn't respond, just smiled to herself as they walked up the stairs at a steady pace. It was nice—in a foreign kind of way—to have someone other than Diego to talk with.

To have someone new to get to know. To have someone to care about in a way she had wanted since she was a kid.

Mia had lost out on having someone to care for, but with the age difference between them, she could see Winona becoming an important part of their little community. An important part of her life. She tried to shush the part of her brain telling her she was moving too fast, but it was useless. Mia had always loved strongly and swiftly. This girl, something about her quiet reserve of patience and pious excitement at things Mia no longer cared for, was quickly worming into a place in her heart. It was probably her maternal instinct, but that didn't stop her from studying the young woman's face and memorizing it as she guided them to the parked vehicle.

## TRANSCRIPTS FROM STATION 101.5 OUT OF DETROIT

CHRIS FORESTER: Hello, folks. I don't know if anyone can hear this, but I think this needs to be said. Hopefully, this can help anyone who has survived the last flooding in Detroit. There was a time when I thought we would survive this without any effort on our part. There was a time when I thought we were safe from harm. [clears throat] I was wrong. The world isn't safe anymore. If you and your loved ones can still hear me, head for safety. The government's safe zones are still in place and available for refuge if you can make it. It's too late for me and my wonderful producers, but it's not for you. You need to push through and survive to rebuild a better world that we couldn't. [sniffles] I don't think we'll be able to have another transmission.

PRODUCER (OFF MIC): You have one minute of power left.

CHRIS FORESTER: Okay. Folks, I want to thank each and every one of you for listening to me or helping push this show out. I

am so grateful to you. Before we have our final sign-off, I want
to apologize to Dr.—


[END OF TRANSCRIPT]

YEAR 5 AGC, DAY 322

## WINONA

"WHO IS THAT?" the man, she assumed to be Diego, asked as he pointed a finger at her.

"That is Winona, and she'll be coming home with us," Mia said. She put a hand on her hip, challenging Diego with a withering look.

Diego balked, his eyes wildly searching Mia's for something she didn't know and wasn't sure she wanted to. But Mia's confident presence made her think that Diego's opinion wasn't quite as important as she had implied earlier. Especially when, in the silence after her statement, Diego's shoulders slumped as he processed whatever her eyes told him. Mia elbowed him, muttering something under her breath, and jerked her head in Winona's direction.

He turned to Winona with a weak smile and held out his hand. His hand, much like his body, was slender to the point that she thought they might not be as well off as she had hoped. Not only could she see the veins that ran up his arm, but with the tight shirt he was wearing, she could make out most of his rib cage. He looked sicker and thinner than Mia. She added that to her con list as she took his hand and shook it.

"I'm Diego, as I'm sure Mia has told you. This may be a ridiculous question, but why exactly are you coming home with us?" He gave them both a wide-eyed look.

Winona turned to Mia, unsure of how to handle the situation. It had been easy to fall into step with Mia; she was poised and friendly. Most importantly, she had this confidence that seeped into Winona with such force she couldn't imagine letting go of that. They were becoming fast friends in the same way she had with Jeremy, though more familial. Both of those had been the points that tipped the pro list into action.

Mia sighed as she grabbed his arm and pulled him aside. She watched as Mia flailed her hands around as Diego just stood there with his mouth agape. She couldn't catch most of what Mia was hissing at him, but she caught enough to know that Winona was just what they were looking for. She added the exception to the con list. A small part of her wanted to scream that she was not as great as they thought. That she alone forced the most important person in her life away because she couldn't handle it. But she shoved it aside in the name of self-preservation. She needed a place to land, she needed a home, and she needed more than to just survive. She wished she realized that lesson before leaving Jeremy behind.

"Fine," Diego said, his voice echoing against the buildings. The two of them walked back to her. "Here's the deal. We will take you in if you promise to help us grow something edible. You will need to pull your weight to be a part of our group."

Winona stifled a laugh at the irony of his words. How weird it felt to be in Jeremy's shoes. "What about waiting for my friend?"

Mia smiled softly at her. "We agreed that we would stay until dusk today and help you search the general area before we leave. If we don't find him, we will come back in a week's time and try to find him again."

It hurt her to abandon the idea of waiting for Jeremy. The

idea itself wasn't the most unreasonable thing she'd heard. She had spent the last two nights roaming the college with no luck. She searched for hours and found that there was nothing edible or drinkable within a couple of hours' walk. She would need to replenish her reserves if she even wanted to be alive when Jeremy showed up. She couldn't give up hope that he was coming.

"I think that's reasonable," she finally said.

Mia's smile widened. "Wonderful. I thought we could walk the college on foot, starting from the center and walking to the edges, and then if we don't find him, we can hop in the car and circle for a mile radius. Does that sound okay?"

Winona shrugged. She wasn't sure what the best way to find Jeremy was, but following the pair down the cracked pathway was better than nothing. As they walked, she studied them. The pair were like magnets, rigid as they walked barely far enough away to keep from touching. It reminded her of the way Maeve and Jenna acted. Something itched at her brain.

She scoffed at herself. That was why she thought their being sisters was weird and why Jenna seemed so fazed by Jeremy and Maeve's closeness. This revelation colored her memory, pinpointing every moment she missed.

"Is everything okay back there?" Mia called.

Absolutely nothing was okay because she was the biggest idiot on this planet, not that there was a long list of people to compare herself to. How had she not realized this before? Maeve would never take Jeremy from her because Maeve was in love with fucking Jenna. She wanted to smack herself. Instead, she nodded at Mia and shoved her thoughts back into the box of bad decisions that were starting to pour over. "Everything is fine."

"I'm not sure I believe you," Diego said. "But I'm not sure that matters. Is anyone really fine in the after?"

His words echoed in the open space they had stopped in, and he grimaced. Mia shot him a withering look.

"Perhaps you should keep your brand of cynicism to yourself until we at least get home?" Mia suggested. Which earned them both an eye roll and forced a laugh from both of them.

"I don't know if I'm going to like being ganged up on by two women," Diego muttered. "This is some top-tier bullshit."

* * *

"Perhaps I could help even that out," a voice said. Tears sprung to her eyes. Her heart hammered in her chest, making her lightheaded and shaky. She tightened her hands into fists to stop her fingers from shaking. She didn't think she'd ever hear that voice again, and the idea that he was there made her dizzy. She batted the tears out of her eyes as she turned in the direction of the voice.

Without giving herself a chance to second-guess her emotions, she ran to the voice and wrapped her arms around him. She was squeezing so tightly that a small part of her thought she might be hurting him, but she didn't care. She couldn't believe she was wrapped in his arms again. He still had the woody smell that she remembered.

Then his arms pulled her close, resting his chin on her head, and her heart felt like it was bursting. She felt the tears soaking into his shirt, and a pang of guilt hit her. As if reading her mind, he ran a gentle hand over her cheek.

"I'm so sorry," they said in unison. Her voice was thick.

"I shouldn't have left," she mumbled into his ratty shirt. Being that close, the musky smell mixed with the dirt made her heart jump. It felt like they were back home, curled up on the couch after hours of gardening. The memory made her chest warm.

"I shouldn't have made you feel like you needed to go," Jeremy said, kissing her forehead.

Someone cleared their throat. Winona untangled herself from Jeremy and turned to the group with an awkward smile.

"So this must be your friend," Mia said. "But who are they?"

Winona followed her finger to the girls who were off to the side of the plaza, deep in conversation. "That would be Maeve and Jenna," she said, gesturing to each of them and raising her voice to get their attention. They turned to look at the group. "Maeve is an extremely skilled hunter, and Jenna is a very capable tracker. We found them in Idaho before we separated."

Jeremy cleared his throat. "Winona and I were barely surviving off the crops she was growing in Washington, but with the help of these two, we were able to add a wider variety of foods. We've agreed to sit together as long as everyone pulls their weight. I hope that will work here as well." Jeremy looked at her expectantly, and she nodded.

Winona wanted to tell him everything, all the words fighting to spill out, but she clamped her mouth shut. They could talk later. Now that she wasn't attached to him, she could get a good look at him. He looked so much healthier than he did back at the house, even though he looked so much better at the house than when she found him. His rib cage wasn't showing anymore, and his face had filled out. He was better looking than the memory she was holding close.

She turned to look at her new companions. They were looking at each other with such intensity that she knew they were having another silent conversation. It was clear they had been together for decades with how easily they conveyed their thoughts with simple facial expressions. Hopefully, Jeremy and she would get there.

"Fine," Diego said. His voice made it sound so final her heart jumped in shock.

Mia turned to Winona. "We think, if you and your friends

want to come back with us, we would be willing to welcome them. Of course, as we had originally agreed, everyone will need to pull their weight."

Jeremy snorted, and she stopped herself from elbowing him as he whispered, "I see you've found like-minded people."

"No one needs your sass," she muttered.

"We're more than happy to join and help," Jenna said. Jeremy was looking at them with wide eyes. She watched the interaction as Jenna nodded to him despite Maeve's clear annoyance. Something was going on there, and it wasn't helping that the small part of her still didn't like the two of them. Jeremy shrugged, turning to pull Winona back into a hug. The warmth silenced it as the group started to introduce themselves around them.

## WINONA

ONCE EVERYONE HAD BEEN INTRODUCED, Mia pulled Diego off to the side. Winona watched the two of them square off in a stance she realized was normal for them. Their hands were flying in the air between them so quickly that they blurred. She turned away from them to look at Jeremy and the girls. Jeremy was hovering between her and the girls as if trying to create a wall between herself and the two girls who were whispering angrily at each other. The two locked eyes, silently trying to figure out which situation required attention more before Jeremy closed his eyes in resignation. He turned toward the girls, dragging his feet to where they stood, and left her to deal with the adults. She didn't want to deal with it either. She wanted to curl into Jeremy's arms and never leave again.

She sighed softly before focusing her attention on the pair. They were arguing about getting home. She inched herself close enough to distinguish their words. Neither of them acknowledged her.

"I understand that you want to help these teenagers, but there's no way we can get them all the way back to our place safely." Diego ran his hands through the thick black hair falling into his face.

Mia rolled her eyes. "You don't get a say anymore. Not after the years of nonaction I've put up with. Besides, we need them."

"Need?" Diego asked. His voice rose with panic. "We've never needed anyone. What is so special about them?"

Mia barked out a laugh. "Needing a bottle is just the same as needing someone. It's just a poor outlet for your anger."

Winona winced at the bite in her words. Diego scoffed at Mia as if the words meant nothing. "When did you become so patronizing? It's not like you don't need it too."

"I'm the only one trying to change that." Mia let out a long breath. "The girl, Winona."

Both of them turned to see her watching them curiously. She tried to avert her eyes, but it was useless. They knew she had been eavesdropping. She gave them a little wave.

"What about her?" Diego gestured at her. Annoyance rippled off him in waves.

She wanted to jump in, ask the same question, accuse them of hiding things. But before she could speak up, Mia let a smile creep across her face as she slid next to her.

Mia wrapped an arm around Winona. It felt weird but comfortable, so she didn't roll it off. "This amazing teenager not only has heirloom seeds, but before she hiked her way out here, Winona had a full garden growing in the middle of the burnt, destroyed northwest. Surrounded by wildfires, she was able to make things grow well enough that she could survive. Thrive even."

Winona tensed. She knew Diego needed to know, knew Jeremy had already given it away, but she still hated to talk about it. Mia gave her shoulders a squeeze, helping to release some of the tension, as Diego's eyes widened. He studied her, his eyes slowly registering the words. "Is that true?"

"It's not a lie," she finally said, after contemplating whether or not she wanted anyone to know what she told Mia on their drive over to meet him. She needed to get over her fear of other people. Her father had come from a place of love, but people weren't as scary as he'd said. These people around her were genuine and caring in ways she'd never expected.

Jeremy laughed from behind them, inserting himself into the group with a grumpy-looking Maeve and a neutral Jenna. "Winona, can you ever just take credit? Had I not burned down the house, we could have lived the rest of our lives there."

"You burned down her house?" Mia asked, turning to give Jeremy an incredulous look.

Jeremy squirmed. "Well, uh. I mean. Yes."

"I'm sorry that all of that happened to you. It seems that this group could really benefit from each other," Diego said, giving Winona a pitying glance. "But none of this solves the real problem."

Maeve cleared her throat. "What exactly is the real problem if it's not the bickering and disagreement within this poorly formed group?"

Jenna elbowed her but didn't open her mouth to correct her.

"The problem is that there's a cult we need to pass to leave Denver and return home," Diego said casually. Everyone's attention snapped to him, with varying degrees of concern written on their faces.

"A cult?" Jeremy asked, his voice higher than usual.

"Cult isn't the word I would use. It's just a group of angry people who won't let you cross without giving them something." Mia looked sheepish. "Regardless, it's not a problem. Diego is being overly dramatic because he has concerns about the other option. We can go the long way, and it will be fine."

"With what battery? We don't even have enough space for everyone. This many people will deplete our battery well before we get home."

Jenna raised her hand. "I can sit on Maeve's lap!"

Winona tuned out the rest of the discussion, focusing on Jenna's statement over and over again in her head. The confirmation made the tension in her neck release. She looked at Jeremy, who gave her a pointed look. She drew her mouth into a thin line. All of that for nothing. She was lucky Jeremy didn't rub it in her face. Instead, when the conversation died out, a plan determined to circumvent the weird, cultlike group, and the group was ready to set out, Jeremy just linked their arms. He pulled her close enough to feel the warmth of his breath and didn't let go until she needed to crawl into the car before him.

Once in the car, he wrapped an arm around her and pulled her into his chest. Her body relaxed into him, and she sighed happily. She'd missed this more than she knew.

WHEN THE CAR HAD STOPPED, the group was parked outside a large house trimmed with black panels. It was planted at the center of a small neighborhood that bordered a large, healthy-looking forest. She admired the lush green against the yellow of the house. Despite the chipping yellow paint, the house appeared in good condition. Diego had explained on the way out there how they had found the house, cleaned it up, and lived in it for the better half of a decade. With the solar panels Mia had described, the house made sense. She'd never seen solar panels outside of books, and she was surprised by how large they were up close.

Winona peered around the neighborhood as the group gathered their belongings from the cramped vehicle. There were maybe five other houses in the circle, three of which were already outfitted with the same solar panels on Mia's home. They didn't look as well maintained, vines growing across many of them, but without her home, this would be better than sleeping on the forest floor. She would take anything over the hard dirt.

"We have two bedrooms available in the house, so the four of you can decide who will bunk with who," Diego said. He turned the knob on the door and flung it open to reveal a well-kept living room that opened to a dining room and kitchen. "Bedrooms are on the second floor."

Mia smiled without her eyes and waved at the staircase to the left of the room. "Diego and I each have a bedroom at the end of the hall, so the two front bedrooms are free to pick from."

Jenna and Maeve took the stairs two at a time, racing ahead of Jeremy and Winona, and claimed the bedroom with one extra-large bed in it. Jeremy grumbled at them. Turning to the other bedroom, Winona took in the small bed that filled the last room. It was barely the size of the bed she grew up in. She took a gingerly step into the room, placing her backpack on the wood floor by the one window, and eyed the space warily.

Jeremy, all smiles, plopped himself on the bed. "This bed is way better than the forest floor."

She nodded, giving him a weak smile. "It looks nice."

Jeremy turned to look at her, and she watched realization dawn across his face. The sparkle in his eyes disappearing, replaced by worry. He rolled off the bed. "I can sleep on the floor."

She bit her lip. It was silly to be so concerned when they had shared a tent together, but this felt different. Everything between them was different and new. "No, it's okay. I'll go see if I can sleep on the couch."

"No!" Jeremy said quickly.

"Umm." She fought at the fluttering in her chest. They hadn't had a chance to talk since reuniting, but her mind ran to the ever hopeful thought she'd dreamed about during her hike across the countryside.

"It's fine. Take the bed. Really." Jeremy walked over to the small closet, rifling around, and pulled out a faded blue quilt. He spread it out next to the bed, dropped one of the few pillows on the bed next to it, and then sat on the floor. "I'll be fine down here."

She looked at him. She was filled with guilt at the forced smile on his face. "We can alternate until we find a better situation."

When Jeremy didn't argue, they headed downstairs to work on getting dinner started for the group. Jeremy had offered in the car to make dinner the first night. Since everyone but Mia and Diego knew how good his cooking really was, no one fought him.

They spent dinner avoiding the obvious tension and awkwardness radiating between them. The differentness of their tentative relationship was like a giant boulder between them. It was easier than she expected because the group was chatty as everyone utilized the time to learn about Diego and Mia. The pair had been living there longer than she'd been without her parents but surviving worse than she had in her time alone. It was clear that they were trying to appear nonchalant about the issues they faced, but it was just as clear that they were just barely surviving and needed the group of travelers.

Even Jeremy had noticed the looks Mia gave Diego as they picked at the food on their plates. Food, she had learned after several frustrating one-word responses, that neither of them could eat. Everything dinner was made with had come from Jeremy's and the girls' backpacks. Most of which, besides the meat, was foraged or collected from empty houses.

By the time Diego and Mia had finished their story, the sun had set and left the sky in a darker purple color that was cut only by the soft glow of the lights in the house spilling out the back door.

"I think we should all get some sleep. We can start planning how we'll divvy out tasks tomorrow," Diego finally said when the conversation had sputtered out. Everyone but Winona agreed, moving away from the table and toward the house.

She wasn't ready to deal with so much silence between herself and Jeremy in the cramped room they had to share. She didn't want to mess this up again, and the anxiety that came with that was crippling.

"Are you not tired?" Jeremy asked. He was waiting a few paces ahead of her. The rest of the group was already inside.

Winona shrugged. "I am. It's just been a weird day. That's all."

"We should get some rest. Why don't you tell me about your day when we get into bed? Tomorrow is going to be a long day, so I don't want to be too tired." He held out a hand to her.

She nodded, grabbing his hand and following him through the house to their room. The silence rang in her ears as they settled down into their own beds. Jeremy made a few attempts to talk, but she had clammed up, and he had started to fall asleep. She tried to focus on the soft breathing coming from the floor as Jeremy slid steadily into sleep and reassured herself they had all the time in the world now to talk.

"I missed you," she whispered into the air once she thought he was asleep. Saying it out loud, even just to herself, made her heart ache. She more than missed him, but there weren't words for it.

The sound of his voice whispering, "Missing you doesn't cut it," dug into her chest so deeply she coughed on the suddenly charged air.

A small part of her thought she had imagined hearing his voice. But she couldn't ignore the hope in her chest, whether or not it was her imagination.

"Why did you leave?" His voice was raw as it floated up to her. "Did I do something wrong?"

She didn't have a good answer. She had thought she did when she had walked away, and by the time she realized she was running from something she should have held on to with her life, it was too late. The longer she spent mulling over that night, she realized she didn't run away because of Maeve. She had left because she didn't think she deserved the good in Jeremy because she wasn't capable of giving him the same.

She bit her lip. "I thought you were better off without me..." She trailed off to the sound of his sharp intake of breath.

He laughed humorlessly. "The idea that I would ever be better off without you is fucking trash. How could you possibly think that?"

"You said... I can't. I felt like I couldn't give you what you wanted." The truth burned through her. The air was heavy with everything unspoken.

"I said what? I said that I didn't want Maeve over you." His voice was heated, passionate. It stripped her of any argument. "What do you mean give me what I wanted? I had everything I wanted right in fucking front of me. I had it all within an arm's reach, and then it was all gone. It felt like you had just hit your head and forgot about me. It felt like everything was my fault, just like when I killed my family."

His last few words were softer, like he was trying to hide them. But she heard them, felt the sting of them, and wanted nothing more than to take that sting away.

"You shouldn't have left," he finally said, his mouth suddenly so close she could feel it radiating. The bed shifted under his weight as he lay down next to her. He tilted his head so their foreheads were pressed together. "I never wanted you to go. I never wanted anymore from you than you were already giving me."

He grabbed her hand and squeezed it. It felt like it was

squeezing her heart instead. "I never want you to go anywhere ever again. Promise me."

She swallowed the lump in her throat. "Okay."

"Promise me, Nona. Promise me you'll talk to me instead of running away. Promise me, please." His voice was intense and husky.

"I promise," she said softly.

"Good," Jeremy murmured. "Now that we've settled that. I want to hear everything. I don't care how tired I am. I've missed the sound of your voice."

She pressed herself closer to him and let it all out. She told him about the coyote, the long days and nights alone without him, the way she had crumbled under the weight of everything she was running from when she was inches from the college.

He listened, soft hums of acknowledgment scattered throughout her story until she trailed off and asked him about his travels. She listened intently to how he described Maeve's mounting frustration with him until she finally snapped. How they had searched and searched for her, finding where he now knew was the place she had been cornered by the coyote, and how Maeve thought she was dead. What he didn't say, what he didn't need to say, was that no matter how bad it got, he hadn't given up on her. That he had fought to find her for weeks. The mere thought made her eyes sting with unshed tears.

When he finally finished, he pulled her into a hug, wrapping his arms around her from the back. She let herself relax in his arms. "Thank you for finding me."

"Thank you for being found," he murmured back, pressing a soft kiss into her hair.

They lay like that, curled together like two halves of a whole, until they both fell into the darkness their bodies desperately needed to recover. Sleep came easily with the comfort of Jeremy's arms around her.

## DEE

AFTER SEVERAL DEBATES, Dee had convinced Rowan that entering the city might not be the safest option despite her earlier thoughts. She had never been able to shake the idea that Denver would be bad for both of them. Rowan had begged her, reminding her how their father had spoken highly about Denver when he told stories of the past, but eventually, she got him on board. She had almost given in, she was so tired of fighting with Rowan, but he had cracked first. She had almost cried she was so grateful.

Rowan made sure to remind her daily that he was placating her silly concerns. They had managed to find a middle ground on the lying to her for years issue, which mostly consisted of them avoiding the subject, and she was happy about that. But it's impossible to spend this much alone time with your sibling and not want to wring their neck. Especially when he had been making the same five or six jokes for the last two weeks.

City versus forest was just another instance where her hands itched to shake him into submission. Another time when she felt she knew better, but she couldn't force it on him. It was like their mother was still there, reminding her that he was fragile and that she needed to protect him. She was so tired of protecting him.

Dee took a deep breath, centering her mind, and pressed her thighs into her horse. The horse took off in the direction they had agreed on. She focused on the path as she listened to the steady thumping of their horses in time. It was relaxing to just ride in silence instead of listening to Rowan make the worst jokes she'd ever heard. Even more than that, she was grateful they weren't starting another argument. The arguments over their parents' mistakes were making her break out and her stomach knot.

If she heard him giggle after calling out Route 69, if she heard his condescending snort when she expressed her annoyance, she wouldn't be able to keep her hands to herself. Rowan would have one hell of a black eye. Luckily, she had managed to keep the anger at bay despite the circumstances.

When she had made it into the forest, covered by the thick trees, she slowed down. She was finally able to calm the warring emotions inside of her, so she let him catch up. Dee flashed a smile when they were in line with each other.

"You could wait for me, you know that, right?" Rowan grumbled.

Dee shrugged. "I could. I could also push you off your horse and leave you behind. Speeding up seemed to be the safest option."

"I'm not that annoying," Rowan whined.

She looked at him, his face barely matching the protest in his words. "Even you know that's a lie. Don't bullshit me."

Rowan rolled his eyes, blowing out a long breath. "This whole trip has been so boring. I'm just trying to entertain us!"

"Entertain us into hating each other?" The words came out harsher than she'd planned. She bit her lip, waiting for him to call her out on it. The silence made her ears ring. When he didn't make a comment, she dared to peek at him. He wasn't looking at her but staring straight ahead with a frozen mask of frustration. "Listen—"

"No, you listen," Rowan cut her off. "You can't sit over there on your high horse as if you've never damaged our relationship. Because that would be a lie, and you know it. I understand you are still hurt and frustrated, but you can't place all the blame on me. I thought we were done with this. Our parents made me promise. Do you think I wanted that?"

She shuddered.

He flung his hand into the air with annoyance. "Would you have told me if the roles were reversed?"

She slowed her horse down as she thought it over. He was right, and she hated that. With a heavy sigh, she said, "You're right." She made a noise in the back of her throat. "Ugh, I hope I never have to say that again."

Rowan pulled himself next to her and reached across to elbow her. "We can't change what they did and how they handled the situation. But at the end of the day, we're responsible for each other. We're responsible for fixing the damage they created. We can't just spend all our time quietly hating the other one."

Dee frowned at him, her chest tightening. The idea that Rowan hated her was more upsetting than she was willing to admit to herself, let alone him. "Do you hate me?"

"I mean, for someone to not find me funny? Fuck yeah." Rowan elbowed her again. She winced, letting out a high-pitched screech.

"Stop it," she said, whacking him.

Rowan laughed before pulling his horse to a stop. He hopped off, grabbed the reins, and tied his horse to a tree. "Can we just stop and talk about this? Finally end this fight?"

Dee paused. She knew it was better to talk than be mad, but the idea of sitting down and dealing with it made her break out in a cold sweat. Rowan made a point of sitting on a nearby log.

She took a deep breath before jumping off her horse and joining him. "What is there to talk about? Our parents built our home on a lie and forced you to keep it. We've lived a lie our whole lives, and it's destroyed the relationship they spent years cultivating between us."

"Well, yes. That's obvious. But that can't be all you're feeling." Rowan wrapped an arm around her shoulders and gave them a squeeze.

"Okay, okay." She pushed his arm off gently. She needed some degree of separation, or she would lose it. "I guess. They had always made it so fucking important that we feel like siblings. That when they died, we would take care of each other. Why was that so important they had to lie? Did they think after spending seventeen years in the same fucking house wasn't enough to feel like family? Does you being my half brother make you not my brother? I just don't understand why it felt worth it to them. I read that journal, and all I could figure out was they were trying to protect us."

Dee blew out her breath. "Why the fuck did it matter? That's what I can't wrap my head around. Why? Do you know why?"

Rowan studied her, not replying to the question. She bristled, gripping the log and pulling off a chunk of bark. It crumbled in her hand, and she flung it out in front of them. She turned and shoved her shoulder into him. "This is not a time to stay silent, you little shit."

He shrugged. "You're right, it's a time to start talking again, but you're not done. Let it all out, Dee."

"Yes, I am." She pouted, fingering the hole in the bark she created.

Rowan gave her a pointed look. She wanted to smack it off his smug face.

"Fine. Maybe I'm not. I just…if they were so worried about this…why would they want me to hate them after they were gone? Because they're gone, Rowan. Never coming back. And every memory I have of them is marred by this lifelong secret. Every happy memory we've ever shared is now tinted with the ugly brown of deceit and lies." Dee felt it crawling out of her only a second before she was hysterical. She let out a low whine, tears sprouting and burning her eyes. Before she could even process it, she was a blubbering mess of snot and tears.

Rowan pulled her into a hug and let her sob into his shirt. She rubbed her face clean on the soft, worn fabric and ignored how his teeth ground together. He hated getting grimy with her tears or snot, had begged her to use a rag so many times, but she didn't care. All she cared about was that being wrapped in Rowan's arms felt like being wrapped in their mother's. Her heart ached for their parents, ached for what their family used to be, ached for the past. She would do anything for one more chance to ask them why they left them like this.

It wasn't long until she could feel Rowan's chest heaving with his own tears. It moved in time with hers as if they were one person crying. It felt so close to the lie of them being twins she just cried harder. They sat there, crying out everything they hadn't after they'd buried their parents and Rowan told her the truth. How they had gone this long without dealing with it was a testament to how strong-willed the two of them were.

She hiccuped, her tears drying out, and sat up to look at Rowan's red-rimmed eyes and tear-streaked face. She probably looked just as disheveled. She gave him a weak smile as she smoothed out her curls. "I didn't realize…"

He nodded. "We were never going to move past this until we let out all the hurt. Mom and Dad left us with a lot of baggage, but it's not ours. It doesn't matter to me if you are my twin or not. It's been us against the world since we were infants. I don't plan to change that because of an inconvenient truth."

"When did you get so fucking wise?" she asked, shaking her head.

Rowan laughed, his smile lopsided but half-hearted. "Don't

get used to it. This is the last time I'm being nice to your sorry ass. I've said what I needed to. Memorize it for the next time you want to give me shit." Rowan flicked his dreads. "I've never met someone who has single-handedly made me gray from annoyance."

"You've barely met anyone besides me and our parents," she said.

"Whatever," Rowan said.

"Don't whatever me, you little pain in my ass." She hugged him, squeezing just a little extra tight, before sticking her tongue out. Dee stood up, rubbed her hand over her face, and untied her horse. She looked back at him before hopping up. "Let's go. We have places to be, and your ass is slowing us down."

Rowan rolled his eyes but gave her a genuine smile. Rowan may not be her twin, may not be her full brother, but he was the only brother she would ever need. No lies would change that, and Dee would always be grateful for that.

# YEAR 6 AGC, DAY 20

## WINONA

WINONA KNEELED in front of the baby stalk of soybean, gently kneading the soil in hopes of giving the plants some extra oxygen. She mimicked the way her father had taught her to separate the dirt in their home garden when she was a kid. She had planted more than half of her seeds across the large planter boxes between their temporary home and Mia's house. This house didn't have solar panels, so it wouldn't work long term, but it was better than being holed up in Diego and Mia's house. Jeremy had worked with Mia to help create, fill with soil, and prep the boxes for her, but she had taken the time to carefully recreate the trellis system she had back home out of vines and branches Maeve and Jenna brought back from their hunting trips.

The garden looked much better than her old one, and yet it was lacking. Thank goodness the girls had managed to get enough meat to sustain everyone but Mia and Diego. They were relying on her plants as their last efforts to find a solution to their inability to keep down anything but the bathtub gin that Mia made. They learned early on that the meat from the hunting trips wasn't edible for them, something to do with their artificial stomachs, and since she couldn't get her garden to grow as healthy as they had in Washington, they were using inedible foraged ingredients instead. She felt guilty that they were still suffering after all this time.

The seed pods in her hand were ready to be pulled off the plant, but she wasn't sure the plants would survive after this initial pull. The stalks were thinner than she was used to, and she was worried they wouldn't produce again. It didn't help that she was running out of seeds, and creating new seeds from these weak plants was a poor choice.

She hadn't told anyone but Jeremy about her concerns. Instead, she kept a secret garden in the basement of their future house in hopes that she could replace these plants if they died. Those plants were growing stronger, with more vibrant greens and thicker stalks, despite only getting filtered sunlight from the small windows. The plants were closer to what she remembered, but they wouldn't produce pods. It was infuriating that she couldn't provide what she was supposed to.

Jeremy was fixing up the houses for everyone.

Jenna and Maeve were bringing home the food.

Mia and Jeremy cooked for everyone.

And she was staring at a plot of useless plants.

"Are you trying to will the plants into submission?" a voice said from behind her.

She looked up at Mia and gave her a forced smile. "Just making sure that there's enough oxygen in the soil."

Mia lifted a brow and kneeled next to her. She touched one of the pods. It snapped off in her hand, causing Winona to cringe. "What's wrong with them?"

Winona huffed, ripped a different pod off the vine, and pried it open. She showed Mia the small beans inside. "These beans, the ones my family has cultivated for years, were twice the size. I don't know why they aren't growing as well. Everything about these plants doesn't look right."

"Why does it matter?" she asked, rolling the pod over in her hands. "Wouldn't these be good enough to cook with?"

She lifted one shoulder. The idea of pulling these to cook with made her uncomfortable. "Yeah. We could pull them now and make tofu or let them dry out for wax and oils. But I don't know if the plants will survive another growth cycle. I don't know if those will be the last seeds."

Mia frowned. She pried the pod open and inspected the inside. Winona didn't know what she would find that she hadn't. "Do we have extra seeds? Can we save some seeds for replanting?"

Winona shifted back and forth on the balls of her feet. "I have a few extra seeds but not many. And if we need to use seeds from this plant, they most likely will not end up growing to size, just like these. It'll just perpetuate this bad trait."

"Having something"—Mia placed her hand on Winona's shoulder and gave her a smile—"is better than having nothing. I think you're being too hard on yourself. Look at this garden."

She brushed her hand off in annoyance. Mia didn't know what she was talking about. Winona had seen what she could grow, and this was not it. Mia wasn't slacking like she was. "Easy for you to say. You're the backbone of this entire community. Without you, none of this would even exist. I'm just mooching off of everyone."

Mia laughed, her voice breathless and tears springing to her eyes.

"It's not fucking funny," she muttered.

Mia wiped her eyes. "You're right. It's hilarious. You, of all people, think you are contributing nothing. You've built this entire community. Diego and I were on our own, and you're the one who is pulling this group together. You're the one out here every day gardening, producing food for the group. For fuck's sake, you should have seen the pitiful garden Diego had tried to make. Ten years and that man couldn't even make a seed sprout, and here you have a whole garden."

"Do you know how much he would have given for what you call measly?" she asked, sobering up and gesturing to the plants.

She didn't know. She had never not been able to grow plants. She had always been capable of making magic that even her parents were surprised about. She shook her head.

Mia sat down on the ground and scooted next to Winona. "Sit down and let me explain something to you." She patted the ground when Winona didn't move. "Please."

Winona sat down begrudgingly. "Fine, but don't expect it to make me feel better."

"No one is going to force you to be or do anything." She turned to look at her home and blew out her breath. "Diego and I have been struggling since the collapse. In the before, Diego was a world-famous scientist, and I was his assistant. We worked day and night to help fix the problems of the world, but it wasn't possible. No one wanted to listen to us." Her eyes glossed over as if she was reliving it. "Eventually, everything we said would happen did. Diego started to spiral out of control, and we've been in that spiral for over a decade."

"Diego lost the one thing he thought he was good at, and then we found this place. He rebuilt the grid in our home to link with the solar panels. It took two weeks and a lot of mistakes, but when he was done, he smiled for days. It bolstered him to try solving our alcohol problem." Mia sighed. Winona watched her carefully, the pain and sadness written all over. "It didn't work. Then he tried again. And again. Until he finally gave up and gave in to the alcohol."

Mia shook her head and turned to look at Winona. "Diego has lost everything, feels like he can't accomplish anything."

"I don't understand," she said when it was clear Mia wasn't going to continue.

"The point I'm getting at is that you've lost everything, your parents, your home. Yet here you sit, having still accomplished the one thing you are good at. The one thing you feel makes you special. There are people who would kill for that. You should never look down on yourself because your accomplishment doesn't feel as good or important as you think it should be. There is always someone who will think otherwise, and that's the person you should listen to."

"But—" Winona said.

Mia cut her off. "There is no but here. You need to learn how special you are and how amazing this accomplishment is." Mia put an arm over her shoulder, and this time, Winona didn't fight it. "Everyone here thinks what you are doing is amazing. Everyone here is proud of you."

Winona gave her a weak smile. "It doesn't feel amazing."

"Trust me, it is." Mia looked around, finding Jeremy walking between houses, and pointed toward him. "That man right there spends every minute he can doting on you or gushing about your skills. You need to spend more time listening to him and less time listening to the demons in your head. Now, give me a hug and show me how to help oxygenate the soil."

Winona laughed the tears back before hugging Mia. Their hug felt so much like what her mother's used to feel like that a few tears escaped anyway. When she pulled away, she quickly wiped them away before moving to kneel in front of a new plant. She stuck in fingers in the soil. "This is how my dad used to do it. Here's how he showed me."

Mia watched carefully, mimicking the movements of the plant next to her. When she felt Mia didn't need guidance anymore, they worked in silence. The silence was comfortable, happy even. She tried not to spend too much time looking up at Mia and wondering why she felt so motherly. Instead, she focused on the rhythm of their movements and enjoyed the company.

# YEAR 6 AGC, DAY 25

## DIEGO

"This is the best meal you've made so far," Winona said, placing the tasting spoon down on the counter. She smiled over at Jeremy, and Diego frowned at them. He was glad Winona and Jeremy were so enamored with each other. He really was. But he couldn't look at them and not feel the stab of jealousy. All this time, all this effort, and he still couldn't tell Mia how he felt. How could he when he saw the disappointment in her eyes every time she looked over at him?

"Do you want to try?" Jeremy asked, cutting into Diego's thoughts. He was holding out a small cup filled with a reddish-brown liquid. Small veggies floated in it. Diego made a face despite the scent of savory, spicy soup invading his nose. He hadn't kept down food in years, and he was not enticed by the idea of spending another night bent over the trashcan covered in sweat. Once was more than enough, let alone once a week as they tried but didn't find solutions to the problem.

"I don't know. I doubt I'll be able to eat it." He took the cup regardless. He swished it around, letting the smell and steam wash over him. It smelled heavenly. Jeremy was, according to the rest of the group, a prolific chef. He wished he could experience it.

"This is the first meal that has come only from the garden," Winona said. He looked up at her soft smile and sighed. Winona had softened in the weeks after she and Jeremy were reunited. He didn't know what she was like before, but the girl who showed up with Mia was angry, hard, and the girl in front of him had much softer edges.

"Well, I'd rather get sick than let Mia try it." He grabbed a spoonful, blew on it for a second, and slurped it up. The soup was better than it smelled. He hadn't tasted flavors like this in over a decade. The spicy heat from the peppers, the savory tang of the mushroom. Even the fragrance of the rosemary elevated the flavor of the potatoes. Jeremy was a wizard in the kitchen, just like everyone had said.

They stood there, locked into their positions, until Diego had finished the cup. He placed it down on the counter softly and waited. And waited. Until Jeremy finally took the cup to put it in the sink.

"Well?" Jeremy prodded.

Diego looked at him incredulously. "Nothing. No pain, no gurgling, not even slight discomfort."

How long had they been standing there waiting for him to feel anything? Most definitely, it was the longest he had kept anything other than gin down. A laugh bubbled out. Then another. Until he was laughing so hard his eyes stung with tears. He felt delirious with excitement.

"What's so funny?" Mia asked. Diego turned to where she was entering the kitchen with wide eyes. Her eyes flicked between the pot of soup and Diego's beaming face. "No. Really? Don't fucking lie to me, Diego."

"Really," he said. Diego practically skipped to Mia, lifting her off the ground and spinning her into the empty dining room. He placed her down but didn't let go. Their eyes locked in excitement and shock. He could feel her lean into him but knew it was probably just a fluke.

"I want to try." She pulled herself out of Diego's hands to stride over to the pot. Diego ignored the slight pang of how easily she pushed him away in what he felt was an important moment. Another reminder that she did not feel the same way about him.

By the time he had pulled himself out of his own misery, Mia had finished a similar portion. He watched her smile spread across her face. "No shit."

Jeremy laughed. "Now that we've established that you can eat. Go get the table ready, so I can serve dinner."

DIEGO STUDIED Mia as she put out bowls and silverware. Diego was supposed to be putting cups out, but he couldn't stop smiling like an idiot. They could eat. They could finally eat. He couldn't understand why Mia looked so calm, was not screaming from the rooftops like he wanted to. There was finally sun peeking out from the horizon, and he was ready to explode.

"Is there a reason you are staring at me instead of doing your part?" She waved a spoon at him in annoyance.

He put down the cups and searched her eyes. "Why aren't you excited? We've been working toward this for almost ten years."

She didn't respond, just placed her remaining plates out in silence. Diego wanted to shake her. When her hands were free, she sat down on the corner of the bench and gave him a sad look. "I've never been more excited."

"But?"

"BUT. That's just it. There shouldn't be a but. Except there is. Because no matter how much progress we make, I still have to spend most of my time worrying about you." Her voice cracked. In the dim candlelight, it was hard to tell, but he was confident she was crying or at least starting to. He wanted to reach out. Wanted to wipe away the tears. But he'd never been that guy, and he was confident she wouldn't want him to touch her. His affection for her was only one way.

He studied her. The wrinkles he didn't realize she had developed. The tufts of gray hair at her temples that were expanding. The way her mouth had started to dip downward, creating frown lines. The way she stopped joking with him as much. He did this. He ruined her. He ruined the only person who had ever cared about him. It was his fault. He batted at the burning in his eyes. "I never wanted you to spend your time worrying about me."

She laughed harshly. "That means fucking nothing, Diego. We've always been a partnership. For years you were the reason I got up in the morning. The reason I fought for my degree and our research. Your passion didn't just drive you. It drove me. You pushed me through my darkest days. I have never wanted to give up on you the way you didn't give up on me. But now you just drink and whine. You lost all your passion when you realized the world didn't want to listen to you, didn't want to save itself. You left me to do it all alone. To carry the weight of both of us, and I'm exhausted."

Mia turned her face away from him, her body shaking with silent sobs. He tried to place his hand on her shoulder, but she smacked it away.

"Don't." Her voice was firm and harsh.

He shoved his hands into his pockets and dug his nails into his thighs. How had he ruined the one person who meant so much to him? "I never meant for you to feel like this. I shouldn't have let this happen. I'm so sorry. All of this is my fault."

She let out an annoyed huff followed by a sniffle. "You can be sorry all you want, but you can't expect me to trust you again. Not when you haven't proven you can change. Not after all these years of this…" She waved a hand in his direction.

He circled the table and sat across from her. She wouldn't look at him, but at least she didn't turn away. "I'm going to change. I swear to you." He placed a soft hand on her chin and gently brought her eyes up to look at him. "I won't let you down again. I don't expect you to believe that, but I am hoping you'll give me a chance to prove it. Just one chance."

She closed her eyes and let herself sink into his hand. "I would give the world to see the guy who loved his research so much he wouldn't give up on it no matter what. I would love to see the guy who spun me in circles." She laughed softly, her eyes lighting up as she searched the woods. "Do you remember when you won the grant for your research?"

He gave her a weak smile. He remembered everything about that moment. It was when he realized that no matter what happened or how Mia felt about him, he would want her in his life. Whether it be a mentee, a confidante, or only his friend. She had become a part of his world, and he couldn't see it without her after that. "Of course I remember."

"That guy, the one I saw that day, he's the one I…"

"Are you guys okay?" Jenna asked, interrupting them to sit at the table.

Mia sniffled, using her sleeve to wipe her face, as she turned to smile at Jenna. "Of course not. We're just so excited. We were finally able to keep some food down."

Mia shot him a look. Biting back his hurt and annoyance, he nodded enthusiastically at Jenna. "She's right. We'll finally be able to eat dinner with everyone tonight. It's a big night."

* * *

DIEGO FILLED his bowl with seconds despite Mia's whispered warning that he shouldn't indulge so much so fast. But Diego felt good, better than he had in years. Everything was sharper, the colors brighter, and he actually felt the warmth of the firepit a couple of feet away from the table. He felt like he was on top of the world. Like he could tackle Mia's disappointment in him head-on and prove to her he was still the guy she knew back then.

"You're going to make yourself sick," Mia chided as he took the last few slurps.

He turned to smile at her, but when he saw the concern swimming in her eyes, he frowned. "Don't worry about it. You don't need to. I can take care of myself." He leaned toward her, and whispered, "I promise."

She didn't respond, standing up to start clearing the table with Winona. The pair of them whispered to each other as they walked away. Diego watched them walk away longingly. He had replayed his conversation with Mia over and over again. He wanted to finish it, to prove himself.

Jenna and Maeve grabbed their own dishes and excused themselves from the table, leaving him alone with Jeremy.

"So…how are you feeling?" Jeremy asked.

Diego chuckled. "I've never felt better. I'm so grateful to you and Winona for making this happen. It's truly a miracle."

"Happy to hear it," Jeremy said. "Hopefully, this will give you a chance to focus on getting the solar panels up and running for the other houses. I don't know much about electricity since we didn't have it growing up."

Diego tried to ignore the guilt. Mia was right about him. He had let so much slide in the last few years and given so little to their efforts to stay alive. He had been practically useless, but he wasn't going to be useless anymore. He was going to contribute and prove to her he could be everything she expected and wanted from him. "I'll get started first thing tomorrow. I'll teach you everything I know. Everyone needs to have their own place to truly be settled in the community."

"It would be nice to have a place to spread out and settle into. I'll get up early and make us breakfast." Jeremy took a deep breath. "I'm excited to learn how to do this. It's important these skills get passed down."

Diego cocked an eyebrow at him. "You know, I don't think many people give you enough credit for how wise you are."

"The people that matter know, and that's all that matters to me," Jeremy said as he stood up. His eyes flicked to Winona in the window, and he smiled. He grabbed his plate and turned from the table. "Get some sleep, Diego. Tomorrow will be a long day for us."

Diego watched him leave as his stomach started to churn. He wasn't sure if it was the overeating or just the immense pressure to get his act together, but all of a sudden, he could feel bile rising in his throat. Sweat broke out on his forehead. Everything Mia warned was coming true, and he had to confess that he once again screwed up.

He darted into the woods just in time to throw up his second bowl of soup. He dropped to his knees and hiccuped.

"Fucking shit," he mumbled. He threw up again and tried to hold back the tears as his throat burned. He leaned his forehead against the cold bark of the tree next to him. His body didn't stop until he was emptied out and drained of all his energy.

By the time he pulled himself together, the lights in the house were all off except the patio light. They must have assumed he went for a walk after dinner and would be home late. It wouldn't have been the first time, and today would be a day he needed the clarity. He mumbled a curse. He had wanted to talk to Mia, wanted to finish their conversation before it was interrupted, and now she was probably asleep.

He trekked back to the house, shoulders slumped, and dragged himself into his bed. He looked up, studying the ceiling, and replayed the conversation with Mia until he tired his mind into a restless sleep.

## THE FOREST PERSON

THE LOW RUMBLE of one of the coyotes had dragged their attention, along with the two coyotes that were curled up with them, toward the soft burnt orange on their right. The sun was just barely peeking out over the mountains, casting a soft glow behind the trees and turning their leaves a murky brown instead of their midday vivid dark green. One of the coyotes nudged their shoulder, and they let it pull them off the floor.

They watched it kick off, spraying dead leaves into their face. The coyote arced over the fallen trees that surrounded their home, landing a couple of feet away before taking off in a sprint. They weren't as fast as any of the pack, but they'd been there long enough to build up the leg muscles to keep up, even if they showed up last. By the time they made it across the forest to the small clearing the coyotes were circling, the damage was already done. They hadn't been fast enough to stop anything, which meant they needed to problem solve. Fast.

A boy no older than they were was whimpering under the snarl of their alpha, who must have found him on patrol. Their alpha had made it clear this boy wasn't welcome, but he was still unharmed. It was the smell of blood, the faint iron taste of the air, that forced their eyes onto their beta. He was almost as large as the alpha but was pure instinct. The alpha was more likely to pause, hold a trespasser hostage, whereas their beta was known for jumping head-first into danger. It was the reason he was the beta, not the alpha.

His teeth were clamped around the middle section of a young girl who looked eerily similar to the boy. The girl was breathing shallowly, her eyes shut as her head dangled in the air. The sharp fangs dug into her stomach, causing small rivers of her blood to slide down her body. Now that they were there, the only sound was the drip of her blood landing in the puddle growing underneath them.

They pushed past two of the female coyotes in front of them, their backs straight with a ridge of fur standing up to the sky and their mouths pulled back to show their impressive teeth. They tried to keep them from entering the circle, it wasn't safe for them to interrupt the leaders when they were so feral, but they didn't care. The sound of the blood dripping, the boy whimpering, and the groaning from the girl were cascading in their head so loudly it hurt. The sounds lay on top of each other until they forced a shiver across their back. They shook out their shoulders. And focused past the sounds.

"What in the fuck?" they finally said, their voice pitched two octaves lower for the coyotes' benefit. Their eyes snapped to them, the alpha taking a step back to keep them and the boy in his view and the beta turning with the girl still ensnared. The girl shrieked, her eyes flashing white briefly as his teeth ripped more flesh, but it was cut short with the look they shot her. Shrieking would not help her case right now, and if she managed to stay silent, they might be able to salvage the situation.

The alpha grumbled, his eyes calming down from the swirling anger that was there moments before. They raised an eyebrow as they let out a low, annoyed growl, and he lowered his lip to show fewer teeth. It was the closest they would get. Then he yipped out a whine, just one, and they rolled their eyes. The gesture was lost on the coyotes, but the boy gave them an annoyed look.

"You're not starving, Alpha. Let these poor people go." Their voice was low and grunted out, but the alpha's eyes made it clear he understood.

He whined at her, a high-pitched noise that made them shiver, but nudged his beta to release the girl. The beta growled but dropped her onto the ground so hard that her head snapped against the ground. The sound reverberated across the meadow, and they cringed. They were becoming less and less sure the girl would survive. With the two teenagers out of immediate harm, they spun to address the rest of them. "Oh, stop it. These teenagers have done nothing to you. Have they, Alpha?"

They gave him a look, their shoulders pulled back and teeth bared, and he blew out a breath close enough to a huff that they assumed their point had been made. When they turned to focus on the pack, they were all standing calmly without a pair of fangs in sight. What had been so tense and vicious became soft and complacent. "Okay then. Everyone but Beta can get the fuck out of here."

None of the coyotes moved, and they growled, pointing their finger out into the forest.

Finally, the alpha started to walk away, and the group slowly filed after him. No doubt they would make them sleep alone tonight for saving some kids from their bellies, but they could live without that. Who cared about the cold nights when they could save someone? What they couldn't live with was a replaying of what happened to their parents before they realized they were able to save them. Their parents had been in the same place, almost the same meadow, and they had just been playing in the grass behind their house. They had been so close, had the same pull over the coyotes that they did now, but they didn't know. Didn't know how much power they had bubbling up inside.

If only they had been close enough to their parents. If only they had been close enough to the realization of how strong they really were.

When the coyotes' footsteps were far enough away, they turned to inspect the girl. The boy, still shaking, was frozen as he stared at their beta. It didn't help that the beta still looked like he was going to eat them. His teeth weren't bared anymore, but his eyes still held the same anger. They whacked him on the nose and pointed at the ground. He clicked his teeth together, annoyed, but lay down anyway.

"Fucking coyotes, man," they said, giving the boy a shrug. Before he could get his bearings, now that their beta was on the ground, they ripped off their shirt and the girl's. Her stomach looked much worse up close than it did when they originally got there; even with the dried blood, it was clear it would be hard for her to survive.

Without Beta's teeth to hold it together, the blood was pouring out faster than ever. What used to be streams had turned into floods. They pulled her shirt apart, creating one long bandage, and wrapped it around the girl's torso. For a second, it was almost as if nothing happened.

It soaked quickly with the blood, but when it didn't seep out, they breathed out a sigh of relief. The girl's eyes fluttered for a few seconds before shutting again. The only thing keeping hope was that her chest still moved. It looked laborious, but moving was better than not moving. They held their fingers to the girl's neck and felt the weak pulse. She would need more than they could give her right now. She needed a doctor.

But there were only two people they knew who might be able to help. They turned to the boy, ready to tell him that they needed to get help, but he was crawling toward the girl with tears streaking the dirt caked on his face. His brown eyes flicked between them and the girl. Their heart tinged, feeling guilty that they weren't confident they could save the girl.

"She needs more help," they told him when he finally was kneeling next to them. He was shaking with tears and rubbing the girl's face soothingly. They squeezed his shoulder, feeling him give into their presence.

"Whatever you need to do to save her. She's all I have left." The boy hiccuped.

They snapped their fingers at the beta, letting a harsh growl leave their lips as they signaled him to stand in front of them. They clamored on top of him before grabbing two tufts of his fur and pressing their knees into his abdomen. He shot off, running at a speed they'd never seen before or even expected after his performance earlier, and they did their best to guide him through the forest to the house that used to be theirs. The house that held the only people she'd seen walking around in lab coats like the doctors in the books their parents read to them as a child.

No matter how weak the woman seemed, they knew if anyone could save the girl, it would be her or her husband.

When they made it to the edge of the forest, they saw the woman sitting on the back porch with a mug. She was sipping it and staring out at the sunrise with a grimace. They got off the coyote, giving him a soft pat, before running down the hill between the forest's edge and the house. They were almost across the field when the woman noticed them. She jumped to her feet, spilling her drink on the ground, and mumbled something as she tried to back up. The fear in her eyes was obscured by concern.

"Wait. Please. Wait," they said, pleading. They held their hands up in the air.

The woman narrowed her eyes but stopped moving. "You're the girl in the forest Diego is always talking about. I thought he was losing his mind."

They paused, cocking their head in confusion. Didn't she recognize them? They brushed the thought away as quickly as it came. "Please. Someone is hurt. She needs help."

"I'm not a doctor. At least, not that kind." The woman placed her mug on the table as she studied her. Something changed as she looked at them. With a sigh, she nodded. "Okay. Fine. We'll help. Let me go wake Diego."

"We don't have time," they said. The woman gave them a look but didn't argue.

"Let me at least get some of our first aid supplies." She slipped back into the house. They tapped their foot impatiently, turning every few seconds to make sure Beta was still there and to check on how far the sun had risen. Luckily, both were where they had been just minutes before. Their chest deflated as they stopped tapping. The woman was going to help. It would be okay.

When the woman emerged, she was holding a backpack and a shirt. "This is for you. It appears Diego has been giving you my clothing, and you're half naked, so just get this on, and we'll head out. How far is it?"

They slipped the new shirt over their head, fingering the soft fabric before focusing on the woman. "It shouldn't take more than a few minutes. We have a ride."

The woman stared at them, her eyes wide. "A ride?"

They whistled for Beta, who came loping down the hillside faster than they expected. The woman's sharp intake was the only sign she was concerned. Even with the ragged breath coming from the woman, she climbed on behind them and wrapped her arms around their torso tightly. Once settled, they guided them back to the meadow as quickly as Beta would take them, making sure the woman didn't fall off the back from the way Beta whipped himself around bends. When they slowed to a stop, both of them had to pause to gain their baring. They scratched his ears before waving him out of the meadow.

The woman ran to the girl, her covered stomach a dark, vivid red with browning edges, so quickly it made their head spin. They followed her into the heart of the clearing, Beta moving near the edge of the forest and kneeling next to the boy. He hovered so close to the girl that the two were almost touching. For a second, they didn't know where one ended and the other began.

The woman reached out to check the girl's pulse, angling herself around the boy with a muffled grunt of frustration. They linked her elbow with the boy, lifting him off the girl and dragging him a couple of feet back. He whined, fighting them the whole way, but they moved him easily. When they had given the woman enough space to start fidgeting with the shirts wrapped around the girl, they faced the boy with a softness they never expected.

"Getting into her face won't help your"—they waved a hand uselessly—"person."

"Sister. She's my twin sister. Well, half sister. It's a long story." The boy gave them a weak smile and continued to babble. "Her name is Dee. I'm Rowan. We grew up on the East Coast in a small town in Upstate New York, but Dee wanted to move. Wanted to leave the past behind and look at what it brought us. I knew we shouldn't have moved. I told her. I told her."

They listened to him, his voice turning to whispers that repeated themselves in a haunting manner they'd never seen before. Coyotes didn't dwell on the past, and they couldn't barely remember their parents, let alone their actions. His moaning was disconcerting. Less about him and more about the way it dug at their core with just fervor that they felt emptied out.

When he finally stopped, he bit his lip and gestured at the woman. "Do you know her?"

They shrugged, trying to piece together everything they'd

learned from the supplies left for them and the one time they'd gone into the house. "As much as I know anyone else. She's a scientist. So is her husband."

"He's not my husband," the woman grumbled from her position crouched on the ground. Her annoyance bit, making them curious. "We're chemists. He was my mentor in the before. My name's Mia by the way."

"A chemist? Are you even capable of saving my sister?" Rowan balked.

They rolled their eyes. "Do you have any other options?"

"I'm as capable or more than you look to be," Mia said.

He sighed, running a hand across his face. "I don't... It's just..."

"I get it. I would be just as hysterical if something happened to Diego. Was as upset when I lost my family all those years ago." She brushed her dirty hands against her jeans and stood up. "Your sister is stable. I don't know if she can survive this blood loss, and without knowing her or your blood types, I don't know if we can give her a transfusion. I'm not even sure I could manage something like that. I've only seen it when my parents were sick."

Rowan breathed out in relief. "Thank you. Thank you for trying, Mia, and thank you for getting her..." He gave them a look. "I don't think I ever got your name?"

She shrugged. "Don't have one anymore."

They both gave them a look.

"I grew up out here with them." They pointed to Beta, who was sleeping in a ball away from them. "I'm sure my parents named me, but they've been gone for a long time. You can just call me..."

They bit their lip. They'd never tried to name themself. Names weren't something the coyotes used. Weren't something they needed to communicate. They didn't know any names other than the ones shared today. They didn't know if they related more to the boy or the girl. They were just a person who existed.

"How about Parker?" Mia suggested. "It means protector of the forest."

Rowan nodded in agreement.

They didn't think a name was necessary, but it seemed to please them, so they gave in. "Parker, fine." The name felt good in their mouth. Brushing that aside, they focused on the group. "Now that we've settled that, we should get Dee in a safe place and covered while she recovers."

The group settled on building a fire nearby and creating a protective circle around the girl. They called Beta and a few other coyotes to stand guard around the group.

Once the fire was sparking to life, they focused on the sound of the girl's breathing. It was shallow and ragged, mimicking the sounds of a dying deer when the coyotes pounced on dinner. It didn't give them a warm feeling about Dee's survival, but they weren't willing to ruin Rowan's hope. At least, not yet.

Besides, who knew, they could be wrong.

It wouldn't be the first time.

# YEAR 6 AGC, DAY 26

## WINONA

DIEGO'S SCREAMS startled her out of Jeremy's arms and onto the floor next to their temporary bed. She rubbed her tailbone, wincing in pain, before looking up to find Jeremy still fast asleep. He could sleep through a tree falling. She stood up to shake him awake. Even that took genuine effort and a pang of jealousy. She wished she could sleep like that. When his eyes opened a fraction, she snapped her fingers in his face. He opened his eyes a little more and looked at her.

"Wake up, Jeremy. Something is wrong." His eyes shot open, looking at her with bewilderment. She felt bad that this was how he had to wake up, but it didn't change the circumstances. She locked eyes with him briefly, wordlessly conveying her worries and concerns, before saying, "I don't know what's wrong, but I'm going down to see why Diego is screeching."

She gave him one last lingering look before slipping out the door and down the stairs to the living room. Diego wasn't wailing anymore, but she could still hear a low whine coming from where he was pacing the length of the dining room. Winona eyed him as she cautiously approached Diego's shaking body. She'd never seen him so distraught. Most of the time,

Diego was drunk and tipsy, so he was easygoing. "What's wrong?"

His eyes bored into her, wild and crazed, as he turned toward her. She took an involuntary step backward, raising her hands. He mumbled something incoherent.

"Diego. We can't help if you don't tell us what is wrong." Seeing Diego like this made her nervous. Where was Jeremy? He would know how to help. Diego had been completely stoic after years and years of just barely surviving. Mia said he used to be funny but lost it a few years ago. This version of him was unnatural, disjointed. He wasn't the stoic person she knew or the funny person she wanted to get to know. This Diego was almost rabid.

"She's right," Jeremy said, his voice carrying from the bottom of the stairs. He walked into the kitchen and brought over a small glass of amber liquid. Diego paused long enough to rip it out of his hands and gulp it greedily. Well, at least she recognized that version of him, no matter how upsetting it was.

"Mia." The word was slurred, but it was clear that drink was his first. It was as if he was talking through tears that she couldn't see. What was going on with them for him to be this insane?

* * *

Winona looked around, expecting the woman to come out of the basement with her usual placating smile. She lingered on the basement door, hoping she would appear and deal with Diego. She focused back on Diego's pacing form. "What about Mia?"

"She's fucking missing. Mia is fucking missing," Diego snapped. His voice was screechy, higher than she'd ever heard it. It forced a shiver through her body.

"Where would she have gone? Are you sure? Maybe she went for a walk," Jeremy said, shrugging in an effort to look nonchalant. But his shoulders didn't move equally, and she knew better. He was just as concerned as she felt. Not just that Mia was gone, but the sudden frantic energy wafting off Diego. Everything felt off-kilter this morning, and neither of them was equipped to deal with it.

She took a calming breath to steady her voice. If Diego heard her concern, he would most likely spiral more than he already was. "Jeremy's right. Have you checked the rest of the houses? We're still working out the issues for everyone to move into their homes. She could be anywhere in the neighborhood. She had a long list of chores to complete."

Diego gave her a hopeful look, and she plastered a smile on her face. It was strained, but Diego bought it. He slowed to a stop and nodded with confidence that felt misplaced. Perhaps she should have been more direct instead of hopeful. Mia could be dead for all she knew.

Diego strode between them, heading toward the front door. He looked over his shoulder at them when he swung the door open. He shot them a wide smile, his eyes gleaming with hope as he said, "I'll check the girls' house. You can check yours."

"You got it," Jeremy said, his voice the fake upbeat he used when she had cooked their meals. It had taken her a long time to figure it out, but now it felt so obvious. When she had called him out on it, he had shrugged as he told her that he didn't want to upset her. She had stopped that in its tracks immediately.

Once Diego had left, Winona gave Jeremy a weary look. "I feel bad for giving him hope. Do you think she's hurt or...?"

Jeremy shivered. "She wouldn't have just left. We just need to hope she makes it back before Diego goes overboard. I don't know if we can handle that."

"Are you sure he's not already overboard? Had they not been able to eat dinner last night, I was confident we would have lost him to insanity." Winona frowned. She leaned her forehead against Jeremy's chest with a sigh. She mumbled into the fabric of his shirt, "Well. We might as well go take a look at our future house. Maybe she'll show up."

* * *

"WE'VE BEEN STANDING HERE for thirty minutes. She's not here," Jeremy said once they completed their search and were sitting in the dim living room. Without the solar panels set up and properly linked to the house, the room was only lit by the sun that was high in the sky. It was just enough lighting to make out the wrinkles of concern on his face. She wanted to smooth them away, but it wouldn't fix anything.

Winona picked at a loose string on the dark-blue chair she was sitting in. "I don't want to tell him. It's going to crush him."

"We don't have a choice. The sooner we tell him, the sooner he can come to terms with it," Jeremy said. He reached out and placed his hand over hers. She stopped picking to link their fingers. He gave her a weak smile. "Delaying this will only hurt him more."

Winona narrowed her eyes at him. "When exactly did you become so wise?"

"I always have been. It's just whether or not you listen to me." He stuck his tongue out at her. "Maybe you should listen to me more often."

She grabbed the pillow out from behind her with her free hand and chucked it at him. "Whatever. You can tell him, Mr. Wise Guy."

"Tell who what?" Diego said from the doorway, startling them. Jeremy dropped her hand as if it had burned him, and she tried not to let it hurt. Instead, she focused on the open doorway and Diego. They hadn't closed it when they came in, so it wasn't surprising that neither of them heard him show up, but that didn't change the sudden discomfort in the room. The tension was so thick she felt like she was choking.

"Did you find her?" Winona asked, trying to shift him away from their useless search. Maybe Diego had better luck.

"No." The word hung in the air. It felt final and hard. She wanted to punt it across the room and never think about the implication again. "Did you?"

Jeremy's face slipped into a grimace for a brief second before he plastered the same fake smile on his face. She tried to do the same while he addressed Diego's question. "We didn't. But she might be out in the woods? There are other places to check."

Diego deflated, his body shrinking into itself and making him look three feet tall. "Yeah. Maybe."

Winona stood up to try to comfort the older man, but by the time she made it to the door, Diego had left the house. Jeremy came up behind her, and the two of them watched him drag his feet across the neighborhood and enter their house. It looked as if someone was dragging him home instead of him moving himself.

"Should we go after him?" she asked. Winona waved her hand vaguely in his direction.

Jeremy shook his head and wrapped an arm around her. She smiled into his chest when he pulled her close. "Let's give him some time. We can take a look at your garden and then look at our solar grid. We'll check on him around dinner time."

Winona agreed, nodding into his chest, but something felt wrong. Her stomach rolled with concern that Jeremy's soft forehead kiss and hug couldn't stop. Mia wasn't one to just give up or leave. It just didn't match everything she'd learned about the woman in the last few months. She tried to push past the mounting fears, but even when she was pulling weeds in her garden, her mind returned to the moment Mia had made her feel special. Her thoughts lingered on Mia for the rest of the day, distracting her to the point that Jeremy told her to focus on the garden while he dealt with the other chores.

All she wanted was for Mia to be okay. Winona was

confident the group wouldn't stick together without her. There was something in the way Mia spoke with everyone, the way everyone seemed to want her opinion or have her involved with their activities, that made her the glue no one else could be. No one else could bring this ragtag group of survivors together the way Mia could.

# YEAR 6 AGC, DAY 27

## WINONA

By THE TIME the sun was peeking out, Winona had been awake for an hour. After another dream about Mia getting hurt in the forest, she wasn't able to fall back asleep. She needed to do something about the situation, or she would feel the guilt until she died. The squeak of the girl's door across the hall forced her out of bed. She crawled over Jeremy, who slept like a rock, and followed the sounds into the kitchen where Jenna and Maeve were trying to heat up leftovers.

"Are you guys heading out for another hunt?" she asked. Jenna looked up, unfazed, as Maeve jumped in her seat.

"Shit. Why are you so quiet?" Maeve muttered, shaking her shoulders out and stabbing a piece of potato.

"Ignore her. She's not a morning person." Jenna rolled her eyes. "We're heading out as soon as Maeve gets some breakfast in her. Otherwise, her stomach will give us away."

"Oh. Okay." Winona sat down across from them. "Are we running out of meat?"

Jenna shook her head. "No, just making sure we stay stocked…" She raised an eyebrow at Winona. "What's wrong? You don't normally talk to us without Jeremy around."

"That's because she's stuck up," Maeve added.

Jenna sighed. "Can you not pick a fight, just this once?"

"Fuck that. I'm not helping her." Maeve stabbed the air in between them with a fork. "I still remember what she did to Jeremy."

"Stop it."

"No, she's right. I understand your annoyance with me," Winona said. She uncrossed her arms and placed her palms on the table. "I deserve this, but this isn't about me."

Maeve narrowed her eyes. "Did something happen to Jeremy?"

"No," Winona said, bristling. All Maeve ever cared about was Jeremy. Didn't that upset Jenna? It would upset her if they were to switch roles.

"Then don't bother me."

"Maeve, can you stop? Listen." Jenna placed a soft hand on hers. "I think if you just apologized, we could all move past this."

Winona bit her lip. Apologize? How ridiculous. "Fine. I'm sorry for leaving you guys to deal with Jeremy."

Maeve barked out a laugh. "That's so fucked up. How could you not apologize for what you did to that poor sweet boy? He's obsessed with you. Not to mention, Jeremy has done anything and everything he can to take care of you, and you're fucking sorry for leaving us with him?"

"Maeve," Jenna warned.

"Don't." Maeve stood up and stormed across the room as waves of hot anger filled the space between them. "You don't deserve him."

"You're right. I never have," Winona said calmly. She'd known it for a long time but wasn't willing to deal with it.

Spinning on her heel, Maeve stared her down. "So you know, and you're still dragging him around?"

"Dragging isn't the word I'd use." Winona let out a long breath. She didn't want to drag him along; she just wasn't willing to give him up. She could barely imagine a life without him. "I owe Jeremy everything right now. It's something I have to deal with, something I have to make right. It's not something you can make poof away."

Maeve growled but stayed silent, choosing to focus her eyes on Jenna. "Well, what do you want from us?"

"Mia is missing, and I hoped you two would help find her," Winona said, turning to focus on Jenna. "I don't know why you chose to stay, but your skills are unmatched, and she needs you."

"We didn't stay for you, that's for fucking sure," Maeve muttered.

"That's enough, Maeve." Jenna gave Winona a weak smile. "It was my choice to stay, and I stand by it."

"Damn right."

Jenna shot Maeve another look. "What Maeve is trying to say is that she didn't want to come here and is only here because I asked her to."

"If you don't want to be here, no one will make you feel bad if you leave. But if you could just help with Mia before you go?" Winona tried to keep her tone neutral, but it was obvious she was doing a shit job.

"We're not going anywhere. Despite all of Maeve's whining, we're both happy here. It's the first home we've had since my mom passed away that feels like a home." Jenna raised an eyebrow at Maeve. "Right?"

"Fine. Whatever. Happy?"

Jenna chuckled. "That's the best we're getting from her, trust me."

Winona let the silence ring for a minute before turning to address Maeve. "Listen, I'm sorry we started on the wrong foot. I'm sorry I hurt Jeremy. I'm sorry you feel this way. I can't change the past; I can't be somebody I'm not, but I can try to do better. I want you both to feel welcomed, to feel appreciated, and to feel like I'm making the same amount of effort you are."

She stood up and crossed the kitchen with a hand out for Maeve. When they clasped hands, she continued. "I promise, from now on, I will do my best to address your concerns and continue to ask for your input so you don't feel this way again."

Maeve shook her hand. "I'll take it."

Winona laughed. "That's better than you punching me in the stomach."

"It wouldn't be the first time she's done that," Jenna said.

"I can still do it if that's what you want."

Winona held up her hands. "No thanks. I'm okay." Heading back to the table, she focused on Jenna. "What do you need to help find Mia?"

Jenna's face turned serious. "I need some of her clothing to track the smell."

"I can grab you some. Anything else?"

"Lunch," Maeve said, smiling as she strode back to the table. Jenna rolled her eyes. "What? I get hungry, and who knows how long this will take?"

"I can manage some lunch. Do you want me to make it, or should I get Jeremy when I grab Mia's things?"

"Jeremy," they said in unison with a laugh.

"My cooking isn't that bad!" she protested. They didn't relent. "Okay, fine. I'll be back."

She left the girls to start planning their trip as she made her way up the stairs. Despite the circumstances and her concerns over Mia, the conversation with the girls had lifted a weight off her shoulders she didn't know was holding her down. They would never be best friends, would probably only be casual acquaintances, but she didn't want to keep building this home for everyone without fixing that relationship. No one deserved to feel how she imagined they did.

# YEAR 6 AGC, DAY 27

## DIEGO

DIEGO ROLLED off the bed and stood up for the first time in half a day. He grabbed the first two things he found to wear and beelined to Mia's door. He knocked, listening for movement, but the only sounds he heard were the soft rustling coming from down the hall. He felt himself deflate. He knew it wasn't likely, but he expected Mia to just reappear.

When he heard the squeak of a door open, he slid away from the door and turned to smile at Winona. "Good morning," he said with forced enthusiasm.

Winona narrowed her eyes at him in what looked like an effort to hide the pity that he wished he didn't see. "Don't lie to me. I know you were hoping she was there. I was too." She frowned. "I've checked a few times since the sun rose, but no sign of her. I asked the girls to see if they could track her down with one of her old shirts. Hopefully, that helps."

"I can't believe I didn't think of that." He sighed. "Thank you."

"Don't thank me. Why don't you go and help Jeremy with the solar panels? Be the person Mia thinks you are so when she gets back, she won't be as miserable as she looked the other night."

He stared at her, mouth agape. "You heard that?"

"Diego, if you think anyone in this community didn't hear that, you would be stupider than I thought. For such a smart person, you sure can be a huge dumbass."

He dug his nails into his palm. "I'm not a fucking dumbass. I'm fucking broken. I was a world-fucking-renowned chemist. I was in the fucking news, warning people about this." He waved his fist in the air. "I won grants to help people. I tried to help people for years. Now look at me. I'm a disappointment to the only person who has ever fucking cared about me."

Winona softened, the pity shining stronger than before, and Diego resented it. She walked down the hall and wrapped him in her arms. The simple gesture made him soften. "There is not a single person here who does not care about you, Diego. None of us would be so angry if we didn't care."

He bit back the tears but let himself collapse in her arms. She rubbed his back soothingly. "I am trying," he protested weakly.

"No one thinks you aren't." She pulled back and locked their eyes. "Jenna is going to find Mia. She's going to bring her home. You need to focus on proving you are still the man she agreed to follow to the ends of the earth all those years ago."

He gave her a weak smile. "I don't think I am."

"Well, of course not, you shit. It's been twenty years. If you were that exact same guy, I'd be far more concerned about zombies than I am." Winona rolled her eyes.

Diego snorted, a soft chuckle escaping his lips. "That's fucking rude."

"Did you know that we have a house rule about being upset?"

He shook his head, eyeing Winona's smug face.

"If you laugh, you can't be upset anymore. Sorry." She shrugged. "Those are the rules. I don't make them. I just enforce them. Well, I do make them, but it doesn't matter. Go get your ass in gear. Jeremy has been poking at those solar panels since the sun rose, and I don't want him to get hurt."

Diego gave her a tight squeeze, whispering into her ear, "Thank you. Jeremy is lucky to have you."

She didn't respond, just marched down the stairs. He listened to the door slam before he let his tears run silently. He had never been much of a crier, so they didn't last long after a few rough scrubbings of his eyes, but it felt good to let it out. Everything since the collapse had been too much for him to care about whether or not crying was something he was supposed to be doing.

He took a deep breath. "I can do this. I can fucking do this."

* * *

"I CAN'T DO THIS," Jeremy grumbled. He pushed himself off the ground roughly. Diego looked up at him. Then back to the wiring in front of them. Jeremy had been doing a great job, better than Diego had done the first time he tried to fix their house. Mia had laughed at him when he showed up in the kitchen with his hair sticking straight up. The fact that no one had been electrocuted was a huge feat.

Ignoring the pinch of sadness, he patted the ground next to him. "You're doing great."

"That's a lie," Jeremy said.

"Let me tell you something." He patted the ground again, shifting so he was facing Jeremy. Jeremy huffed but sat down anyway. Diego squeezed his shoulder. "When we first made it out here, our house was completely off the grid, and our car had finished up all of its power reserves. We didn't pick this neighborhood on purpose. It was more like the neighborhood picked us."

"I remember Mia's bright smile when we realized most of

the houses had solar panels. We'd grown up in what used to be Florida, most of which doesn't exist now, and solar panels were rare. They shouldn't have been with all the sun we got, but people didn't care about things the way we do." He smiled softly. Mia's eyes had glowed that day, wide and excited, as she took in the house. She'd run inside each of them until she finally stepped out onto the front porch and proclaimed that this was their house. He couldn't even fight her with how infectious her excitement had been.

"We were never expecting this. It wasn't until the sun had dipped below the forest that we realized none of the panels worked." He pulled out a few blades of grass and threw them into the wind. "We spent our first two weeks trying to remember how wiring worked. Both of our chemistry degrees included physics, so we had some basic understanding. Plus, when you're a young research assistant without a grant, you learn how to build your instruments from the ground up to save money. So we weren't helpless, but man did we feel it."

Jeremy rolled his eyes. "Save your bullshit. I don't need a pep talk."

"Shut up and fucking listen, you shit." Diego laughed as Jeremy made a face. "This isn't a pep talk. It's a bonding moment. Bond with me, you pain in the ass."

"Fine. Keep going," he said. Diego ignored his snarky tone. Jeremy had picked up some of Winona's snark, but he was still the sweet boy they first met.

"As I was saying, we weren't helpless. I got up every morning, cup of gin in hand, and walked in at lunch electrocuted." Jeremy gave him a blank stare. "You've probably never had to deal with it, but when you work on this kind of stuff without the right protective gear and precautions, you can get really hurt. And I just kept going back for more."

"His hair didn't lay flat again for a month," a voice said. He snapped his head toward the group that had appeared in the open field. Mia smiled at him. His heart started hammering in his chest, his vision blurring from tears. He moved on autopilot, his brain not processing as he jumped off the ground, bounded across the space between them, and lifted Mia up. He pulled her close, pressing his lips against hers with force.

When she didn't immediately respond, it snapped his brain awake. He started to pull away, to apologize for his brash actions, but she snaked her hand up his back and into his hair. She returned his kiss with the same fervor. For a split second, Diego thought he had died. There was no way this was happening, no way this was real life. He had to have electrocuted himself. He had finally pushed his skills too far, and he had somehow ended up in heaven.

He pulled back for air long enough to catch the stares of the newcomers. He placed Mia on the ground awkwardly, wrapped an arm around her waist, and let out a long breath. "You're alive."

Mia laughed lightly. "Why wouldn't I be?"

"I-I…," Diego stuttered. "I was so worried."

Mia squeezed his hand. "Let's talk about this in private. For now, let me introduce Parker and Rowan."

The pair looked at them. The boy stood hunched over with heavy bags and a pale complexion washed over his deep-brown skin. The girl gave him one short wave without smiling. She looked healthier. She looked familiar. He narrowed his eyes at her as recognition dawned. "You're the forest girl."

She frowned. "I don't particularly like the word girl, but yes, I am the one who lives in the forest. I've been meaning to…" They cleared their throat. "Now that you both are here, I wanted to thank you for the clothing. I'd been living there for most of my life. I'd forgotten how much better the world was with the comfort of something soft."

He smiled. "I'm glad they meant something to you. I was worried the first night that you would throw them out."

Parker shrugged. "I should have come talk to you guys before. You moved into my parents' home. It's nice to see someone caring for it again. It's been over a decade since they've been gone. I couldn't bear the memories, so I haven't been back." They blew out a breath. "Sorry, I don't normally blabber like this. I just… It meant a lot. That's all."

Diego nodded. "I'm happy to help." Under his breath, he added, "Even if that's all I did to help."

Mia elbowed him. He turned as she watched him with knitted brows. "Parker and Rowan would like to stay with us. Rowan just lost his sister, and I think we should give him some time to mourn before we make any decisions. I told them we should all have a vote, but at the very least, they could stay for the next few days."

Jeremy nodded. "I'm making deer stew, thanks to Maeve here."

Maeve blushed, calling Diego's attention to the girls who had probably found Mia. He mouthed a thank you. They gave him a nod.

"It was nothing," Maeve added.

"It's not nothing," Jeremy cut in. He gestured to the girls. "Maeve here is a great hunter. Jenna is her tracker. I do most of the cooking. Mia is our mother hen and all-over motivator. Diego is filled with the answer to any question you could come up with. Winona." Jeremy broke into a soft smile. "She's not here, but there's nothing she can't do, but she is mostly in charge of growing everything. She can make magic happen with some dirt and a pile of seeds."

Mia nodded. "We all play our roles." She pulled out of Diego's arms but twined their hands while gesturing at Parker. "Parker grew up with the coyotes in the woods. I'm sure the protection will serve the group well."

He watched Rowan flinch before locking eyes with Parker. Parker turned to face the group. "Yes, I'm sure they will be happy to help." They squeezed Rowan's shoulder. "Rowan can find water anywhere. Perhaps that will be helpful."

"That's fantastic. The other houses need wells put in, so we can set up the plumbing," Jeremy said, holding a hand out for a high five. Rowan just looked at him, then at Parker. Parker shrugged before smacking Jeremy's hand uncomfortably. "Well, if we're going to have more people. I need to find Winona and figure out if she has a few more potatoes."

Everyone mumbled their agreement, their eyes glued to Diego and Mia. He tried to ignore it, but his skin crawled with their scrutiny. "We'll meet up first thing tomorrow and finish that panel," he said, gesturing to the wide-open wiring cabinet. Jeremy agreed before jogging off. Jenna and Maeve offered to show the newcomers around, leaving Mia and Diego alone.

Diego shivered. The tension was claustrophobic. He let go of Mia's hand and sat down on the grass. "I guess we should talk."

"We should have talked a long time ago," she said, her voice softer than he expected.

"I'm so sorry for letting you down," he said as she said, "I should have told you this a long time ago."

They made eye contact and laughed.

"You can go first," she said.

He took her hands in his. "You mean the world to me. Had I known I was hurting you so much, I would have apologized a long time ago." She opened her mouth to speak. "Please let me finish," she snapped it shut. "I never meant to be such a disappointment. I promise that I won't be anymore. I'll prove to you that I'm the same guy you met all those years ago."

He let go of her hands and placed his hands on either side of her face softly. "I don't know why it took me so long to realize this. I should have known the minute you bounced into my office, smile plastered on your face, and told me you had decided to work with me. As if that was how things worked. It's not, by the way."

He laughed. "Mia Cruz, I love you. I have loved you for more than half my life." He fought back the tingling in his eyes. "You don't need to love me back. I can't imagine you would with how badly I've fucked up. Just promise me you'll stay my friend. I can't picture growing old without you."

Diego's heart pinched with every silent second as he studied her face for anything. He worried for a moment that he had upset her so much she was stunned. Then she lifted her face to his and pressed her lips on his.

"You. Dumb. Oblivious. Pain. In. My. Butt," she said between kisses. "Do you remember the last thing I said before I left?"

He nodded. The words still hung in the air. *That guy, the one I saw that day, he's the one I…*

"That guy. He was the one I fell in love with." She kissed him again. "I know he's still in there. I saw him today." A tear slid down her cheek, and he wiped it away. "I watched you with Jeremy. I almost didn't cut in. I was so proud to see you showing your potential. That was the man I fell in love with."

He laughed. All this time, they had just been moons circling the same planet. He pulled her to the ground and stared up at the sky as she curled against him. They stayed like that, letting the tension wash away like the clouds moving through the sky. He was positive they fell asleep for a little while, but he didn't care. All he cared about was that Mia was finally his. He wasn't going to mess up again. He propped himself up, and she blinked up at him. He brushed a curl off her face.

"Are you ready to tell me what happened yesterday?"

She nodded, launching into how she had tried to save Rowan's sister and how they couldn't move her. "She hadn't made it, and Rowan turned to stone. He's been silent ever since, but he seemed willing to talk to Parker. The pair seem to be building a fast friendship."

He listened, focusing on every word and locking it away as she detailed every moment he missed. He wouldn't take her for granted again. He memorized her features, from the blue of her eyes to the one dimple on her right cheek she got when she laughed too hard. There wasn't a part of her that wasn't beautiful, inside and out.

Diego always wondered how he had gotten so lucky.

# YEAR 6 AGC, DAY 27

## WINONA

WINONA SPENT most of dinner silently watching the newcomers with apprehension. Rowan thinner than Jeremy was when he had shown up all those months ago but formidable. And Parker, lithe with an improbable softness that butted up against the swirling heat of their brown eyes. They took seats next to each other at the end of the long, smooshed-together set of tables and stayed mostly silent despite the constant prodding from the rest of the group. Rowan didn't look away from his food for longer than the few seconds it took to look at Parker. She was confident he hadn't spoken a word since showing up.

Parker, on the other hand, was willing to answer most questions, albeit they were a little short. The more concerning trait was the way they kept surveying the room warily. It wasn't until their eyes connected with her own that she noticed the hardness in them.

They narrowed their eyes, the swirling fire burning her insides as they locked with her curious glances. She thought about looking away, but the demeanor of this person made her skin crawl. Winona wouldn't back down and give the appearance of giving in. These two newcomers were as concerning as when she'd met the two girls, except it was clear they were not the secret-keeping type, just overly quiet. Jeremy had made it clear they were safe, just as Mia had about this disjointed pair, and Jeremy had been right. Except some days, they didn't feel safe, and that unease was similar to her feeling about the pair. The silence that resonated with them was uncomfortable. Rowan hadn't said a single word, choosing to just look at Parker with some silent communication, and Parker had given small, one-word answers for the both of them.

Eventually, Parker brushed her off and went back to eating the food she'd dished for both theirself and Rowan. Another interesting interaction she added to her list of concerns. Winona wanted to shake them, to pull out the details of who they were, but instead, she turned her body away from the silent pair and placed her forehead against Jeremy's shoulder. His earthy smell and radiating warmth calmed the spinning voices in her head.

She let her body move with him as he laughed heartily at a joke Jenna had made when she wasn't paying attention. The gentle pressure of his hand on her waist, pulling her into his arms, warmed her from the inside out, wiping her mind off the rest of her concerns. His lips brushed the crown of her head, and he murmured, "You're worrying too much again."

She chuckled into his shoulder and poked his side. "When do I not?"

She expected him to laugh or poke her back like usual, but the sound of his sigh cut through her temporary ease. She hated it when he treated her like an insolent child, even when she knew that was how she was acting.

"I don't need a lecture, Jer," she hissed, untangling herself and standing up. She plastered on a fake smile and focused her eyes just above Mia's head to give the impression she was looking at them without her eyes locking with anyone. "Dinner was great, everyone. It looks to be getting a little late, so I'm going to start on dishes."

She grabbed her still-full plate, forcing her face to stay fake happy, and offered her hand out for any other plates. Diego and Mia, still reveling in the fact that they could eat from the vegetarian food Jeremy cooked, had cleaned their plates to the point she didn't think they needed to be washed. She picked them up, stacking them under hers, and spun to hike back into the house. Halfway across the grass, she could hear the rise in whispers between one end of the table. The words weren't audible, but it was no doubt a hushed conversation between Mia and Jeremy about her.

She closed her eyes and took a deep breath. She needed to be calm when someone inevitably checked up on her. Sure enough, by the time she reached for the door handle, there was a soft rushing sound as someone stepped away from the table. She couldn't tell if it was Jeremy or Mia, so she mentally prepared for either.

Without looking to see who was following her, Winona slipped into the house. She dumped her food into the trash as anxiety zapped her appetite. Standing at the sink with the dirty plates, she steeled herself as she caught sight of Jeremy reaching for the glass doors to her right. She should have guessed he would be the one to come.

He sat down silently on one of the stools that butted up against the counter. He made a point of scraping the chair loudly to get her attention. Rolling her eyes, she kept her face trained toward the sink. Without budging, she said, "I don't need a lecture about not worrying so much. This is who I am. Either you accept it, or you don't."

Jeremy's sigh was longer this time, the weight of his thoughts obvious. "No one wants to lecture you, Winona."

She shot him a sidelong glance while fighting to keep her face neutral. "Yeah? Then what is it you all want from me that you were sent to speak with me? I know it's not to tell me I can skip the dishes tonight."

She listened to his chair scrape across the floor, followed by the sound of his soft footsteps, and braced herself as he spun her around and into a hug. She tried to fight, but it was a weak attempt. He squeezed her so tight she struggled to breathe until she collapsed into him. She didn't want to give in to him again, but she couldn't avoid it. At some point, Jeremy had just figured her out and knew exactly how to get to her. Her body melted into his, tears pricking her eyes. He whispered soft, kind words into her hair.

"Damn you for knowing me this well," she grumbled into his shirt. His soft laugh drove her nuts.

"You don't need to worry for everyone around you. No one is telling you that you shouldn't worry. We're living in the after. Everything is a low hum of worry. But you are surrounded by people who care about you, who worry about you as much as you worry about them. You can't hold all the burden. You need to let the rest of them do some of the work."

She mumbled into his shirt, but it was just a bunch of words that didn't make sense. Some days she hated how much Jeremy got to her. He was always right.

"No. Winona." He pulled back, holding her face in his calloused hands. "I know that your parents forced this independence on you, and when I came into the picture, I didn't make it any better on you. But now we don't need you to hold everything on your shoulders. We need you to be the happy person I saw peeking out before we moved."

She nodded, tears running down her face and into her mouth with a sharp, salty taste.

"Do I think you're going to be able to do that?" Jeremy

laughed, forcing a hiccuped laugh out of her. "Absolutely not. But I'm going to remind you every day for the rest of our lives until your shoulders don't tense to the sound of a door opening and you loosen the tight frown you think you hide from everyone. You're very bad at hiding that, in case you were wondering. Your emotions are all over your face."

Winona snorted out a laugh, pulling her head away from Jeremy and wiping a rag over her face. The tears were still running, but she felt the tension start to release. "Whatever."

The word had no bite, and Jeremy knew it. He leaned against the counter, pulled a rag from the stack next to the sink, and grabbed a wet, clean plate to dry it. He didn't push her anymore, and she loved that about him. He let her process her feelings in any way that worked for her, and he would be there every step of the way. She studied him, his soft smile across his face that lit up his eyes and the way his body curled as if waiting for her to snuggle back into it, and flicked suds from the soap in the filled sink at him.

It was the closest she would get to admitting he was probably right.

He gave her a look, softly placing the plate on the counter, and scooped a handful of suds. Before she could stop him, they covered her face. He laughed, and she knew he accepted her peace offering.

She broke out in laughter, throwing more suds at him until he reached out to pull her close. A shiver ran through her body, and she couldn't help the sudden thumping of her heart. How far they had come. Grabbing a handful of her hair, he brought his lips to hers to brush them lightly across each other. Her body tingled with anticipation. Winona breathed out a sigh, melting into Jeremy's arms, and tried to close the kiss.

Jeremy pulled away just long enough for her to give him puppy-dog eyes. Using his free hand, he ran his thumb over her cheek and lips. She bit her lip, and he finally closed the distance. She felt like putty in his hands.

The world had more worries than pleasantries, but having Jeremy there to navigate their new future would make everything just that much better.

# YEAR 6 AGC, DAY 40

## WINONA

WINONA SHUFFLED the wicker basket she was holding to her other hip as she walked to where Jeremy was preparing dinner. It was the heaviest harvest from the garden to date. With an actual kitchen full of tools, he had jumped at the chance to cook for everyone, and Winona was happy to give him the supplies he needed. No one admitted it, but Jeremy was the only person who could cook a decent meal worth anything. They had tried shifting the work from person to person for a while. Jeremy had insisted, and no one argued with him after Jenna gave everyone food poisoning.

She finally accepted her crops for what they were and harvested them on a regular basis. Now that they had power in their home, Winona spent a lot of her time cultivating seedlings in the basement with the grow lights they'd tracked down. She woke up early to start her day caring for the plants and loved the reminder as the sun rose that she was making her parents proud. That she wasn't just surviving but thriving in this little community alongside someone who made her heart happy. She still wished they were there, but she had finally accepted their absence and taken charge of her life. Despite her fears about traveling, Jeremy burning down her home and forcing her out into the world was one of the best things to happen to her.

Jeremy was the best thing to happen to her, and she did her best to tell him every chance she got. She didn't want to ever get complacent and fall back into who they were before landing here. She dropped the basket on the counter of their kitchen, a few potatoes rolling out, and reached to give Jeremy a kiss while trying to catch them. It wasn't successful, but she brushed it off to focus on bigger worries. Like the look on Jeremy's face.

"Hi, dear." He didn't look her way as he reached for the basket and plucked two of the biggest potatoes. She watched him slice the potatoes into tiny chunks and drop them into the boiling water. He was eerily calm and focused. He was not the man who made every effort to make her feel safe. She crooked an eyebrow at him.

Peering into the pots he had on each burner, she tried to get his attention. "What's for dinner tonight?"

"Roast duck with mashed potatoes and sautéed spinach," he said, his eyes focused on the counter. "I cooked up some tofu for Mia and Diego."

She looked around the pot at the big book he had his nose stuck in when he was done with the potatoes. "What's that?"

Finally, Jeremy looked up at her. His face split into a huge smile, and she let out a sigh of relief. There was the Jeremy she knew and cared for. Maybe even loved, but she wasn't ready to say it aloud to herself, let alone him. He lifted the book and handed it to her. "Jenna found this old family cookbook in their attic. It's full of hundreds of hand-written recipes from the before. Did you know that people used to collect recipes?"

She pulled the book out of his hands and flipped through it. "I've never seen half of the foods they have in her. Like eggs?" Her voice raised questioningly. She pointed to a yellowing photo of a small roasted bird. "Have you ever had chicken? I don't think I have."

Jeremy shook his head. "I bet Diego and Mia could describe it to us. I'll ask them at dinner. How cool is this?" He pulled the book close to his chest. "There are so many things to try to make."

"It's awesome. I can't wait to make it all. In the meantime"—Winona smiled at him—"I'm just going to...sneak a peek in here." She opened the oven a small bit and inhaled the savory smell of roasted vegetables and duck before Jeremy snapped it shut in her face.

"Oh, come on. Just give me a little taste," she whined, pouting at him playfully.

"You're going to mess up the cooking process," he chided, whacking her hand when she went to open the oven again.

"You're messing up my appetite." She laughed but raised her hands in defeat. She sighed and said, "Fine, fine. I will wait like everyone else."

He eyed her, looking down at her dirty hands. She forgot she hadn't washed them after bringing in the harvest. She gave him a cheeky smile.

Rolling his eyes, he said, "I don't believe you, but it's almost done, so go wash the dirt off your hands so you can help me carry these plates to the table."

"Fine, but I want the first taste before it goes out," she called out as she headed to the bathroom.

She chuckled when he yelled, "Deal but hurry up!"

* * *

THE GROUP HAD FILLED out two tables shoved together for so long that Jeremy and Maeve had spent their spare time building a firepit behind Maeve's house for the group to eat at. It was the first time they got to use it. While it wasn't cold during the day, the nights had turned cooler over the last few months to the point Mia claimed it was cold. Cold enough that Mia had taken to wrapping herself in a blanket that night despite the roaring fire they circled.

Winona wasn't as cold but had pulled a sweatshirt over her shirt to stop herself from shivering. Washington had never gotten this cold. "Is it just me, or is it getting much colder this year?"

Mia put her plate on the ground and pulled her blanket closer. "It hasn't been this cold since I was a kid. And even then, it wasn't nearly as consistent."

"This is a good sign," Diego said, sticking his head out from behind Mia. "All of my research, our research, was on the patterns in our world to help predict how long we had before full destruction and what we could do to help humans survive. We're lucky that it didn't get that far. I didn't think we'd get this cold this fast, but the lack of abuse on the earth has turned things around at lightning speed. It's amazing to see."

"Abuse?" Parker asked from across the circle. Their head was barely visible over the fire.

"Yes. Before any of you were alive, the people who lived in our world had not heeded the warnings of scientists. It's the reason the world is like this. It's why it's so hard to survive now. It was never this hard in the before."

"I always forget that you haven't had a chance to learn of the before as much as the rest of us," Jeremy said.

"I'm not sure that it's a problem. I don't know. I've never seen anything like the stories you all have told, and I don't think I want to," Parker said, giving them an annoyed look.

Winona smiled at her, hoping to soften the mood. "I agree. Having heard all the stories from my parents, I hold more resentment than knowledge of the past. There are so many things I wouldn't have even known existed or thought to create had it not been for those stories." She grabbed her metal canteen filled with water. "Take this canteen. Do you know what they used before this?"

Parker shook their head.

"They made plastic bottles using by-products of the fuel they used in vehicles."

"Not like the electric car we use," Diego added.

Winona nodded at him. "Good point. The plastic bottles were single use only. People would just throw them out or drop them out of their cars. They ended up everywhere. The ocean by my home was littered with them. Jeremy and I used to get them in our fishing net instead of fish on a regular basis. Sometimes I would find dead fish trapped inside." She shivered just thinking about it.

"What's your point?" Parker asked.

"Her point is that while she needed to know about this issue, she wouldn't have even realized they were something people used instead of canteens had she not been forced to deal with it. Sometimes you just need a balance," Mia said.

"Exactly. There is no reason for you to learn about some of the horrendous things people did in the before if it doesn't support a healthier future," Jenna said.

Everyone turned to look at her. Jenna and Maeve didn't normally participate in conversations focused on the past. They tended to stay silent, refusing to even speak of what they knew of the past. Winona had never prodded because it always seemed to be painful for them. But Jenna looked good-natured as she rolled her eyes at the group. "I know I don't normally talk, but I do have opinions."

Parker laughed. "I just always assumed you didn't know that much of the past."

"My mother loved history. I've been listening to stories of the past since I was able to talk. I read every history book she had. I am just so sick of talking or listening or thinking about every shitty thing people did. I used to beg to hear stories of the good things," Jenna said. She flicked her eyes toward Diego. "It's funny, actually. Whenever I asked, my mom told me about this scientist who had interviewed on what they called TV before it became obsolete. He was far ahead of his time, and no one listened to him."

"Shut up," Mia said. "You cannot tell me you knew who Diego was this whole fucking time."

"Excuse you. I was quite memorable in the before," Diego protested as Mia laughed.

"My mom was fascinated by everything you had to say. When you introduced yourself, I knew exactly who you were. Maeve had wanted to leave, keep traveling, but I couldn't give up the chance to get to know you. It took a lot of convincing, but she came around. It's been interesting to see how you've followed your own warnings to survive."

"I don't know if surviving is the best word for what we were doing when we found y'all," Mia said with a shrug. "We would have been lost without each and every one of you. As a community, we are much stronger than before."

Everyone murmured agreement except Rowan, who just nodded in agreement.

"Okay, enough sappy talk. The food is getting cold," Winona said. The group let the silence wash over them, listening to the crackle of the fire and the soft whispering of the wind. Mia was right, each and every one of them was necessary for the group to thrive, and she was once again grateful that Jeremy had pushed her to step outside her comfort zone to be wrapped in the joy of their small community.

# EPILOGUE

# YEAR 10 AGC, DAY 355

## WINONA

WINONA CRACKED her eyes open to the crying of a newborn. It was so high-pitched she wanted to cover her ears to stop the ringing, but she was too tired to lift her arms that high. They felt like she was being held down by boulders. She turned her head and watched the baby that was cradled in a nervous Jeremy's arms as he rocked it. It was a beautiful sight to wake up to. She listened to him coo softly and admired them, the baby with a full head of Jeremy's black hair and Jeremy doing his best to hide his worries in front of Mia.

Mia, however, wasn't paying any mind to them but was quietly studying her. She hadn't alerted Jeremy to her being awake yet, and she was grateful for that. Instead, Mia offered a gentle smile before excusing herself. Jeremy barely looked up, his focus solely on the little child in his arms.

The sound of the door snapped Jeremy's head up just in time to see her try to shut her eyes again. She knew she was caught but squeezed her eyes shut anyway. Her whole body ached, hurt, cried out from the strain of the last several hours of labor. None of that mattered when the baby rolled her small head to show its deep-brown eyes that mirrored her own. They were the exact same shade of chocolate and were watching her curiously.

Just like that, all her fears about motherhood over the last nine months washed away. Sudden, fierce love filled her instead.

"Isn't she cute?" Jeremy said, his voice a low whisper. The baby, their baby girl, watched her as if she was transfixed.

"We had a girl?" Winona couldn't help the excitement. Mia and Diego were capable scientists, but they could only do so much. Without any medical equipment, there was no way for them to find out the baby's sex. It was pure luck that she'd made it through the nine months with no major incidents. Not that any of that mattered now. Winona would love that child no matter what because it was a part of each of them. It was the best part of both of them wrapped in an old throw blanket Mia must have found while she was resting.

Jeremy nodded, his eyes glassy. Her heart swelled as she took in the emotions playing over his face. "Do you want to hold her?" he asked.

She reached out wordlessly, her arms protesting, and Jeremy placed the baby girl in her arms. She was soft, her skin warm and smooth, and her weight was comforting. It made her arms burn in a good way until she leaned the baby's back onto her chest. This tiny being felt like lying under layers of comforters on a cool night. It was reassuring in a way nothing else could be.

"She's beautiful," Winona murmured.

"We'll have to name her before anyone else sees her, or they'll start calling her something, and we won't be able to stop it."

She laughed, wincing in pain.

"Are you okay? I can take her."

"I'm perfectly fine, Jer. Do not take this child away from me while I'm still memorizing her face." She gave him a weak smile and sighed. Jeremy had barely been a man when he showed up on her doorstep, had barely been able to take care of himself, let alone manage even the idea of taking care of someone else. But this Jeremy who stood next to her, the one cooing at the child in her arms, was not the one she'd kicked a rock at.

This Jeremy, the man he grew into, was her most trusted confidant. He had become her safe place, her rock, and she couldn't imagine anyone else she would want by her side. The day two years ago when the community held their makeshift wedding was, until today, the happiest moment in her life.

"Do you have any ideas?" she asked. She looked down at the child finally sleeping in her arms and bent down to kiss the crown of her head softly. When she didn't wake back up, she breathed out a sigh of relief.

"Demetria."

"Are you sure?" she asked. It wasn't an ugly name, but it seemed silly to name their baby after a season that didn't exist anymore. It got cold, sure, but it was just a brief moment between the brisk fall and spring. She would barely call that winter. Winter was only in points.

Looking out the window, she followed Jeremy's line of sight. Small flakes were falling from the sky, dissolving against the window in small droplets. She'd never seen anything like it, only heard about it from the stories her parents and Diego told. Diego had said it would come back as the world healed from the past, but she didn't expect it to be so beautiful. She didn't expect it to be so soon.

"Is that snow?" She knew the answer, but it felt so improbable she needed to ask.

Jeremy nodded. "It started right after she was born. It's not sticking to the ground. According to Mia, it's not cold enough for it to last, but it's still there. Glittering across the sky."

Glittering. What a way to describe it so perfectly. She looked down at their baby with a soft smile. "It's perfect. She's perfect."

# ACKNOWLEDGMENTS

I wrote this book when I never thought it would be published or that I would be published. I was struggling with writing, getting an agent, and, most importantly, the pandemic raging around me. I turned to this piece and poured everything I felt into it. This story means the world to me, and I couldn't be more excited that you took the time to read it.

This story started over a teams chat, and I want to thank the friend I sent that message to. Juan, I don't have words to thank you for being the catalyst for this story. You listened to me for hours. You inspired me. You never made me feel bad for trying to work out the intimate details of this book over the phone at all hours of the night. Thank you for every kind word and thoughtful response. I cherish your friendship and look forward to our next adventure.

I want to thank my husband, Jesse, for encouraging me to pull this novel back out of my forgotten pile and giving it the chance it truly deserved. While Juan encouraged the first draft, you pushed me to get to the final draft. I would be lost without your constant encouragement. Thank you for always being my support system, even when I don't realize I need it.

There are a few other people who influenced this novel who deserve a moment. My editor, Chrissy, for jumping into this story with me and encouraging me to make it the best it can be. My friend, Quinn, for always being there for me and helping me make the hard decisions. And my best friend, Caitlyn, for reading the first draft and encouraging me to keep going. This story would not have happened without each and every one of you, so thank you from the bottom of my heart.

# ABOUT THE AUTHOR

J.C. Warren lives in Raleigh, North Carolina with her husband, their surly cat, and two wild dogs. When she isn't running around trying to keep her house clean, she can be found curled up on the couch with a good book or hunched over her laptop. She loves to watch crime-based TV shows, romantic comedies, and cooking shows.

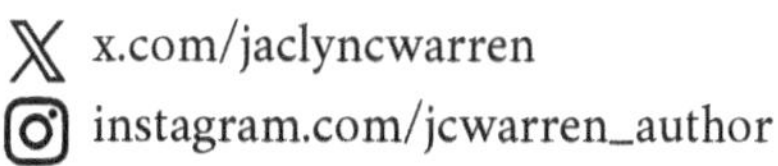

*A SHY, OVERACHIEVING HALF-NYMPH.*

*A DEFIANT AND RECKLESS SHIFTER.*

*A HAUNTED CAMPUS.*

Sixteen-year-old Arya Willow is a Freshman at Gomada Academy, a prestigious boarding school for mythical beings. But she has a secret: she is half-human and half-Nymph. Intense rivals within the school make her question her enrollment – but nothing prepares her for her life-changing encounter with Shifter Cole, who is just as monstrous in human form.

Sophomore Cole Hudson is a full-blooded Shifter with a family secret of his own, indulging in rebellious acts to escape his destiny. All he wants in life is to forge his own path, yet fate continuously pulls him back. But when catastrophe strikes the campus, Cole believes he's right where he belongs.

Arya's timidity and Cole's belligerence clash when they first meet, making the fact that they've been paired up in the school's Mentorship Program all the more unbearable. However, their chemistry is undeniable, and neither one wants to admit it.

Can Arya and Cole put their differences aside to stop a ghost? One thing is for certain...

**Secrets do not survive in Gomada Academy.**

www.ingramcontent.com/pod-product-compliance
Lightning Source LLC
Chambersburg PA
CBHW060810190726
48285CB00002B/608